The

Lost Mother
of Ireland

BOOKS BY SUSANNE O'LEARY

The Road Trip

A Holiday to Remember

SANDY COVE SERIES

Secrets of Willow House

Sisters of Willow House

Dreams of Willow House

Daughters of Wild Rose Bay

Memories of Wild Rose Bay

Miracles in Wild Rose Bay

STARLIGHT COTTAGES SERIES

The Lost Girls of Ireland

The Lost Secret of Ireland

The Lost Promise of Ireland

The Lost House of Ireland

Susanne O'Leary

The
Lost Mother
of Ireland

bookouture

Published by Bookouture in 2023

An imprint of Storyfire Ltd.
Carmelite House
50 Victoria Embankment
London EC4Y oDZ

www.bookouture.com

ISBN: 978-1-83790-194-4
eBook ISBN: 978-1-83790-193-7

1
———

Laura's birthday started with a leisurely breakfast in the kitchen of her little house on the north side of Dublin. She had treated herself to a croissant, a cinnamon bun and a large cup of coffee, topped with frothy milk from the Nespresso machine she had bought as a present to herself the day before. Wrapped in her dressing gown, she shivered as she stared out the window into the tiny garden, where a robin was pecking at the ground looking for a worm. The sky was overcast with a promise of rain. Dublin was cold and dreary in the beginning of February and Laura longed to get away from this city, the traffic and noise. It would be so nice to be somewhere less hectic where people had the time to enjoy life.

She was startled out of her reverie when her phone rang. Without thinking, she picked it up and answered straight away. 'Hello?'

'Laura Keane?'

'Speaking,' she said, frowning at the deep voice she faintly recognised.

'Hello,' the man said. 'This is Michael Monaghan,

Josephine's son. We've met a few times while you were caring for my mother. And at the funeral, of course.'

'Yes, of course I remember you, Michael,' Laura said, the image of Josephine's son drifting into her mind. Tall, blonde and pale with a serious expression, he was not a bit like his beautiful, vivacious mother, who had been in Laura's care for the past two years. A former opera singer with a colourful past, Josephine had been a delightful contrast to Laura's usual patients, and they had formed a close bond during those two years. Her death had been expected, but still felt like a terrible loss for Laura.

'It was a sad day,' he said.

'Very sad. How are you?' Laura added. She absentmindedly twirled a lock of her wild curls while she tried to find the right words to express some kind of sympathy. But all the anger she had felt during Josephine's last years bubbled to the surface. She had only met Michael a handful of times. His visits to his mother had been so rare. 'I'm sure you're still trying to cope with your loss,' she said, having to force out the words.

'Well, yeah, of course. I'm doing my best,' Michael replied. 'But she was ninety-six after all and not very well.'

Laura was taken aback. 'Yes, but still,' she said. 'It's always sad to lose a parent.' She made a face at herself in the little mirror on the opposite wall, her bright blue eyes flashing with sudden anger. She had been told she had a bold face when she was a small child. Well, she felt very bold right now. He had just lost his mother and all he could say was that she was very old, as if her death had been a relief.

'True.' He paused and then his voice took a sharp tone. 'I'd better get to the point. The reason I'm calling you is to tell you that we're going to contest.'

Laura blinked. 'Contest what?'

'The will, of course,' he snapped.

'What will?' Laura asked. And then it dawned on her what he meant. 'You mean Josephine left me something?'

'Yes. We've just come from the reading and found out that she left you... Well, quite a lot. But I'm sure you knew that already,' he added, a nasty tone creeping into his voice.

'No. I had no idea,' Laura said hotly. 'How could I know?'

'She might have told you before she passed away. Or you might have...' He stopped.

'Might have— what?' she asked while her mind reeled. She was a beneficiary of Josephine's will. What was she being left? It had to be something large enough to be worth contesting...

'We're discussing the possibility that your influence over my mother might have persuaded her to leave you this rather valuable property.' Michael's voice cut into Laura's thoughts.

Laura sat up straighter, hot with indignation. 'What do you mean? Are you saying I might have... fooled Josephine in some way? That's very insulting after all I did for her.'

'It was your job,' Michael remarked drily.

'It might have been, yes,' Laura snapped. *But all the extra time I spent with her was not in my job description*, she thought to herself.

'And I never really appreciated all those outings and excursions you took her on. They were quite unnecessary, really.'

'Well, it made her happy,' Laura said, shocked at his attitude, remembering the outings to museums, concerts and the seaside they had been on together, which Josephine had hugely enjoyed.

'Might have been too much for her,' Michael suggested.

'She was ninety-six years old,' Laura protested. 'Surely a moment's happiness would have been good for her?'

'Well, that's debatable,' Michael grunted. 'But I didn't call to discuss your unusual methods.'

'No, you have made that perfectly clear,' Laura retorted. 'But I want you to know that I never discussed her will with her.

It would have been impossible to force Josephine to do anything if she didn't want to.' She suddenly smiled as she remembered the feisty old lady, how she would stand her ground and refuse to budge about even the smallest issues. 'She was as stubborn as a mule,' Laura told Michael.

'Maybe not during her last few months,' Michael argued. 'She might have been a little feeble in her mind then.'

'No, she wasn't,' Laura said hotly. 'Not in the slightest. But how would you know? You never came to visit her until the very end.'

'I was busy.' Michael paused. 'But let's stop this argument. I only called to say that we're contesting the will. I thought if you could simply give up your claim, we could avoid all the hassles of a court case.'

'My claim to what exactly?' Laura asked. 'I have no idea what she left me.'

'A cottage in Kerry,' Michael replied.

'A cottage in—' Laura gasped. She knew instantly what he meant but couldn't quite believe it. 'Kerry?' she croaked when she could get the words out. 'The one she bought two years ago?'

'Yes. You really don't have any right to it at all,' he said sourly. 'We would be prepared to compensate you somewhat of course if you simply agree to hand it over to us.'

'Why should I?' Josephine's sad face drifted into Laura's mind. She had always been so very lonely. She'd always hoped her son and his family would visit more often and she always seemed devastated that he didn't. Michael seemed to think that his absence went unnoticed, but it certainly hadn't.

'We would be willing to pay you half the market value,' Michael suggested. 'Not that you deserve it. We feel you misused your influence over my mother and this is why she left you the house. But we won't make an issue out of it if you just sign it over to me. And then you'll get the money as soon as we can organise it.'

'Really?' Laura's anger turned to rage; she had to stop herself from snapping back at him. 'No thanks,' she said between gritted teeth and swiftly hung up the phone. How dare this man speak to her this way. He was Josephine's son, but he had no right to insult her and insinuate that Laura had cajoled his mother into giving her this cottage.

Laura didn't know what to do. It didn't feel right arguing with someone else's family. She was happy in her work; she didn't need a cottage in Kerry, not really. She wondered if, despite everything Michael had said to her, she should just give it back?

But as her thoughts twisted and turned, as she sat considering everything, the doorbell rang. A letter had been delivered by courier with the name of Josephine's solicitor on the back. It must be the notification of her inheritance. Laura ripped it open and found a note, and another envelope with her name written on it in Josephine's beautiful handwriting. It smelled faintly of the perfume Josephine always wore, Quelques Fleurs by Houbigant, and it made Laura's eyes well up with tears.

Laura read the note from the solicitor first, clapping her hand to her mouth. She had to read it twice before it sank in. Could this really be true? Had Josephine really left her all this? She read the note again. Apart from the cottage her son wanted so badly, she had been left a large sum of money, an elderly Labrador called Ken and a painting. The mention of the dog made Laura laugh. Typical. Josephine had loved the old thing, but she knew Laura wasn't a doggy person. Ken might be elderly, but he was fit and healthy and had 'several more years in him', the vet had said the last time they went for a check-up. Maybe she wasn't used to dogs, but Laura knew Ken would always remind her of Josephine, which was a comforting thought. She'd just have to get used to having a dog in her life from now on.

She read the rest of the message, which said that probate had been granted and the deeds and keys to the cottage could be picked up from the solicitor's office. It said that a neighbour was looking after Ken temporarily, the painting would be packed and sent to Laura's address and a large sum of money would be lodged into Laura's account as soon as they got her bank details.

Laura put away the note from the solicitor and opened Josephine's letter, holding back her tears as she read the words in Josephine's lovely script.

Dear Laura,

When you read this, I will be gone. I know you will feel very sad and I'm sorry to have left you. But don't grieve, dearest friend, I'll be with my darling Edward, my lover and friend, who I have missed ever since he passed away thirty years ago, as I've told you many times.

You have been my best and most loyal friend these past years and it has been a true pleasure to have someone like you with whom to share the last years of my life. I hope it hasn't been too hard for you and that you will cherish the memories of all the fun and laughs we had. I hope you will try to move on and maybe do something fun now that you don't have an old woman to take care of. The money I'm leaving you will help you do just that. Use it wisely but don't be too sensible. I do hope we can celebrate your birthday in the usual fashion, cracking open a bottle of bubbly and get a little tipsy while eating cake and watching a silly movie. But if not, please do it in my memory. You have given your life so far to help others and you deserve this cottage. I want you to make sure it doesn't return to my family. My son already has so much, but it's important to me that you keep it. It's my final wish that this beautiful home becomes a haven for you.

Sorry about leaving you Ken, but the poor thing will have nobody else to take care of him. I know you'll make sure his last few years are comfortable and happy.

But I'm rambling instead of getting to the most important things: the cottage and the painting. They go together in a way, I've been told, but I never knew exactly how. I bought the painting years ago and then I was told it was painted in Sandy Cove on the Ring of Kerry. So that's why I bought the cottage on a whim, hoping to go there myself and maybe find out what the story was. It was too late for me to go on such a journey, so I'm leaving you the painting and the cottage so that you might be able to find out the story of the woman and the artist who painted her. I'm sure it will be an exciting adventure for you.

Last but not least, I want to tell you what a beautiful woman you are. With your auburn hair, your soulful blue eyes and that radiant smile, you could, like Helena, launch a thousand ships. I know you have been unlucky in love and keep declaring you're happily single, but I'm sure true love will come your way one day. And when it does, don't turn it away but embrace it and be happy. If you don't, I will haunt you till the day you die.

Love,

Josephine

Laura smiled a sad little smile as she read the last lines, then got up from her chair and walked across her small living room. She picked up a framed photo on the mantelpiece. It was of her and Josephine, taken only a few months ago. A selfie they had managed to take as they sat on a bench by the seaside in Howth on a sunny day last October. It had been a warm and pleasant day and Josephine had been unusually energetic, Laura remembered, chatting and smiling.

She studied her own face in the photo, looking for signs of that beauty Josephine had referred to, but found none. Her face was pleasant enough, her features even with a square chin and a wide mouth that often widened further in a happy grin, just like it had that day. Her eyes were her best feature, large and round and startlingly blue. Her hair could be stretched to auburn with a bit of imagination, but to Laura it had always been brown with curls she could never tame even cut into a short bob, often ruffled by the wind. *Not bad, but no beauty*, she decided, and put the photo back. She glanced at herself in the mirror above the fireplace and tried to conjure up that 'radiant smile' Josephine had described. But all she managed was a sad little grin. *Today is not the day for radiant smiles*, she thought with a sigh. One thing in the letter was not true, however. Laura was not 'happily single'; she had just given up on ever finding someone to share her life with. Love had simply never come her way. She had been in relationships a few times but they had never developed into something serious, probably because of her independent spirit. She had never felt that spark, the chemistry described in romantic novels. But maybe, as Josephine had suggested, she just hadn't met her true love? She knew she probably never would, so she had done her best to appear not to care and filled her days with looking after others.

Nursing had been Laura's chosen career and it was all absorbing, especially when staff shortages in the hospital meant long hours, leaving little time for dating or having fun. When the stress had become too much to cope with, Laura handed in her notice, turning to rehab and elder care with an agency. It was less tiring but, in a way, more rewarding than general nursing. She had found that she liked caring for old people, who were often brave and kind and very grateful for everything she did. They appreciated the smallest gesture, a touch, a hand to hold, someone to talk to when nobody else would. It was as if she was filling a void, that lonely place when there was nobody around to inquire after one's health or well-being.

But Josephine was right that it was a long time since she'd had a break. And, if it wasn't for Josephine, there was no way she could afford to own, or even stay, at a cottage like the one she had been left.

She knew exactly where it was as they had often talked about it. In a small village on the edge of the Atlantic, the cottage had sweeping views of the ocean and the islands. 'The most beautiful spot I have ever seen,' Josephine once said.

But what was she going to do? How could she fight Michael Monaghan and all his money? He was a well-known businessman and had a high profile in Dublin society, along with his wife. Laura needed a solicitor. And a plan. Given all Michael had, she couldn't help but wonder, how could a little cottage in Kerry be so important?

2

When Laura's sister Maureen arrived at the front door later that day, Laura couldn't believe how quickly the day had gone. She was almost startled when she opened the door and found Maureen and her daughter Rachel on the doorstep, with a cake and a bunch of flowers, shouting, 'Happy birthday!'

Laura laughed and let them in. 'Hi, you crazy kids,' she said, overwhelmed by their kindness. 'Thanks for coming over. I had nearly forgotten it was my birthday.'

'No you didn't,' her sister argued. 'You were sitting here being miffed about us forgetting.'

Laura laughed again. Little did her sister know that she had been rather distracted. 'I probably would have been in another hour or so. But here you are. Go through to the living room and I'll...' She was about to say she'd make coffee, but then remembered what Josephine had said in her letter. Laura actually had a bottle of champagne that Josephine had given her just before she had taken ill. 'Stick it in your fridge right now, so you won't forget on the day,' she had said, and Laura had done just that and forgotten about it because of what had happened shortly afterwards. 'Who wants a glass of bubbly?' she shouted on her way to the kitchen.

'Me!' Maureen and Rachel shouted in unison from the living room.

Laura laughed, cheered by their good mood, and put three champagne flutes on a tray, along with plates, spoons and a knife to cut the cake. She felt so lucky to have an older sister like Maureen and a lovely niece like Rachel. Both had strawberry blonde hair and the same bright blue eyes as Laura. But Maureen had the confidence her younger sister lacked, and Rachel was the image of her mother both in looks and feisty personality.

Rachel shot up from the sofa in front of the fireplace when Laura entered with the tray. 'Hey, I'll get that. Mum, light the candles and we'll sing.'

Maureen took a small bag with birthday candles out of her tote and started to stick them into the cake she had placed on the coffee table. 'There. Just a few candles, instead of all the fifty-two, I thought. We don't want to start a fire.'

Laura laughed and sat down. 'You should talk. There'll be a lot more candles on your cake next birthday.'

'Don't rub it in.' Maureen took a box of matches from the mantlepiece and lit the candles while Rachel opened the bottle of champagne with a loud, festive pop. Then they sang the birthday song, and Laura blew out the candles before cutting the cake.

Maureen took a sip of champagne. 'This is delicious. Top-class champagne,' she said, glancing at the label on the bottle. 'One of Josephine's?'

'Yes.' Laura ate a spoonful of cake. 'Only the best was worth spending money on, she used to say.'

'She was amazing.' Rachel smiled at Laura. 'You must miss her terribly.'

Laura nodded. 'Oh yes. She was more than just a patient. She was my friend.'

'I know she was.' Maureen patted Laura's hand. 'You're still upset. Understandable after only two months.'

Laura put her plate on the coffee table and grabbed her glass. 'Well, I'm sad. But what is upsetting me today is not Josephine's passing.'

'What happened?' Maureen asked.

'Michael Monaghan, Josephine's son, called me.' Rachel went on to tell them about the phone call and then the inheritance.

They both stared at Laura when she finished her tale. 'What a miserable shit,' Rachel finally said. 'Sorry, Auntie, but he is. Doesn't he have enough money without grabbing your inheritance as well?'

'There must be a reason he wants that cottage,' Maureen pondered.

Laura shrugged. 'Maybe. But Josephine wanted me to have it.'

'Sandy Cove,' Rachel muttered and picked up her phone. 'I've heard that somewhere... Hold on. I'll google it.'

Laura took another sip of champagne. 'Great idea. I haven't had a chance to do that. It all happened so quickly.'

'What are you going to do?' Maureen asked.

'Not sure yet,' Laura replied. 'But I need a solicitor. Could I ask yours for advice? I haven't got one of my own. Never needed one.'

'Of course.' Maureen picked up her phone. 'I'll text you his number and then I'll shoot him a text to explain why you need him.'

'Brilliant,' Laura said with a feeling of relief. 'Then I'll send that oaf Michael the contact details. Tell him to speak to them from now on.'

'Sandy Cove is a gorgeous place,' Rachel interrupted. 'Right on the edge of the Ring of Kerry. Lovely little village with stunning views. And...' She paused. 'What did you say those cottages were called?'

'Starlight-something,' Laura said.

'Starlight Cottages,' Rachel read from her phone. 'It's an old coastguard station with four cottages that were completely renovated around two years ago, and then two of the cottages were sold for astronomical prices. The third one is for rent, but it doesn't say anything about the first cottage. Probably occupied by the owner. And yours, of course, was the one Josephine bought.'

'Not mine yet,' Laura argued.

'But didn't that note from her solicitor say your name is on the deeds?' Rachel asked, her eyes on the screen. 'Hey, just look at this place, Auntie Laura,' she continued, handing Laura the phone.

Laura studied the images of a pretty village that appeared to be on the edge of the Atlantic coast. The views were indeed spectacular and the village itself like something from a story book, with old-fashioned lamp posts and quaint shop fronts. 'Oh, what a beautiful place,' she said as she scrolled through the photos. 'And those cottages are gorgeous,' she added as she looked at a picture of a row of whitewashed houses on the edge of a cliff. Each of the houses had a front door painted a pastel colour: pink, light blue, yellow or pale green with matching window frames. The ocean glinted behind them, and she could nearly smell the salt-laden air. 'This is just what I've been dreaming of,' she mumbled.

'Show me,' Maureen said, taking the phone from Laura. 'Oh my God,' she exclaimed. 'That's the most beautiful place I've ever seen. But of course these are from the tourist office so they were taken on a beautiful summer's day. I'd say it's different right now, in February. Stormy and wet, would be my guess.'

'Wild and spectacular,' Rachel filled in. 'The winters are so mild in Kerry that the rhododendrons and camellias are in bloom at this time, I've heard.' She looked at Laura. 'You know what I'd do if I were you?'

'What?' Laura asked. 'Fight for my inheritance in court?'

'No,' Rachel said with a wave of her hand. 'Forget that. I'd go down there to Kerry and just move in. Then I'd call that guy's bluff. I bet he thought he could just buy you off or scare you a bit and you'd just give in and take his money to save him all those legal fees.'

Laura looked thoughtfully at Rachel. 'You know what? I'm nearly tempted to do that. To just go there when I get the deeds and the keys, load old Ken and my stuff into my car and take off.'

'It's the beginning of February,' Maureen protested. 'Kerry would not be ideal right now. It can be very wet and windy there this time of year.'

Laura wasn't listening to Maureen's warnings. The image of that little village she had seen only briefly on Rachel's phone was still on her mind. 'Yes, but it's better than just sitting here being miserable.' She was about to tell them about the painting Josephine had left her, but decided to keep quiet about it for now. She hadn't seen it yet, and she didn't know how valuable it was.

'Oh yes, it is.' Rachel's eyes glittered with excitement as she looked at Laura. 'Auntie Laura, you have always been looking after other people and putting yourself last. Isn't it time for you to live a little and have some me-time? You deserve this inheritance, every bit of it. Don't let that miserable so-and-so win. Stand up for yourself and fight your corner. And then go to Kerry just for the craic and the adventure. That's what Josephine would have wanted you to do.'

Laura could nearly see Josephine cheering her on while she looked at Rachel's determined face. Rachel had often called in to Josephine and they had got on really well from the start.

Fired by the challenge and the urge to do something to break her sadness, Laura nodded, taking a deep gulp of champagne. Then she lifted her glass. 'Cheers to Josephine!' she exclaimed. 'She gave me a gift and a challenge that I must accept or she will haunt me forever.'

Rachel laughed and clinked Laura's glass. 'That's the spirit, darling Auntie. Next stop, Sandy Cove!'

3

It all happened so fast. Once Laura had decided to stand her ground and claim her right to the cottage, everything fell into place. Josephine's solicitor had been surprisingly helpful when she phoned him, declaring that he knew the old lady had been fully aware of what she was doing and not at all 'feeble' as her son had insinuated. He had also told Laura that Josephine had calculated exactly how much inheritance tax Laura would have to pay and made sure that there would be enough left of the money to give Laura some financial security. That didn't sound like someone who wasn't in possession of all her faculties, he said, and he would stand up in court and swear to that, if necessary.

And then, at the end of the conversation, he said something strange in a near whisper.

'I beg your pardon?' Laura said, startled.

'Keep it quiet,' he said a little louder. 'This is what Josephine asked me to tell you. She didn't want to put it into the letter in case it fell into the wrong hands. She said to tell you not to show the painting to *anyone*. It's apparently worth a lot but she insisted you were to have it because she trusted you to give it to the rightful owner once you found him... or her.' Then he had said goodbye very quickly and hung up, leaving Laura standing in her living room, surrounded by boxes, feeling both puzzled and worried.

So the painting was valuable? Did Michael know this? Possibly not. And what had Josephine meant by 'the rightful owner'? How could Laura find that out? The answer to all those questions would be found in that little village, she felt, and she couldn't wait to get there.

The painting, which was quite large, was delivered the following day. Laura immediately unwrapped it and propped it against the wall of her living room. With old Ken, the big black Labrador, who had arrived the day before, she looked at it in amazement. It was truly stunning, the colours so vivid she could nearly feel the wind and the sun and hear the seagulls gliding around in the blue sky. And the scene looked as if it had a fascinating story.

It depicted a young woman sitting on a rock on a beach, looking at the artist over her shoulder, as if he had just called her name. She wore a white broderie anglaise dress and the sun glinted on her raven hair that she wore in a long plait down her back. Her hooded, hazel eyes had a dreamy faraway expression and she looked as if she was trying to overcome some kind of sadness or difficulty. But there was also something in her expression that said there was a close connection between her and the artist.

It wasn't just the woman that intrigued Laura, however, it was the backdrop of a hill covered in wild roses and the ocean glinting in the distance. A beautiful painting by all accounts, but now that she knew it had been painted in or near that little village called Sandy Cove, it intrigued Laura even more. She had never seen this painting in Josephine's house, but then she hadn't been in every room.

She looked at the woman and met her eyes. *Who are you?*

Laura thought. *Why do you look so sad and forlorn even though there is a glint in your eyes?* The more she looked at the beautiful young woman, the more she wanted to find out the story. She was sure Josephine had felt the same but had not had the strength to investigate further. And now she had given the task to Laura, who realised that this painting was not hers to keep but to pass on in order to find peace for the woman and the painter. She was sure that there was some kind of love story there. But how was she going to find out? It seemed an impossible task.

Laura wrapped the painting up again and carried it to her car, which was already loaded with two suitcases full of her clothes, two cardboard boxes with kitchen equipment, a bag with bed linen and towels, and now the painting that had to be wedged in beside all that. Ken would travel in style on the back seat wearing a safety harness that he seemed to hate.

'Tough luck,' Laura said to him as she got him into the back seat. 'It's for your safety. And mine,' she added, patting his head. 'We'll stop a few times on the way,' she promised him before she closed the door and started the car, ready for the trip to the south-west and Sandy Cove, where she would take possession of her cottage.

She had given notice to her landlord and said she wouldn't be back for a long time; it hadn't taken him long to find a new tenant. She felt a dart of fear as she thought about it. Was she really leaving her Dublin life behind for a place she had never been to? The south-west – wild and windy and remote, was this really going to be her home from now on? She was sacrificing everything for something new and different, which seemed a little unwise at her age. She had grown up in Dublin and was used to city life. Even though she loved nature and outdoor pursuits, she had never actually lived in the country.

Then fear was replaced by excitement. It was an adventure. She had a new home to go to and enough money to live on for a while. She didn't have to decide anything right now, but could simply follow the road ahead and see where it led. Josephine had given her this chance for a new life, a new beginning. She had to at least give it a chance. She owed Josephine that. Who knew what would happen next?

As Laura drove up the street and saw her little house disappear in the rear-view mirror, she felt a pang of sadness as she left it behind. She had been happy there, if a little lonely. But now she was going to a home that was all hers, and that gave her a buzz of excitement. It all now seemed like a huge adventure because of the painting and Josephine's cryptical message. Whatever the future held, the cottage was a solid base to fall back on. It was full of promise.

After a long and tiring drive with many stops, Laura finally arrived in Sandy Cove. The village was quiet as she drove down the main street. Its mixture of cottages and Victorian houses spilled pools of light onto well-tended front gardens, as lamps were lit in the windows one by one in the gathering darkness.

Despite the failing daylight, Laura noticed to her delight camellia bushes with deep pink flowers already in full bloom, and a glimmer of the distant sea at the end of the street. A group of children in school uniforms alighted from the school bus and walked up the street, chatting to each other, before they parted to go home. There was a smell of turf in the air and Laura could see smoke rising from some of the chimneys. She had the impression of a cosy, close-knit community, and she was looking forward to meeting them all once she had settled in.

And then, in what seemed like no time at all, she was finally there, standing in a fine drizzle as dusk fell, in front of the quaint whitewashed cottage, with its little front garden, a tub of red geraniums providing a splash of colour. Laura took a deep breath of the air that smelled of seaweed and salt and opened

the little garden gate. Then she stood at the pale pink front door
for a moment, the key in her hand, Ken at her side, ready to go
inside her new home.

Laura looked up at the dormer window, the surround of
which was painted the same pink as the front door. She knew it
belonged to one of the bedrooms, of which there were three, the
master with its ensuite shower room downstairs, the other two
and the bigger bathroom upstairs, according to the plans the
solicitor had kindly provided. She had also been told that the
house had been looked after by someone in the village, who'd
kept an eye on the place ever since Josephine had bought it. She
had spent a few days there, she had told Laura, and then bought
the cottage fully furnished, hoping to come back the following
summer. But then she had fallen ill and nobody had lived there
since then, so it might be a bit dank and cold.

Laura hesitated for a moment, then put the key in the door,
pushed it open and entered a small hall with an antique hall-
stand against the wainscoting, which had been stripped and
painted a distressed white. She hung up her jacket and, with
Ken at her heels, went through the next door and down a corridor, where the stairs with their beautifully carved banister led
to the upper floor. Then she came into a small sitting room with
wide wooden floorboards on which stood a chintz sofa, a deep
blue shagpile rug in front of the pretty period fireplace that had
been stacked with logs and kindling ready to be lit. Two wicker
armchairs with embroidered cushions flanked the sofa. The
coffee table was a work of art, with blue and green tiles forming
swirls and circles in an intricate pattern. Laura had never seen
such a beautiful little table, and she ran her fingers over the
smooth surface, wondering how it had been made. At the end of
the living room was a glass door that led to a sunroom, which
would have beautiful sea views, according to what Josephine
had told her. But, right now, it was too dark to admire those
views.

Laura looked around the living room, breathing in the faint smell of damp, and shivered, pulling her cardigan tighter around her. She had been sent instructions on how to turn on the heating, so she walked back down the corridor and into the kitchen. Laura turned on the light, looking for the switch that was supposed to be situated just below the fuse box beside the door.

It was a gorgeous country kitchen with both an electric cooker and a small woodburning stove. The cupboards were of some kind of bleached wood and looked as if they had been made especially for the house. Then Laura noticed a basket with fresh bread on the table with a sticker that said 'Gino's Village Bakery'. How kind of whoever had put it there, and who must also have stacked the wood and kindling in the fireplace. It made her feel instantly welcomed by some invisible thoughtful person, probably the caretaker.

Laura found the switch to the heating and turned it on, comforted by the immediate little hum that told her the house was being heated. She turned on the fridge-freezer and more lights as she went back out to the car to unload her things. She would make dinner once she had got everything inside and lit the fire, which would make the living room more cheerful.

It didn't take long to bring everything in, and after three trips all that was left was the painting. Laura had wrapped it in several layers of brown paper and an old blanket to protect it from any knocks during the journey. She now knew it was valuable but to her it was worth more than money because Josephine had given it to her. It was quite big, and the gold frame added to its weight. Laura had nearly managed to get it out of the back of the car when a hand shot out of the dark.

'Hey, I'll give you a hand with that,' a pleasant man's voice said.

Laura nearly dropped the painting. 'Oh,' she exclaimed. 'You gave me a fright.' She turned to peer at the man in the dim light from the lamp over the door, and discovered he was tall with unruly dark hair and brown eyes.

'Sorry,' he said. 'I just arrived home and saw you struggle with that thing. I'm your next-door neighbour.' Then he stopped and stared at her in shock. 'Oh my God,' he said at the same time as Laura recognised him.

She couldn't believe her eyes. Was this her next-door neighbour? That man she knew so well...

4

'Shane?' Laura stammered. 'Dr Flaherty? I mean...'

'Laura Keane? Is it really you?' he asked, looking as shocked as she felt.

Laura blinked and tried to take in that it really was Shane Flaherty standing there outside her new cottage. 'Yes,' she mumbled. 'But what on earth are you doing here? The last time we met...'

'We were in the A&E department in Limerick hospital,' he filled in. 'And there was a huge emergency after a massive pile-up on the motorway. God, you were magnificent.'

'So were you,' Laura said, taken aback by the compliment. The memory of that night tumbled through her mind. They'd worked together from time to time but that night she had been head nurse and Shane the consultant on duty. They and the whole team had worked hard all night taking care of badly injured people. 'Thank God everyone was all right in the end,' she said.

'All thanks to you,' he remarked.

'And you and all the other nurses and doctors on duty that night. I'll never forget it.'

'Nor will I.' Shane pushed the hair out of his eyes. 'It was a tough night...'

'It was.' Laura struggled to hold on to the painting.

'Let's get this thing inside and then you can explain what you're doing here of all places in the whole world,' Shane suggested.

'Yes. I really could use some help. It's quite a big painting. And then you could tell me what you're doing here too,' Laura said, laughing.

'Let's get going then.' Shane pulled the painting out of the car and, with Laura's help, carried it into the house, where Ken greeted him enthusiastically, furiously wagging his tail. They propped the painting against the wall of the living room. Then Shane stood back and stared at Laura. 'Holy God, it's so weird. What was it – ten years ago since that night?'

'Yes. Something like that.'

'You look the same, only less tired.'

Laura studied him for a moment. 'You look much better. I remember how exhausted you were. I was worried about you to be honest. But now you seem to have landed here – but how?' She shook her head, trying to take it in while he stood there smiling at her. 'Hey, how about a cup of tea?' she finally asked.

'That would be lovely,' Shane replied.

'I'll go and put the kettle on.' Laura walked down the corridor to the kitchen, with Shane and Ken following behind her.

'I'm one of the GPs in this village,' Shane said once they were sitting at the kitchen table, mugs of tea in front of them. 'I run the surgery with another doctor. And I live next door with my wife, Edwina.' He paused. 'How about you? I'm guessing you are the mystery heir to this cottage everyone is talking about. The woman Josephine Clarke left it to.'

'How did you know?' Laura asked as she sipped the hot tea.

Shane laughed and poured milk from the jug into his mug.

'We all knew you'd be here soon. There are no secrets in this village. But it was Gino who told Edwina and she told me the new owner was on her way. But that it would my old friend and colleague Laura Keane is a huge surprise. How did you know Josephine?' he asked, peering at her.

Laura put her mug down. 'That's a long story. I left Limerick not long after I last saw you and went back to Dublin and did a training course in rehab. I realised I wanted to do something a little less stressful.'

'Good idea,' Shane agreed. 'So that's how you ended up looking after Josephine for a while?'

'Until she died,' Laura replied. 'Did you just mention someone called Gino?'

'Yes. He's the village baker.'

'So I gather.' She pointed at the basket of bread on the table. 'He left this for me. Would you like a bread roll? Or a muffin?'

Shane shook his head. 'Thanks, but I'll be having dinner soon. Nice of Gino to leave it for you, though. He's not only the village baker but also the person who has been looking after this cottage ever since Josephine Clarke bought it.' Shane paused. 'And that was just as the renovations were finished so she was the first owner of the refurbished cottage. She bought it fully furnished and then we thought she'd move in, or at least spend the summer here. We were looking forward to meeting a famous opera singer. But she never came back after that first visit just after she bought it. I heard she had taken ill shortly afterwards.'

Laura nodded. 'Yes, that's right. She had a stroke. She never really recovered physically so she couldn't come even for a visit, which was very sad for her. I was looking after her until the end.'

'I heard she passed away a few months ago,' Shane said with sympathy in his voice. 'Must have been very sad for you.'

'Yes. We had become very close.'

'Is that why she left you the cottage?'

'I think so.'

'She was a lovely woman by all accounts,' Shane remarked gently. 'You must miss her.'

'I do.' Laura put her empty mug on the table. 'Very much. In a way that's why I came. I needed something to distract me from the sadness. Mad to come here in the middle of winter, I know. But I like a challenge.'

Shane smiled. 'I know you do, Laura. But Kerry weather is unpredictable. You can have a summer's day in February and winter storms in July. But that's the charm of it. We love it here, but then I'm from Kerry, as you might remember. I'm so happy I came back. Wouldn't live anywhere else.' He checked his watch and got up. 'I have to go. Edwina will be home soon and I promised to make dinner. Welcome to Starlight Cottages, by the way. Let us know if you need anything. And maybe you'd like to join us for dinner soon?'

'That would be lovely,' Laura said, touched by his kindness. 'And thanks for your help with the painting.'

'You're welcome,' Shane said as they walked together to the front door. 'Give me a shout if you need help to hang it.'

'Thanks, I will,' Laura said, knowing she wouldn't. She would put it in her bedroom, where nobody would see it, and just lean it against the wall so she could see it every morning when she woke up. She didn't want to show it to anyone because that's what Josephine had wanted, at least not until she had found the rightful owner, if ever she found out who that was.

'Great. Lovely to meet you again, Laura. Thanks for the tea,' Shane said before he left.

Laura said goodbye to Shane, closed the door behind him and went back to the living room to sort out the boxes and suitcases she had brought, still amazed at meeting someone from her past like this. She suddenly realised she hadn't seen the rest of the house and proceeded to walk around, looking into every room and every cupboard to get her bearings and familiarise herself with her new home. She was amazed by the gentle way the cottage had been renovated. It had all the mod-cons of a modern house, but all controls were discreetly hidden behind panels and wainscotings.

The furniture was a mixture of old and new and a cross between country chic and beachcomber relaxed. The master bedroom had a double bed with a headboard shaped like an enormous shell. It would have sea views, so Laura decided at once that this would be her bedroom, as she fell in love with the bed and the ensuite shower tiled in white and turquoise, with two blue ceramic dolphins on one of the walls. She was making the bed with the sheets she had brought when the doorbell rang, making Ken bark loudly from the living room where he had settled on the rug in front of the fireplace.

Startled, Laura ran to the door and opened it a crack to discover a chubby woman with grey curly hair on the doorstep.

'Yes?' Laura said.

'Oh hello,' the woman said. 'I saw the light in the window and thought I'd pop in to say welcome. I was actually calling in to the doctor here with some papers for him to sign, but thought I might as well introduce myself. I'm Bridget McCarthy, surgery nurse among other things.'

Laura smiled. 'Hi, Bridget. I've just met my next-door neighbour and discovered to my huge surprise that we know each other from way back. We used to work together at the same hospital.'

'You know Doctor Shane?' Bridget exclaimed. 'That's amazing. So then you already know that he's one half of the medical practice, Dr Kate being the other one. And I'm the piggy in the middle,' she ended with a laugh.

'I see.' Laura held out her hand. 'I'm Laura Keane. Nice to meet you, Bridget.' She paused. 'We're colleagues, of course.'

'I thought so when you said you worked with Shane a while

ago.' Bridget looked at Laura with interest. 'What kind of nursing do you do now?'

'I became a carer a while ago. But I've done all kinds of nursing, even midwifery.'

Bridget looked impressed. 'Gosh that's a lot of experience you have there. But now you're here, will you be looking for a job?'

'No, not at the moment,' Laura replied. 'I'm just going to settle in and have a break. I was left this cottage by the lovely lady I was caring for and I'm not really sure what I'm going to do with it, to be honest.'

Bridget nodded. 'Yes, it was Josephine Clarke, wasn't it? I saw her on TV many years ago. Lovely voice. And of course she was here when she bought the cottage. Everyone loved her.' She stepped back. 'But I'm holding you up and I have to get home to my husband, who'll want his tea. Nice to meet you, Laura. Welcome to our village.'

'Thank you. Lovely to meet you too, Bridget.'

'Don't forget to pop into Gino's when you have a minute,' Bridget said as she walked to the house next door. 'He's been dying to meet you ever since we heard you were coming. Josephine told him all about you, he says.'

'I will.' Laura slowly closed the door, wondering how on earth Josephine had managed to get to know so many people in the village during the short time she had been here. Her fame as a much-loved opera singer had probably helped a lot. But also her charm and bubbly personality would have made her very popular.

Laura could imagine how Josephine had looked forward to living here. And then she hadn't been able to get back but had left the cottage to Laura in her will, which could change her life forever. She suddenly had a feeling that Josephine had somehow mapped out her future, or at least tried her best to make sure Laura was happy and secure. The money, the cottage and the painting felt like some grand plan, or a path marked with arrows showing her the direction Josephine wanted her to go.

The thought made Laura shiver as she went back to the living room. Ken lifted his head and looked at her with his sad doggy eyes. Laura patted his back. 'I suppose you are also part of this grand plan Josephine had for me,' she mumbled. 'Just to make sure I had company.' Ken let out a little grunt before he went back to sleep, snoring softly. 'I see you agree,' Laura said with a laugh. 'Okay, I get it. Josephine planned it all and now I have to go forward following this mysterious path. But do I really want to, do you think, Ken? I might do the direct opposite.' She yawned and realised she was exhausted. And also hungry. She would have some soup and bread and then go to sleep in that amazing bed and wake up wondering what else Josephine had planned for her.

5

It was still dark when a cold wet nose pushed at Laura's face. She let out a little moan and then realised it was Ken. She reached out a hand and patted his head. 'Morning, Ken,' she mumbled. 'You're awake far too early. But I suppose you want to go outside.'

Ken let out a whine and wagged his tail.

'Oh, okay, then.' Yawning, Laura sat up and pushed the duvet away, realising to her surprise that she had slept all night without waking up.

That was a first for a very long time. It had to be the distant sound of the waves that had lulled her to sleep. That and the feeling of peace in this house, where she knew the neighbours were close by and the village only minutes away. A much nicer feeling than the anonymity of the city where neighbours preferred to keep themselves to themselves. Last night the cup of tea with the next-door neighbour, who had turned to be someone she knew, and then the nice nurse coming to her door had given her a feeling of being among friends, chasing away the loneliness that she had been struggling with ever since Josephine's death. She had realised then that the reason she loved looking after older people was that she was never alone and was always needed by people who were grateful for everything she did for them. It was also nice to make a difference and make life a little easier for someone at the end of their lives.

'Not that I'm a saint,' she said to Ken as she pulled on her tracksuit and put on her waterproof walking shoes, which she had retrieved from her suitcase. 'Old people can be quite difficult, you know. Just like old dogs who wake up at the crack of dawn.' She smiled at the old dog, who looked at her with his melting brown eyes. She was warming to him, feeling that he was her last link to Josephine, who had loved the old dog with all her heart. 'I think we're bonding,' she told him.

Ken wagged his tail and went to the French door that led out to the terrace, poking his nose at the curtains, which Laura pulled back to open the door. What met her eyes through the window made stop and hold her breath. What a stunning view, especially now at sunrise, where the bay below was bathed in a rosy light, tiny rippling waves glittering and the clouds coloured pink. Far out at sea, she spotted the jagged outlines of the Skellig Islands where flocks of sea birds hovered around the peaks.

This was truly heavenly on a morning like today despite the cold wind that howled around her as she opened the door to let Ken out. She had to run to the hall to get her warm jacket and find his lead before she went back out onto the deck and looked around, wondering where she could take him for a walk. Then she saw the fence and the gate, behind which she discovered a steep path with steps that looked as if they led down to a tiny beach below. Perfect. The key to that gate was on the keyring she had been given, so she went back in and picked that up from her bedside table where she had left it the night before. Then she clipped the lead onto Ken's collar and made her way to the gate.

They climbed slowly down the steep steps, Ken as careful

as Laura, as if he sensed that she could easily slip on the wet stone steps hewn out of the rock. Buffeted by the wind, she clung to the rope that served as a handrail and was relieved to finally jump down onto the flat sand.

'Wow,' she exclaimed, looking around. 'Ken, what do you think of this, then? Isn't it wonderful?'

Ken seemed to agree and strained at the lead until Laura unclipped it and he was free to run ahead, his nose to the ground, sniffing at the shells and bits of crab, seemingly enjoying the fishy smells.

While the dog disappeared behind some boulders, Laura breathed in the salt-laden air and felt a sudden lightness of spirit, the cold wind ruffling her hair and bringing tears to her eyes. She looked across the beach and suddenly recognised the slope on the other side, which would connect it to the headland to the west and the main beach on the opposite side. No longer covered in wild roses, it was nevertheless very similar to the slope in the painting with the woman sitting on a rock.

Laura walked a few steps ahead and tried to figure out exactly where the woman had been sitting. There was a rock jutting up from the sand a little further ahead, which had a flat surface and would be quite comfortable to sit on. Laura made her way to it and sat down, pulling her knees up just like the girl in the picture. She looked over her shoulder, wondering where the painter had been standing and surmised it had to be just a few metres away, on the flat bit of sand that would be perfect for an easel. The painting was so detailed, which made Laura think he had been standing quite close to his subject. She could nearly see them both: her sitting here looking at him and he just over there... What had been going on between them that day?

The sound of barking in the distance woke Laura up from her daydream. She had completely forgotten about Ken and now it sounded as if he was in trouble. She jumped up from the rock and started to run in the direction of the barking, which now sounded like two dogs instead of one. Another dog must be around. But Ken was old and a little nervous and needed reassurance from time to time. Laura ran faster and when she came to the end of the little beach, she discovered Ken standing on a large boulder and a black and white Jack Russell below him, barking furiously.

'Stop it,' Laura ordered the angry-looking little terrier. 'Stop scaring my dog, you little rascal.'

The small dog turned and barked at Laura in reply.

'You're a feisty little thing, aren't you?' Laura said to the terrier. She was about to put the lead on Ken, to pull him away from the strange dog that might bite him, when she heard footsteps behind her and turned to discover a man running towards them. When he came closer, she saw he was dressed in a dark green jacket over a black tracksuit and had short dark hair and a close-cropped beard.

He came to a stop in front of Laura, and she noticed he was only slightly taller than her five foot eight. 'What are you doing to my dog?' he asked angrily.

'What is he doing to mine?' she retorted, suddenly irritated despite feeling a tiny dart of attraction. 'Look at him, he's terrified.'

'And a big chicken by the looks of it,' the man remarked. 'Stop that racket, Anne-Marie,' he ordered and picked up the terrier. 'You're scaring the old gentleman.'

'That's right,' Laura said, clipping the lead on a shaking Ken and getting him to jump down. 'He's old and nervous and that's not his fault. You could teach your dog some manners, by the looks of it,' she remarked, glaring at him.

'Well, Anne-Marie is a little feisty. She doesn't mean any harm. She just likes to assert herself with new dogs. Just to make sure they know who's boss.' The man peered at Laura. 'You've just arrived? I've never seen you here before.'

'That's right. I came yesterday.' Her anger dissipated as he smiled at her.

'And you're...' He paused. 'Oh, I see now. You must be Laura, the new owner of Josephine's cottage. And that must be Ken.' He held out his hand, the dog tucked under his other arm. 'Hi there. I'm Gino.'

'Laura Keane,' she said and shook his hand. 'Are you the Gino who runs the bakery?'

'That's right. And I do a bit of caretaking for houses that are unoccupied during the winter months. Like your cottage that Josephine asked me to mind.'

'Did you know her well?' Laura asked, her irritation disappearing completely as she met his warm gaze.

'Yeah, I did. Very well. I met her when she bought the cottage. She was supposed to come back and stay here in the summer, but she fell ill and couldn't make it. Pity. She was so looking forward to it. But we were in touch quite often by phone and email. We had some wonderful long conversations, often late at night when we were both awake. She was a lovely woman. So full of life. And her voice was truly outstanding. I have a lot of her records, actually.'

'Really? So you like opera?' Laura began to warm to him as he spoke. He wasn't what she'd normally find attractive, his features being quite rough, with a large nose and a thin mouth. He wore a small gold ring in his left ear, which gave him a slightly bohemian air. His voice was deep and he spoke with a sing-song Kerry accent that she found very beguiling. His eyes were his best feature: grey with thick dark lashes under black brows. They studied her intently while she spoke, which made her feel oddly self-conscious.

'Yes. Love it,' he said, his smile lighting up his face. 'I'm part Italian, so that might explain it.' He paused and smiled. 'So you're the Laura who looked after Josephine all through her illness?'

'Yes, that's me,' Laura said quietly. 'I didn't know she was talking to anyone late at night. But then I only stayed the night with her occasionally.'

'She mentioned you often. She said you were the best thing that happened to her in her old age.'

Laura smiled, feeling a surge of warmth at his words. 'Thank you. That's lovely to hear.'

'I'm sorry for your loss,' he said with sympathy that sounded genuine. 'It must be hard to lose someone you're so close to.'

'Yes. Very hard.' Laura tried to swallow the lump in her throat. She twitched Ken's lead as she felt a smattering of raindrops. 'I'd better get back. It's starting to rain.'

'I know. I have to go and open the shop. Let's walk back together.' Gino put his little dog onto the sand. 'Behave yourself now, Anne-Marie. You've claimed your territory.'

The little terrier let out a short bark, which made Ken back away. But then she was quiet and trotted beside her owner as he started to walk away, Laura and Ken beside them.

'How come you called your dog Anne-Marie?' Laura couldn't help asking as she tried to keep up with Gino's fast pace.

'I named her after a girl in my class when I was fifteen. Had a huge crush on her but she never noticed me. But I never forgot her, so I thought I'd name my dog after her.'

Laura laughed. 'I wonder how she'd feel if she knew?'

'I hope she'd be flattered.'

'I'm sure she would,' Laura said, as they rounded a boulder and continued walking on the flat sand at the water's edge. 'How long have you had her?'

'Five years,' he replied. 'So she's quite a young thing still, which might explain her feisty manner.'

'I'm sure she won't change even when she's older,' Laura suggested.

'I suppose not.' After a moment's silence, Gino continued. 'So how do you like the cottage?'

'It's lovely. Very nicely restored.' Laura jumped away from the waves that threatened to hit her shoes.

'It's really too bijou for my taste,' Gino remarked as they drew near the steps. 'I liked those houses better before they were tarted up. But I'm sure it suits a lady from Dublin. All mod-cons and all that.'

'I'm no lady,' Laura protested. 'But what's wrong with being comfortable?'

'Nothing, but I like battling with the elements,' Gino retorted. He stopped walking and pointed up the slope above the coastguard station. 'See that shack up there?'

Laura followed the direction of his hand and noticed what looked like a log cabin on top of the hill, with a tall chimney sticking out of the roof. 'Yes?'

'That's where I live. Built it myself two years ago when I came here and took over the bakery. I have a bed and a table, a few chairs, a small kitchen, a record player, a lot of books and my little dog to keep me company. And then a view to take my breath away. What more could a man want?'

'I suppose that's enough if you're single,' Laura remarked.

Gino laughed and looked at her. 'Very true. You wouldn't want to bring up a family there. And a woman might not want to live in such a remote spot with no neighbours. Not that I'm interested in all that,' he added with a dismissive shrug. 'But the village is only five minutes away on my quadbike.'

'So you're a bit of a hermit then?' Laura asked.

'I suppose you could say that,' he replied. 'An occasional hermit in a way.' He started walking again.

'Really?' This idea intrigued her. She couldn't imagine living like that, with nobody to talk to except a dog. She was happy the cottage Josephine had bought was in a row with neighbours next door and the village only a few minutes' walk away. But here was a man who seemed to be very self-contained, happy with his life. She judged him to be in his late forties or even a bit older, judging by the lines around his eyes and the sprinkle of grey in his hair and beard.

'I like being on my own, but I also want a bit of craic now and then and some good conversation, which I get in the pub on a Friday night. But...' He stopped walking and looked at her. 'I like people, but nature is my best friend. You know that poem by Byron?'

'Byron?' she asked, intrigued. She wasn't much into poetry, but he obviously was. 'I'm not familiar with his work,' she confessed. 'Which poem do you mean?'

'This one.' He quoted the passage to her, as he turned his face to the sea.

> 'There is a pleasure in the pathless woods.
>> There is a rapture on the lonely shore.
>> There is society where none intrudes by the
>> deep sea, and music in its roar. I love not
>> man the less, but nature more.'

He drew breath and looked at her. 'That's me in a nutshell.'

'Oh,' she said, suddenly overwhelmed. 'That's beautiful. I love that idea. It's not very me, but understand it.'

'I'm glad you do.' He looked at her with curiosity. 'How about you? Are you one of those happily single women who doesn't need her life validated by having a partner?'

'Eh.' Laura stared, stuck for words. 'I'm single, yes. And I don't mind at all. I certainly don't feel I need my life validated by anyone. Quite happy in my own company. I never met the right person for me, I think.'

'Maybe you will now that you've stopped trying?' Gino suggested. 'Life has a habit of throwing stuff at you when you least expect it.'

Laura smiled and shrugged. 'Well, that would be nice. But I stopped believing in miracles a long time ago.'

Gino looked at her with a glint in his eyes. 'I wouldn't say that someone falling for you would be a miracle. There are plenty of eligible bachelors here I could set you up with,' he suggested as he slowed down.

'Thanks, but I think I'll do my own choosing,' she replied, slightly annoyed at the suggestion. 'I'm not sure you'd know my type anyway.'

'I know more than you think. Josephine told me quite a lot about you. She loved you like a daughter.'

Laura felt a wave of emotion welling up. 'I know,' she said in a quiet voice. 'And she was like a mother to me in a way.'

'You needed each other,' Gino remarked. 'And that was a beautiful relationship. She said she felt energised by your zest for life and the way you made her laugh. And how you treated her like a friend instead of some sad old person who didn't have long to live.'

'How could I treat her any other way?' Laura smiled wistfully. 'She was such fun and so incredibly alive, even though she had that stroke.'

'She was as mad as hell that it happened.'

Laura laughed. 'Oh yes. I think that's why she recovered so quickly against all the odds. She said it wasn't acceptable to be so helpless. She fought so hard to regain her strength. She didn't succeed in getting back to her old self, but she was quite mobile and totally alert in her mind.'

'She certainly was.' Gino stopped walking as they had reached the steps that led to Starlight Cottages. 'After you,' he said politely. 'And you have a key to the gate.'

'You don't?' Laura thought for a moment. 'Strange that there is a locked gate at all. I mean is it really legal to block access to the coastline like this?'

'Probably not.' Gino picked his dog up. 'It was put there to prevent accidents involving small children. But the lock is soon going to be replaced by a latch high up on the gate so anyone under five foot can't reach it. Much better, I think.'

'Oh yes,' Laura agreed. She started to walk up the steep steps, holding on to the rope as Ken, suddenly youthful, bounded ahead, while Anne-Marie barked and tried to wriggle out of Gino's grip. They finally reached the top as the rain started to fall in earnest.

Gino looked up at the sky and laughed. 'There's a storm on the way. Won't last long, one of those short sharp affairs. But I'll have to eat my words about bravely battling the elements.'

'And you have a long climb up to your cabin,' Laura remarked. 'You will get very wet.'

'Not at all,' Gino countered. 'I'm on my way to the shop. I'll be opening in about half an hour. My team has been baking since the early hours and now it's up to me to sell the result of their toil.'

'Oh, of course.' Laura laughed. 'I forgot you're the village baker. And I also forgot to thank you for the lovely bread you left. I had some of the sliced bread last night and I saved the rolls for my breakfast, which I'm looking forward to.'

'I hope you enjoy them. Bye for now, Laura. I'm sure I'll see you soon. I'll run now, if you don't mind. And you'd better go inside and dry off.'

'I will. Bye, Gino, nice to meet you.'

Laura quickly walked up the steps to her terrace as Gino disappeared around the houses at speed, Anne-Marie running behind him. She opened the door to let Ken in, but shrank back as he shook himself, sending a spray of water everywhere. 'Oh please, Ken, couldn't you have done that before we got in?' She brushed off the drops of water and took off her jacket. 'Interesting man,' she said, as if to herself, thinking about her encounter and the ensuing conversation. So, Josephine and this

Gino had been friends? Strange that she had never mentioned him.

That wasn't the only thing that intrigued her about him. He had revealed a lot about himself, like the way he lived. It all seemed quite romantic and eccentric.

But who was he really? What was his story? And what had he and Josephine found to talk about late at night during the years before she died? Laura suspected there was a lot more to Gino than he had told her. She had the distinct feeling there were a lot of layers to peel off before you got to the real person underneath. A mystery to discover, maybe?

6

As Laura made her breakfast and carried it on a tray to the seat in front of the big window overlooking the ocean, her thoughts drifted to Josephine and that very first day they had met.

Josephine had just come home from hospital when Laura arrived at the big Victorian house in Howth, a seaside suburb on Dublin's north side. She was let in by the housekeeper and ushered into a small sitting room, where she found the old lady at the piano trying to pick out a tune. A black Labrador lay on the rug in front of the fireplace; he lifted his head as Laura entered. Then he went back to sleep again.

'That's Ken,' Josephine said. 'My best friend. We're growing old together.' Her thick white hair was gathered in a ponytail and her big brown eyes looked at Laura appraisingly. 'But I should say hello,' she continued and held out her hand that was shaking slightly. 'I'm Josephine Clarke. Who are you? Did you say your name?'

'No, I didn't.' Laura walked further into the room and shook the old lady's hand. 'Hello, Miss Clarke. I'm Laura Keane and I've come to help you while you recover.'

'Oh yes, of course.' Josephine smiled and nodded. 'I

remember now. My son Michael hired you. I'm glad you're here. You seem to be the positive kind, judging by the letter of introduction you wrote to me. Not someone who thinks she's here to care for the elderly in the final stage of their life.'

'Not at all,' Laura replied. 'You had a stroke, but that's not the end of anything. With a little work, you'll be as good as new in no time. But it's all up to you.'

'I know it is.' Josephine turned back to the piano. 'I'm trying to remember how to play this thing. But my fingers don't seem to want to obey me.'

'I'm sure it'll come back to you in time,' Laura assured her. 'Maybe you need to exercise your hands first to get them to work better? You're just out of hospital, so I think it would be best to start slowly and build up your strength and connectivity.'

'Connectivity.' Josephine looked thoughtful. 'Yes, I suppose you're right.' She patted the seat of the piano stool she was sitting on. 'But come and sit beside me. I want to know all about you.'

Laura joined Josephine on the piano stool. Up close, she noticed the effects of the stroke in the left side of the older woman's body. Her face was slightly lopsided as well, but her speech wasn't slurred and she seemed in quite good spirits. There was a mischievous sparkle in her beautiful brown eyes. Her loose silk caftan smelled faintly of some exotic perfume and her soft skin was only slightly wrinkled despite her age. In all she was incredibly attractive, and Laura felt emotional as she realised how brave Josephine was despite being old and frail and obviously very lonely. She resisted the temptation to give this feisty woman a hug.

'So, tell me,' Josephine urged. 'I know your name but nothing else. Are you married?'

'No.' Laura met the probing gaze. 'And I have no children. I'm forty-nine years old and I trained as a nurse at St Vincent's hospital. I love looking after older people, actually, which many people find very odd.'

'Why?' Josephine asked. 'I mean why do you love looking after us oldies? Boring and tedious, I would have thought.'

'Not at all,' Laura protested. 'I find people who have lived a long time really interesting. They are so wise and have so much to share about their experiences. Of course, some can be difficult and grumpy but who can blame them when ageing can cause so much physical discomfort?'

'"Old age sure ain't for sissies," Bette Davis, God rest her, used to say. And that's a huge understatement,' Josephine declared. 'Bette Davis was an old Hollywood film star,' she added.

'I know,' Laura said. 'I love watching old movies. She's one of my favourites. So bold and sassy.'

Josephine looked surprised. 'You really are an old soul.'

Laura laughed. 'I suppose. But I never think of age, mine or anyone else's. People are people and it's the person within that counts, I've always felt.'

'So true.' Josephine looked at the keyboard of the piano and sighed before she closed the lid. 'I suppose I should give up on the music for now. Boring, but there you are. I need to build up my strength slowly, isn't that what you said?'

'That's right.'

'I'm the impatient type, you'll find. I want things to happen yesterday.' Josephine let out a sudden laugh that sounded like little bells. 'Edward used to say I was like a racehorse charging out of the starting gate.' She looked at Laura. 'He was the love of my life, you know. Not my husband. My marriage didn't last very long. We just weren't compatible. And he wanted me to stop singing and become a housewife. Imagine that!'

Laura laughed and shook her head. 'I can't.'

'Of course not. Ridiculous notion. That's what we broke up over. And then I met Edward, who was my manager for a long time, and then we fell in love. But nobody knew. We were lovers until his death thirty years ago, just before I retired from singing. Then everything became very dull.' She sighed and shrugged. 'But that's life. And I have such beautiful memories to make me smile.'

'That's lovely.'

Laura felt suddenly sorry for Josephine, for whom music must mean so much. She had been a famous opera singer in her day and had kept singing until well into her sixties. Then she had disappeared from view and led a quiet life, teaching music and singing to young hopefuls. Then, recently, she had a stroke and ended up in hospital for over a month. But here she was, looking as if she was ready to start the long road to recovery, even though at ninety-four she must be feeling her age. The defiant look in Josephine's eyes was inspirational. She wasn't going to give up. She wanted to go on living and Laura vowed to do her very best to make sure it happened.

'Let's look at your exercise programme,' she suggested. 'I could go through that with you.'

Josephine sat up. 'You mean you'll do them with me? All those little knee bends and standing on tiptoe and all the rest? I find them a bit of a chore to be honest.'

'What if we do them to music?' Laura suggested. 'Like a ballet exercise?'

Josephine nodded, looking a lot brighter. 'What a good idea. But I need to change into leggings and a T-shirt. Could you help me?'

'That's why I'm here,' Laura said.

Josephine held out her hand. 'Help me up. I'm not very steady on my feet yet.'

Laura did as she was asked and assisted Josephine into her bedroom, which was conveniently on the ground floor, and helped her into a pair of loose-fitting jersey trousers and a long-sleeved T-shirt. Then Josephine led the way to the study, where there was a CD player on one of the shelves in a floor-to-ceiling mahogany bookcase. Together they picked out a piano concerto by Tchaikovsky, even though Josephine protested that she was no swan. Nor was she very mobile, but the music seemed to help her get past the pain and stiffness. Laura joined in the exercises and they both started to laugh as they caught sight of themselves in the gilt-framed mirror on the opposite wall.

'Aren't we a pair of klutzes,' Josephine remarked, wiping her brow. 'But you're a lot more graceful than me, of course, which wouldn't be hard.'

'You're doing really well,' Laura argued, helping Josephine to the couch by the window that overlooked the garden. 'But I think we've done enough for today.'

'Yes, but I will do more tomorrow,' Josephine declared. 'You see, I must get strong enough to realise my dream.'

'What dream is that?' Laura asked, startled by the passion in Josephine's eyes.

'You might think it would be impossible for an old woman like me to still have dreams,' Josephine said, sounding impatient. 'But I still do. Before the stroke, I bought a little house in a most enchanting place, a place to grow old among lovely caring people. So that is my dream. To get well enough to move out of this old mausoleum to a little cottage by the sea. Will you help me?'

'I'll do everything I can,' Laura promised.

And she had. During the following two years Laura cared for the old lady, who became very dear to her. Together they worked hard to get Josephine strong enough to realise her dream. But despite all her efforts and Josephine's own hard work, they never managed to get her back to what she had been, or even close to being well enough to move house. Even though they didn't quite succeed, they had wonderful times together with a lot of laughter and delightful chats late into the evenings, Laura listening with rapt attention to Josephine's stories of her long life in the limelight. She often mentioned her dream but became increasingly aware that it might never be realised, even though Laura kept up the pretence that Josephine would one day go and live in that little cottage she had bought just before she became ill.

Oh how amazing those two years were, Laura thought as the memories tumbled through her mind. The laughter and fun and mischief, dressing up in old stage outfits, putting on make-up, singing and dancing as Josephine grew a little stronger, looking at old photographs and listening to recordings of Josephine belting out arias in her wonderful voice. Laura had loved coming to that old house every day not knowing what would happen next, Josephine being wonderful company when she was in the mood to have fun. And her life had been fantastic, of course, travelling to all the capital cities of Europe to sing in those famous opera houses.

Although Josephine often talked about the cottage in that lovely village in Kerry, she never mentioned the painting. Nor had she ever said anything about her friendship with a man called Gino or their late-night telephone conversations. *How strange,* Laura thought as she looked out over the glimmering water of the bay. *Josephine seems to have had a lot of secrets she never shared with anyone.* She sipped her tea and ate the last of the bread Gino had left, and stared, lost in thought, out the window.

Then her eyes focussed on the beautiful vista outside, the light shifting and changing across the sea as the sun peeked through the clouds floating across the sky. Laura felt a surge of pure joy and sent a silent thank you to Josephine. *You knew I'd be happy here,* she thought.

Laura spent the rest of the morning unpacking and exploring the house. She discovered how nice the bedrooms upstairs were and briefly contemplated moving up there. But then Ken would feel lonely, as she knew he would like to sleep by the fire in the living room. In any case, the bed with the amazing shell-shaped headboard was very comfortable and she could hear the pounding of the waves better from there. Maureen and Rachel would love to sleep upstairs when they came for visits, in any case.

Laura made her bed and put her clothes away in the wardrobe, hung her towels in the ensuite bathroom and put her books into the bookcase in the living room. Her photographs in all kinds of different frames looked good on the small chest of drawers by the window in the living room. She looked at each one as she put them down: the cute selfie of herself and Josephine; the photos of her and Maureen as children; the one of her mother and stepfather, who lived in Florida; and then a cute picture of Rachel and her brother Mark sitting in a sandbox in their garden when they were toddlers. Memories of all the people she loved most in the world. Putting them up made her feel at home.

Then Laura looked at the wrapped-up painting still leaning against the wall. She didn't feel like hanging it here, in the living room, where potential visitors could see it. Josephine's post-humous warning through her solicitor still resonated through Laura's mind. 'Don't show the painting to *anyone*,' he had said. 'It's worth a lot of money and you have to give it to the rightful owner...' With those words in mind, Laura unwrapped the painting, dragged it into her bedroom and propped it against the inner wall. Then she sat on her bed and studied it for a long time.

Every time Laura looked at the picture she saw something different. This time, she noticed the little smile hovering on the woman's lips, and the damp patches on the hem of her white dress and that she was barefoot. Had she been walking at the water's edge and got her dress wet? Was that smile mischievous

48 SUSANNE O'LEARY

or maybe flirtatious, despite the faraway look in those eyes? Laura wondered what year it had been painted. The dress was timeless but, on closer inspection, she noticed that the waist was tight and the skirt flared. Could be from the 1950s perhaps?

So many questions, but also a painting that was wonderful to look at as there was so much depth and colour that felt so real. Laura could nearly hear the seagulls and taste the salt in the air. And then there was a sensuality to the beautiful woman who seemed both happy and sad at the same time. As her gaze drifted over the bottom half of the painting, Laura noticed faint letters on the left side. The artist's signature? She got up, crouched in front of the painting and studied the letters up close.

She could see a letter that might be either an *L* or an *I* and a small *d* and a *P* – or *B*? Were they the initials of the painter? Laura couldn't think of any painter with those initials. *I* or *L* – something and then possibly one of those Norman names that had de as a prefix... *de Paor*, maybe? *I de Paor*? Ian? Laura shook her head. No, that didn't sound familiar. Josephine had said in her last letter that the cottage and the painting were connected. But how? And if it was valuable, wouldn't the name be of some famous artist? The questions were like a tease, a puzzle to be solved that would probably take a long time.

But time was not a problem to Laura. *I can stay here as long as I like*, she thought. *Unless Josephine's son succeeds in contesting the will...*

7

Laura didn't venture into the village until the late afternoon. She had brought enough food for lunch, so was happy to stay indoors while the rain beat against the windows and the wind howled in the chimney. She sat by the window of the sunroom eating a sandwich and looking down at the waves crashing against the rocks, a lone seagull sailing on the upstream of the wind, as if it was enjoying itself. Ken stood by her side whimpering and shivering, looking at Laura with his sad doggy eyes.

Laura patted his head. 'This is what the wild west is like in the winter. You'd better get used to it or you'll be a nervous wreck. This is no place for a city slicker like you. Or me,' she added, wondering if that wind was increasing and if the roof would hold. But then the sound eased, the rain stopped and she could see a blue patch in the sky. The storm had abated and it seemed safe to go out. Laura finished her sandwich and put on her rain jacket and sturdy walking shoes, grabbing a shopping bag as she went through the kitchen. Ken had settled back on the rug by the fireplace and gone to sleep, so she left him there and opened the front door, excited to explore the village and meet its inhabitants at last.

There was still a stiff breeze and a few raindrops hit Laura's face as she walked up the street. She was again enchanted with the quaint old cottages and larger houses, the beautifully painted shop signs and the old-fashioned lamp posts. She met the postman as he went in and out of front gardens, pushing post through letterboxes. He smiled at her as she passed him and said, 'A grand day, thank God.' That made Laura smile as it sounded as if he was glad to be alive, even if the weather was a bit wild and wet.

The light was on in the little grocery shop and bells tinkled as Laura opened the door. She went inside and felt instantly that she had been transported back in time as she breathed in the smell of apples and dried herbs, as she felt the warmth from a little woodburning stove in the far corner. Three small round tables stood around the stove and she saw two women having coffee and chatting animatedly. They looked at her and smiled and nodded.

Laura smiled back, grabbed a basket and started to fill it with items she would need for the next few days. When she had everything she wanted, she went to the checkout counter where a dark-haired young woman was sitting reading a book.

She looked up when Laura put her basket on the counter. 'Oh, you gave me a fright! It's such a quiet day, I thought I'd catch up on my reading.' She peered at Laura. 'You must be the woman who's going to live in Miss Clarke's cottage. We have been waiting for you.'

'You have?' Laura said, startled. 'How did you know I was coming?'

'Gino told us.' The girl started to check Laura's shopping through the till. 'My name is Pauline and I run this shop with the owner, Sorcha.'

Laure held out her hand. 'I'm Laura. Nice to meet you, Pauline.'

Pauline grabbed Laura's hand in a tight grip. 'Hi, Laura.

Welcome to Sandy Cove. Sorry about the weather. It got a bit wild there earlier. But they say there will be an improvement later this week.'

'Sure it's a grand day,' Laura replied as she put her shopping into her bag. 'That's what the postman said anyway.'

Pauline rolled her eyes. 'He always does even if it's bucketing down. That's Paddy O'Shea for you. Thinks it's a sin to complain about anything. Drives me nuts.'

'I know what you mean. Jolly people like that can be a pain.' Laura took her wallet from her bag. 'How much do I owe you?'

'That'll be twenty-seven euros.'

Laura paid, thanked Pauline and was about to walk out of the shop when one of the women at the coffee corner stood up and waved. 'Hello,' she called. 'Would you like to join us? We'd like to treat you to a cup of coffee.'

Laura approached the coffee corner. 'That's very kind. I'd love a coffee, actually.'

'Brilliant.' The woman, who had blonde hair and small round dark eyes in a chubby face, pulled out a chair. 'Please. Sit down and I'll get you a— what would you like?'

'An Americano, please.' Laura put her bag of shopping on the floor and sat down. 'I really need a shot of caffeine right now, actually.'

'And we need someone new and fresh to chat to,' said the other woman, who had dark hair with grey streaks and sparkly green eyes. 'I'm Becky, by the way, and that's Elaine getting you a coffee at the machine.'

Elaine turned around. 'Sorry. Should have introduced myself. Hi, Laura. So nice to meet you.'

Laura smiled. 'Lovely to meet you too.' She noticed that Becky was a very attractive woman with lovely eyes in a very pretty face. Her friend Elaine was quite plain in comparison but had a nice smile and a warm expression in her eyes. 'I just arrived here, as you probably know.'

Becky nodded. 'Oh yes, we know everything that goes on here, which is not much at the moment as it's the middle of winter. It's more fun in the summer when all the people who have holiday homes are around. The place is hopping then. But right now we need new blood, so we're delighted to meet you.'

Elaine placed a brimming paper mug of coffee in front of Laura. 'It's very hot, so be careful.'

'Do you want a cookie?' Becky asked, pushing a plate of biscuits across the table. 'Gino's bakery does all the baked goods here. You should try the lemon and almond ones. Really yummy.'

Laura laughed and picked a cookie from the plate. 'Okay, I'll try one of them.'

'He gets a lot of his recipes from his granny in Sicily,' Elaine said.

Laura took a bite. 'Delicious,' she declared while she munched.

'They really are.' Elaine looked at Laura for a moment. 'So, you knew Josephine Clarke? That's what Gino said, anyway.'

Laura nodded. 'Yes, I did. I looked after her for the past two years. Until she died,' she ended, a feeling of immense sadness welling up in her chest.

Becky looked at Laura with sympathy in her lovely eyes. 'You must miss her. We were so sad to hear she had passed away. We'll never forget her, will we, Elaine?'

Elaine sighed. 'No, we won't. She only spent about two weeks here, but she managed to charm everyone in the village. She wanted to move here and spend the last years of her life in that cottage. We were so excited that she'd be one of us. But then...'

'Then she had a stroke,' Laura filled in. 'And I was her carer from the day she came home from hospital. She worked so hard to get her strength back so she could move here. But she never managed to get back to what she was despite all her hard work. That broke my heart, to be honest.'

'She must have wanted you to do what she never could,' Becky suggested. 'As if she wanted you to pick up her mantle.' Laura smiled. People in this town were very observant, she thought.

Elaine smirked. 'Becky is a writer, so she gets a little carried away sometimes.'

Becky sighed. 'Yes, I suppose I do. I write children's stories and poetry, so they say I live in fantasy-land in some way. Maybe it's true. I do love a good fairy-tale.'

'Who doesn't?' Elaine checked her watch and gave a little squeal. 'Holy mother, it's nearly five o'clock! I must get home and get cooking. The kids will be roaring for their dinner. I have four of them,' she said. 'All in secondary school in Cahersiveen and they'll have just got off the school bus. What was I thinking, sitting here blathering?' She got up and picked up her bag from the back of the chair. 'So lovely to meet you, Laura. We'll have to catch up soon.' She tapped Becky on the shoulder. 'See ya, Becks.' Then she walked swiftly out of the shop, the bells on the door tinkling as she banged it shut.

'Oh, wow,' Becky said with a laugh. 'That's typical of Elaine. Forgetting about the kids while she's chatting and then rushing around like a whirlwind.'

Laura finished her coffee. 'She seems like a lot of fun. I suppose I'd better go too. The shop must be closing soon.'

'They close at seven,' Becky said, sitting back. 'And it's only five o'clock now. Relax and talk to me for a bit. I'm single and have no children, just a cat and an old mother, who is quite active at seventy-six. She'll be getting dinner ready later, so I'm a real lady of leisure, except for the occasional scribbling. How about you?'

'I'm on a kind of break from nursing. I've been working with a care agency for about five years. I specialise in rehab for stroke victims.'

'So that's how you came to look after Josephine?'

Laura nodded. 'Yes. I should have left when she got a bit better, but she asked me to stay as she felt so comfortable with me.'

'She must have been so disappointed that her recovery was slow going,' Becky said with sympathy in her voice.

'Yes, but she didn't let that get her down.' Laura smiled at the memories. 'We had a lot of fun most of the time. We danced and sang and she tried her best to play the piano and she often found an occasion to celebrate with a glass of champagne. And I took her to a spa hotel to swim and have a massage and have her hair done. She was so full of life all the time despite her disability. She said you have to live in the moment and not fret about the rest.'

Becky nodded. 'She was right. My mam is like that.' Becky paused. 'Would you like to come over to my house and meet her?'

'You mean right now?' Laura asked, startled.

'Yes.' Becky laughed and got up. 'Let's live in the moment, isn't that what you said? Mam always makes enough food for an army, so you're very welcome to join us for dinner.'

'Thanks, but... Oh, eh...' Laura hesitated. 'I left Ken on his own. He'll be lonely if I leave him there all night.'

'Who's Ken?' Laura asked, looking confused. 'I thought you said you were single.'

Laura let out a giggle. 'Ken is Josephine's old dog. He was left to me in her will.'

'Oh.' Becky joined in the laughter. 'The cheeky thing. I mean Josephine, not the old dog. But hey, why don't you go and get him and bring him over to us? My mam loves dogs. And the cat does too, strangely enough. I have a feeling she thinks she *is* a dog, to be honest.'

'Okay.' Laura gathered up her shopping. 'I'll go and get him, so. Where is your house?'

'It's at the top of the street near the library. A white two-storey house with a green door. I'll leave the door open so you can just go inside.'

'Great. See you in a minute then.' Laura walked ahead of Becky out the door, waving at Pauline, who was preparing to close the shop.

As Laura made her way to the cottage, she thought of Elaine and Becky and how welcoming they had been, inviting her to have coffee with them, then being so friendly and accepting of her, a total stranger who had only just arrived. The three of them had clicked instantly, even though Laura felt more of an affinity with Becky, who looked to be around the same age as her. Someone who could be a true friend.

Ken greeted Laura enthusiastically when she came in. She quickly put away her groceries and clipped the lead on his collar. 'We're going out to dinner,' she told him. He wagged his tail and trotted to the door, pressing his nose against it. He'd been cooped up here a long time and was dying to get outside. He bounded out the door when Laura opened it and nearly pulled her down. They walked up the street as darkness fell and they reached Becky's house in a matter of minutes.

The green door was wide open and the light from the hall spilled into the front garden with its gravel path across the lawn. As she walked inside, Laura could hear music and a choir singing 'That's Amore' along with Dean Martin, which she assumed was from a radio. She discovered it was not sung by a choir but two people dancing around the cosy living room, their arms around each other.

Laura stopped and stared at them, then felt a spark of delight as she recognised the man with his arms around an older woman with short-cropped white hair.

8

They stopped dancing as they noticed Laura.

'Hello there,' Gino said, waving a wooden spoon in the air. 'We meet again.'

'Hi, Gino,' Laura said, her cheeks hot as he smiled broadly at her.

The woman turned around and smiled at Laura. 'Oh goodness, you're here already.' She pulled away from Gino and held out her hand. 'You must be Laura. I'm Fidelma, Becky's mother. Welcome to this madhouse. Gino, turn down the music, please.'

'Okay,' Gino said, as he crossed the room. The radio was perched on a chest of drawers by a green velvet sofa, beside which logs blazed in the fireplace. He beamed a smile at Laura as he turned off the radio. 'Sorry about that. We just couldn't help getting carried away by old Dino singing that song.'

'But we should get back into the kitchen,' Fidelma said. 'That lasagne won't cook itself.'

'I'll finish it,' Gino promised, walking to an open door at the far side of the room. 'You and Laura should get to know each other. And I'll be back out with a glass of wine for you both,' he added before he disappeared.

'Darling boy,' Fidelma said and sat down on the sofa. 'Come here, Laura, and sit beside me. Becky is having a bath and Gino is cooking so we can have a little chat before dinner. He comes here to cook for us sometimes. We're not closely related but family all the same.'

'Oh, eh...' Laura sat down beside Fidelma while Ken sank down on the floor at their feet, only to jump up again as Anne-Marie trotted into the room, barking, closely followed by a black cat. Ken backed away and then wagged his tail as Anne-Marie stopped, sniffed at his nose and then seemed to be happy to see him. The cat sat down and started to clean its face, looking at the dogs with a haughty stare.

'That's Sheba,' Fidelma explained, pointing at the cat. 'Very sure of her own superiority. But she likes dogs, so there's no need to worry,' she said to Ken, who was eyeing the cat with suspicion.

'That's Ken,' Laura said. 'A big chicken, really.'

'Ah, he's old,' Fidelma soothed, reaching down to pat the old dog. 'We all get a little anxious with age, don't we, Ken?'

Laura studied the pleasant woman, who looked neither old nor anxious. Laura found it hard to believe she was seventy-six. She looked both fit and feisty and not at all elderly in any way. Then Laura looked around the warmly lit living room. 'This is such a nice room. I love a house with a lot of books,' she said, pointing at the floor-to-ceiling bookcase crammed with books of all shapes and sizes. There were also a number of framed photos sitting on some of the shelves. 'And I love all these old photos,' she added, getting up. 'Do you mind if I look at them?'

'Not at all,' Fidelma replied. 'Those are mostly groups from family occasions that I don't even remember. Some of them are from my parents' time here before I was born. It's a bit of a mishmash, really.'

Laura picked up a group photo of what looked like a family occasion. There were around twenty people gathered in front of a church and everyone looked happy and smiley. The men wore suits and the women wore wool coats and hats, some with a feather sticking up. *Sandy Cove harvest festival 1952* it said in faint writing at the bottom of the photo. 'This one is nice,' Laura remarked. 'Are you in it?'

Fidelma joined Laura at the bookcase and studied the photo. 'No. I would have been six at the time.' She pointed at a couple standing at the front. 'That's my parents. My mother was so proud of her new coat. And look at my father in a suit and tie. He was a fisherman so that would be his Sunday best.'

'Ah, that's lovely.' Laura put the photo back and picked up another one. It pictured a group of young women in long flowing dresses in front of what looked like a large hotel. 'This one looks like a wedding or something. Or a ball maybe?'

Fidelma smiled as she looked at the photo. 'A spring ball in Killarney. At the Great Southern. I'm the one on the far left in a chiffon dress and goosebumps on the arms. It was a very chilly evening and we nearly froze to death posing for that photographer. I think it must have been in 1964. I was eighteen and it was my first ball.'

Laura looked at the girl in the picture and could immediately recognise Fidelma's large round eyes in a square face and her dimply smile. 'You haven't changed a bit since then.'

'Ah go on,' Fidelma protested. 'I was just a slip of a girl. Now I'm a lot older but not much wiser. It was a fun night though. I think I danced until my feet bled. We did all sorts of dances, the waltz, the rhumba, the cha-cha, the jive and we even had a go at that new-fangled twist. I still have the dress. Green chiffon. Becky wore it for her debs.'

'It's very pretty.' Laura was about to put the photo back on the shelf, when she noticed a face in the back row. A face she knew she had seen recently in another setting. Was it... could it be? Her heart beat faster as she stared at the young woman with dark hair put up in a chignon, the contemplative gaze from the beautiful eyes and the upturned nose and heart-shaped face. 'Who's this?' she asked, pointing at the young woman.

Fidelma looked at the woman in the photo. 'That girl? She looks familiar but it was so long ago. I have a vague memory of her coming here after the ball. But I can't remember where she stayed and how long or what she did here.' Fidelma thought for a moment and then shook her head. 'No, it won't come to me.'

'What won't come, Mam?' Becky asked as she entered the room, dressed in black trousers and a green sweater, her hair still damp from the bath.

'That girl in the photo,' Fidelma replied. 'I recognise her, but I can't remember her name or what she did here.'

Becky took the photo from Laura. 'Who are you talking about?'

Laura pointed at the girl in the back row. 'Her. I was wondering who she was, but your mother can't remember.' She waited with bated breath for some kind of reply. She wasn't sure, but when she had caught sight of that face in the photo, her thoughts immediately sprang to the woman in the painting. The same eyes, heart-shaped face and black hair...

Becky studied the photo for a moment. 'Well, that really was a long time ago. Way before I was born. You were so pretty, Mam. I always thought so. And I loved wearing your dress at my debs. But that girl in the back row... I think I've seen her in some other photo somewhere. Maybe at the library? They have a lot of photos from the old days in their archive. Hmm...' Becky kept staring at the woman in the photo. And then her face brightened. 'I know! It just came to me. She was a teacher at the primary school sometime in the Sixties. I remember seeing her in one of the class photos from the late Sixties when we did a brochure for the one hundredth anniversary of the school. She was only in that one photo but her face caught my interest because she was so beautiful. She must have been teaching here for a while and then gone on somewhere else because she was only in that one photo. What do you think, Mam?'

Fidelma looked thoughtful. 'You could be right. Must have been when I was away in England working, so I wouldn't have known her.'

'But she was at that ball,' Laura remarked, now sure that the woman in the photo was the one in the painting. 'Maybe she went to school with you?'

Fidelma shook her head. 'No, because there were girls from several schools at that event. We had all just graduated. If she had been in my class I would remember her. She could have been from another village.' She looked curiously at Laura. 'But why do you ask? Have you seen her in another photo somewhere else?'

'No,' Laura replied, trying her best to think of an explanation. 'I just thought she was unusual. Quite striking really.'

'That's true,' Becky said as she replaced the photo. 'Stunning girl. She looks somehow exotic. I'll go to the library soon and see if I can find out more. Do you want to come, Laura?'

'I'd love to,' Laura replied, feeling excited at the prospect of finding out more about the mystery woman she was sure was the one in the painting.

'But why that woman?' Fidelma asked. 'I mean you looked quite startled when you looked at the photo. Does she remind you of someone?'

'Eh, in a way,' Laura said, trying to think of a plausible explanation. 'She is the spit of someone I saw in a picture recently. But that could be a coincidence, of course.'

'Probably,' Becky remarked. 'Maybe some kind of doppelganger? We must find out who she is and then do some research.'

Gino stuck his head in the door. 'Hey, girls. Dinner's ready. Get it before the dogs do.'

Becky laughed. 'I love the way you announce dinner. But that smells so delicious that I can't wait to taste it.'

'It's just lasagne,' Gino said. 'But I hope you'll like it.'

'We'll love it,' Fidelma said and walked to the door. 'Come on, girls, let's eat.'

Gino held the door open as they walked through, and when Laura passed him their eyes met for an instant. She felt a sudden dart, like an electric shock, as she looked into those grey eyes. But she couldn't quite decipher what that look meant or if it was negative or positive. She had got the impression earlier that he loved living alone, but here he was socialising and looking as if he enjoyed it. Was it just Laura he wanted to avoid? Maybe he thought that she didn't deserve the cottage and that Josephine had been foolish to give it to her.

With all those thoughts whirling around in her head, she walked into the large bright country kitchen and joined Fidelma and Becky at the table, while Gino went to the stove and started to load plates with lasagne and vegetables. He handed the plates around while Becky poured wine and passed around salad in a big bowl.

The lasagne was delicious, but Laura hardly tasted it as she stole glances in Gino's direction. But he seemed oblivious to her eyes on him, chatting and laughing and cracking jokes. Had she imagined that dart of attraction that had felt like a bolt of lightning? But no, she knew it was real and she still felt tiny aftershocks. But he seemed unaware of her in that way, so this was her own folly and she had to do her best to hide how she felt. It wasn't like her to have this kind of reaction to a man she had just met. She was usually quite cool and aloof around men, especially if they were very good-looking. Handsome men made her nervous as they reminded her of her father, who had left her mother when Laura was very young. She was hard to impress and her radar was very sensitive. But Gino appeared completely at ease around women and Laura had felt instantly that he saw everyone as an equal. A man comfortable in his skin, self-contained, happy with his existence, she assumed.

'Gino, your lasagne is the best in the world,' Becky declared, scraping her plate.

'Oh yes,' Laura agreed, swallowing her last bite. 'It's delicious. But how come you're here cooking dinner? Do you do this every night?'

'No,' Gino replied with a laugh. 'Only occasionally. But Fidelma and Becky are kind of family so I sometimes pop in here when I feel the need to cook. Fidelma has a new cooker with a great oven, so I love to use it from time to time. It's especially good for things like lasagne.'

'Kind of family?' Laura asked, remembering what Fidelma had said earlier. 'So you're all related?'

Fidelma nodded. 'That's right. We're all Powers. I was a Power before I was married, you see. Gino's dad was my second cousin.'

'My full name is Gino Patrick Power,' Gino cut in.

'So we're third cousins,' Becky filled in. 'Even though my last name is O'Shea and not Power.'

'And we're all related to Frank Power, the sculptor,' Gino said. 'You know who I mean?'

'Of course,' Laura said. 'I've seen his fabulous sculpture of the Uilleann piper in Killarney. And that gorgeous one of the horses in Dublin. Such a fabulous artist.'

Fidelma nodded. 'Oh yes, he was. He was a distant relative and he wasn't born here, but in Kenmare. But he spent some time here in the Sixties, in one of the Starlight Cottages just for a summer. And then he moved to Dublin where he lived and worked until his death ten years ago.'

'Really?' Laura stared at Fidelma. 'I had no idea he was from Kerry. Did you meet him when he was here?'

Fidelma shook her head. 'No, not then. It was that summer

when I was in England working. But we went to visit his studio in Dublin once. Such a nice man with huge talent.'

'Good-looking too, judging by photos I've seen,' Becky remarked. 'Tall, with fair hair and blazing blue eyes. A real hunk by all accounts.'

'I've seen photos of him in the National Museum,' Laura said. 'And yes, he was really attractive.'

'We're related to the Powers whiskey family, too,' Gino interrupted, obviously not interested in Frank Power's good looks. 'They started the first whiskey distillery in Ireland in 1799.'

'Aren't we the best family?' Fidelma said with a laugh. 'Art and booze.' She raised her glass. 'Power to the Powers!'

'Mam, you're a menace,' Becky exclaimed.

'I'm a Power,' Fidelma retorted. 'It's in my blood to be a menace.'

Becky rolled her eyes and smiled at Laura. 'No wonder I'm a mess with a mother like that.'

Fidelma placed her glass on the table with a bang. 'You're *not* a mess, Becky! You're a wonderful daughter and a talented author. I'm very proud of you.'

'Ah, thank you, Mam,' Becky said. 'You're an amazing mother too, even if you're a bit of a rebel.'

'A bit?' Fidelma said with a laugh. 'I was real trouble when I was younger. Always protesting about something. I once chained myself to the railings of Leinster House in Dublin to protest about fair pay for women in the Sixties. I even got into the papers.'

'I framed that photo and hung it on the wall in my bedroom,' Becky said proudly.

Fidelma laughed. 'Oh yes, what a role model I was. No wonder you never got married and had children.'

Becky sighed. 'I never managed to find a man who'd put up with me. But my brother Jim got married and had a whole bunch of kids so Mam got to be a grandmother after all. I was so glad the pressure was off.' She turned to Laura. 'How about you? Did your mother yearn for grandchildren and chastise you for not producing them?'

'No,' Laura replied. 'My sister got married and had two children so she was happy with that, even if she would have liked more.'

'But you never wanted children?' Fidelma asked.

Laura's face flushed as she felt Gino's eyes on her. 'Oh, I thought about it for a bit, but then I realised I wasn't the motherly type. Never met anyone I wanted to have a family with anyway.'

'And you love your job, I bet,' Fidelma filled in. 'Nursing is all absorbing, I've heard. And the hospital world is so isolating the way you live in a bubble. I had a friend who was a nurse and that's what she told me.'

'I think that has something to do with it,' Laura agreed. 'I love my job. Now I'm taking a break, but I'll get back to it in a while.'

'Around here?' Becky asked. 'I mean, are you going to move here permanently?'

'I haven't decided,' Laura replied after a moment's reflection. 'I prefer to take it one step at a time and see how I feel when I've had a bit of a rest. The past few months have been... difficult.' She stopped suddenly, feeling that familiar dart of sadness and loss, which puzzled her. Josephine had been a patient who had turned into a friend, but not a blood relation. And she had been so old and frail and near the end of her life, so her death had been quite natural. *So why do I feel so sad?* Laura thought as she looked at Fidelma, noticing the empathy in her eyes.

'It's hard to lose a kindred spirit,' Gino said gently, touching Laura's hand across the table. 'It doesn't have to be a close relation or someone you're related to. I can imagine that Josephine would have been a unique and wonderful friend to you. Someone you will always remember. But she wouldn't want you to be sad.'

Surprised and moved by his insightfulness, Laura nodded. 'Thank you,' she said in a near whisper, as the touch of his warm hand made her heart skip a beat. But he was just being kind and she shouldn't read anything else into it, she told herself sternly. 'And you're right,' she said, her voice stronger. 'Josephine wouldn't want me to be sad. If she saw me now, she'd tell me to get a grip, have a drink and try to have fun.'

'And why shouldn't you?' Becky asked. 'It's not a sin to either have a drink or to have fun. In fact...' She paused for a moment. 'I was just about to suggest you come with me to Killarney on Saturday. I'm meeting up with a bunch of friends and we're going clubbing. There are some great hotels there that have dancing at the weekend. How about it? We'll get glammed up and set the town on fire. I've booked a room at Brooke's Hotel. I'm sure they'll have a room for you.'

Laura thought for a moment. Then she laughed. 'That sounds like just the kind of thing Josephine would want me to do. And I never got a chance to celebrate my birthday. Well, I wasn't in the mood, really,' she confessed. 'So yes, I'd love to come with you if I can find someone to mind Ken.'

Becky clapped her hands. 'Brilliant! We'll celebrate in style.' She turned to Gino. 'Do you want to come with us?'

Gino shook his head, smiling. 'I wouldn't want to ruin your girls' night out. In any case, I have to work. I have a big order for a do in Waterville. I cater for events around here,' he explained to Laura. 'This is for a cocktail party at the golf club. Some very posh people are spending the weekend and playing in some kind of tournament.'

'Pity,' Becky said with a sigh. 'A dishy man at our side would have been great for our image.'

Gino laughed. 'You both will be glamorous enough to create a stir all around town. In any case, that's not really my thing.'

Laura silently agreed, thinking that Gino was not the clubbing kind of guy. She had even been surprised to see him here tonight, so obviously at ease in this company. She had thought him to be a complete hermit, shunning any kind of socialising, living alone with his dog in his log cabin up there in the hills. But then they were kind of family and had possibly grown up together. She looked at him as he put foil on top of the lasagne and put it aside, telling Fidelma it would keep in the fridge for a day or two.

'You know what?' he said. 'I'll mind Ken for you. That way Anne-Marie will have company.'

'Are you sure?' Laura asked, surprised by the offer.

'Of course.' He looked at her with great warmth in his grey eyes.

'That's very kind,' Laura mumbled. She realised that this kindness was typical of him and that he was this way with everyone. 'Your lasagne was delicious,' she added to hide her confusion. 'Was there a special, secret ingredient?'

Gino shrugged. 'Not really. Except perhaps I make the tomato sauce from scratch and don't use tinned tomatoes like most people.' He stopped and took off the apron. 'Well, folks, it was fun, but I have to get my dog and leave you now. I'm on the early shift tomorrow, so I'd better get some sleep.'

'Thanks for cooking dinner,' Fidelma said. 'I wasn't really inspired to cook tonight.'

'A pleasure,' Gino said and went to kiss Fidelma on the cheek. 'You know I love to cook on that new cooker. I only have a tiny gas stove in my little mud hut in the hills.'

'And the barbeque where you do the most amazing steaks,' Becky filled in. 'But that's only when the weather allows, of course.'

'Exactly.' Gino took a battered leather jacket from the back of a chair and put it on. 'And the weather certainly did not allow tonight. But the rain has stopped so I can get home on the quadbike, which Anne-Marie adores. I'd offer you a lift, Laura, but I don't think Ken would enjoy the ride.'

'He'd hate it.' Laura laughed, trying to imagine lugging a protesting Labrador onto a quadbike. 'I'm not sure I'd enjoy it either,' she added.

'It's fun,' Becky said. 'But a little scary if you go fast. Gino is a bit of a devil on it, I have to say.'

'You're a big chicken, that's all,' Gino quipped with a mischievous wink. 'I'll see you tomorrow, Laura, when I come to pick Ken up. I'll use the van so he won't have a heart attack. Oh, and give me your phone number so we can connect should there be any problems.'

Laura read out the number and he typed it into his phone, then sent her a brief text so she could put his into her contacts. Then he put his phone away and smiled at them. 'That's it, then. Goodnight, lovely ladies.'

They all said goodnight and Gino walked out, calling Anne-Marie on the way. They could hear her claws on the floor as she ran to follow Gino, and then the door banged shut behind them.

'Like a whirlwind,' Fidelma said with a sigh. 'But what a darling boy he is.'

'He has his little foibles too,' Becky remarked. 'He can be very difficult and moody sometimes. But he's a great friend to me and a son to you, Mam. I think we make up for the family he lost.'

'He lost his family?' Laura asked, sensing a sad story.

'Yes, poor boy.' Fidelma got up and started to tidy away the plates and glasses. 'His parents and his older sister were killed in a car crash when Gino was only four years old. An aunt who lived in Tralee brought him up. She was old and quite strict and not the best person in the world to bring up a small boy. But there was nobody else at the time. He was sent to boarding school when he was twelve and I have a feeling he was a bit of a loner. Didn't fit in with his classmates.'

'And then,' Becky said, 'he went to spend a year or two in Italy with his mother's family, which I think was a very happy period in his life. That's where he got his sense of humour and that zest for life. And a love of cooking and baking, of course, which he turned into a career of sorts.'

'So, a happy ending,' Fidelma said as she loaded the dishwasher. 'Except I think his childhood experiences come back to haunt him from time to time. Those memories are hard to erase.'

'I'm sure they are,' Laura agreed, getting up from her chair. 'I think I'll leave you now. It's been an amazing evening, but I feel very tired and think Ken needs to get out before I put him to bed.'

'Of course,' Fidelma said. 'It was so nice to meet you, Laura. I hope you'll feel free to call in any time. Even when I'm doing the cooking,' she added with a smile.

'I'd love to invite you both for dinner in my cottage soon,' Laura offered. 'I like cooking for friends.'

'That'd be great,' Becky said as she put the remains of the lasagne into the fridge. 'Hang on, I'll see you out.'

'Thanks.' Laura walked across the kitchen to shake Fidelma's hand to say goodbye. 'Thank you so much for this evening. It was lovely and I felt so welcome.'

Fidelma squeezed Laura in a tight hug. 'This is the way we say goodbye around here. Goodnight, Laura. Sweet dreams.'

'Your mother is amazing,' Laura said to Becky as they said goodbye at the door.

'She likes you.' Becky gave Laura a brief hug. 'And so do I. So nice to meet a single woman my age.' She stopped, looking mortified. 'I'm nearly fifty. I assumed you were around that too. Hope you're not insulted.'

Laura laughed and shook her head. 'Not at all. I'm fifty-two, so a little older than you.'

'Phew, what a relief,' Becky remarked. She looked at Laura with a mischievous glint in her eyes. 'We'll paint Killarney red on Saturday. I have a feeling you scrub up well.'

'I'll do my best,' Laura promised.

'Fabulous,' Becky said. 'Bye for now. I'll pick you up around seven.'

'Perfect.'

A little later, Laura walked down the main street with Ken on the lead, her head full of all that had happened that day. Meeting Gino on the beach and then seeing that young woman in the photo, who she was sure was the girl in the painting, had given her a jolt. She didn't quite know how she could explain to Becky why she was so keen to find out the identity of the mystery woman and discover what she had been doing here all those years ago. And even if she did find that out, there was still the mystery of the artist behind the painting. It seemed to Laura that Josephine had given her quite a task – a very difficult puzzle to solve. Laura looked up at the dark sky and the twinkling stars, wondering if she was up there, watching and waiting.

And then, as she was about to open her front door, Laura looked up at the hills shrouded in darkness and saw a pinprick of light up above, where Gino's cabin had to be. More luminous than the stars, that little light burned brightly, and Laura wondered if he was sitting there, feeling lonely – or perhaps cosy and comfortable in his cocoon.

Whatever the answer, she knew she needed to leave him alone. She'd been single by choice for many years and wanted to respect his privacy. Even though he intrigued her more than she cared to admit.

9

Laura spent most of the following Saturday agonising about what she would wear for the night out with Becky. She thought there was nothing very glamorous in her wardrobe but, finally, as she delved into the last suitcase she hadn't yet unpacked, she found a tight-fitting blue silk dress with a V-neck and long sleeves. She had worn it at a wedding and forgotten about it but, as she pulled it out, she remembered wearing it and the compliments she had received. She also remembered the attention of some of the male guests, who had competed to dance with her, which had made her feel quite giddy and a little embarrassed.

The dress was knee-length and made the best of her shapely figure. As she tried it on, she felt again that glow of looking her best. But was it a bit too much? Too revealing, too come-hither, making her look as if she was trying to flaunt herself? *But it makes me look fabulous*, she thought, as she turned this way and that, admiring the shimmer of the silk fabric in front of the full-length mirror in her bedroom. What would Josephine do? *She'd wear it, of course*, Laura answered herself with a laugh. She peeled off the dress and then went into the kitchen to take out the ironing board. The dress only needed a touch with the iron to smooth out the wrinkles from being packed in a plastic bag for so long.

That done, Laura hung the dress on the back of the wardrobe. Then she had a long leisurely bubble bath while Ken snoozed on the mat below the tub, the radio playing soft music on the classical channel. As she lay in the warm lavender-scented water, Laura felt a sense of peace and calm for the first time since Josephine's death. It had been the best thing to come here and take possession of the cottage, despite the threats from Michael Monaghan. She wondered idly if he would stick to his promise of contesting the will and what she could do about it. She had no idea. But she knew one thing: she wanted to stay here for a while to get the comfort she needed after the loss of her dear friend.

She had only been here a few days, but she already felt at home in the cute little house. She had familiarised herself with her surroundings and met a few of the villagers, who greeted her warmly, told her she was welcome and asked that she let them know if she needed help with anything. All this gave her a sense of living in a close-knit community, and even though she was living alone, she wasn't lonely knowing there were helpful, friendly people nearby.

And then she had her old friend Shane next door, which had been an amazing coincidence. His wife, Edwina, had called in to Laura during the week, just to say hello and that she'd be in touch later on when her current project was finished.

'I oversee all kinds of renovations and extensions,' she had explained. 'And sometimes my clients drive me bananas. The stress level is sky high at times, and right now I'm racing to finish an extension over in Glenbeigh. As soon as that's done, I've promised myself to take a break and then I'll be happy to get to know you better. Shane has told me all about you, but I bet there's a lot more for me to discover. And you about me,' she had ended with a smile.

'Well, I know you've done a fantastic job with these houses,' Laura remarked.

'Ah, that was my mother, actually,' Edwina confessed. 'I was ready to give up but then she stepped in and finished it and managed to make the whole row look amazing. She bought the last cottage in the row, but she's only here in the spring and summer. She and her partner are driving through Spain in their campervan right now.'

'Oh? That sounds exciting,' Laura said. 'And what about the cottage next door to me?'

'That is owned by a lovely woman called Vicky and her husband, Peter. They come here from time to time, so you'll probably meet them soon.'

'I'm looking forward to that.'

Edwina nodded. 'Yes, they're great craic. So we'll do a mad dinner and have a good laugh very soon,' she promised.

'Thanks.' Laura looked forward to getting to know Edwina, who seemed very sweet despite her polished exterior. A stylish woman who seemed very much in love with her husband, Laura assumed.

Getting out of the bath, she looked at herself in the mirror, wondering what to do with her hair, which was even more curly in the damp seaside air of Sandy Cove. She would usually scrape it back into a bun, but now she saw how it framed her face in a very youthful way. Why not leave it like that and do smoky eye make-up? It seemed like the best solution, and once she had done just that, Laura was surprised at how great it looked. So she was a little past her sell-by-date, but wasn't fifty the new thirty, or something like that?

She decided it was and quickly dried herself, put on her best underwear and wriggled into the dress that hugged her body in a slightly risqué but very becoming way. The effect was astounding, and Laura nearly gave herself a wolf whistle as she looked in the mirror. She hadn't felt or looked this fabulous for a long time. Now she was looking forward to the evening with both trepidation and excitement. Would it be a fun night or a disaster? What if nobody wanted to dance with her? That had happened far too often in the past, possibly because she sent the wrong signals. But Becky had convinced Laura to go out and enjoy herself and she would do her best to have a good time, if only for Josephine.

Laura's phone pinged, interrupting her thoughts. It was from Gino. Laura smiled as she read the message.

Running a little late. Still have key to your place so will pick Ken up around eight. Have a fun night. Regards, Gino.

Of course. He must have had a key when he was minding the house. She'd ask for it back when she next saw him, but in this case it was handy, as he could pick Ken up when he had finished work.

When the doorbell rang, Laura was ready. She patted Ken on the head and told him to mind the house until Gino came to collect him. She grabbed her coat in the hall and opened the door.

Becky let out a 'wow' as she caught sight of Laura. 'You'll be the talk of Killarney,' she said, looking at Laura with admiration.

'Well, so will you,' Laura countered. Becky looked amazing with her hair sleek and her face made up, her green eyes sparkling.

'Let's get going then. Oh, and don't look too surprised when you see that Mam is in the car all dressed up to the nines. She is meeting friends for dinner in Killarney so she won't be breathing down our necks.'

Laura nodded while she put on her coat. 'Okay.'

'Did you manage to get a room in Brooke's?'

'I did. One of their small doubles,' Laura replied.

'Great.' Becky started to walk to the car.

As she got out of the car, Fidelma looked fabulous, with her white hair in little curls, her eyes outlined with kohl and red lipstick on her generous mouth. She greeted Laura with a hug and then stepped back to get a better look. 'Lovely,' she said approvingly.

'Don't worry,' she added when they were all in the car and on their way up the street. 'I'm not going to go clubbing with you young things. I just didn't want to sit at home with my cat as you were out having fun, so I called a few of my friends and asked them to meet me for dinner. You're only seventy-six once in your life you know,' she added with a wink. 'I might be getting on, but I'm not dead yet.'

'Talk about the merry widow,' Becky quipped. 'But I know dear old Dad wouldn't want you to be sad and lonely.'

'No, he wouldn't,' Fidelma agreed with a sad little sigh. 'He liked to party like there was no tomorrow. And he did right to the end.'

'What happened to him?' Laura asked.

'My darling Sean died suddenly of a heart attack twenty years ago,' Fidelma replied. 'Such a shock for us all, even though I had seen it coming for a while.'

'We were devastated,' Becky filled in. 'But then... well, if you knew my dad, you'd also know that he's still with us in so many ways. He was such a life force.' She stopped and stared ahead into the darkness as she drove down the winding country road. 'It's just like in that poem about not standing by a grave and crying. He's in the wind and the stars and the ocean and all the beautiful things we experience every day.'

'Oh,' Laura said. 'How comforting. And the funny thing is, I'm beginning to think that way about Josephine. I feel her around me ever since I came to Sandy Cove.'

'She loved it here,' Fidelma said. 'So yes, she'd be here in spirit, looking at you from above.'

'And she doesn't want you to be sad,' Becky cut in.

'I know,' Laura whispered. 'And I'm trying.'

They continued in silence until they reached the outskirts of Killarney. The bright lights of the hotels and restaurants spilled into the street, and music could be heard here and there, giving Laura a buzz of excitement for the evening ahead. They were here to have fun and she suddenly felt eager for it all to start. Becky suggested they check into the hotel before they ventured out into town. 'We can walk to the clubs and restaurants from there,' she announced. 'Mam, where are you meeting your friends?'

'At Foley's,' Fidelma replied.

'Great food and not too far,' Becky said approvingly. 'Do you want me to drop you off and then I can check in for us both?'

Fidelma checked her watch. 'Yes, that would be lovely. It's nearly eight o'clock and I think most of my group will be there already. Text me the room number when you've checked in.'

'Okay.' Becky drove slowly up the main street and then pulled up outside a restaurant with a cosy-looking interior. 'Here we are. Have fun, Mam. See you later, but don't worry if it gets a bit late. You know what my friends are like.'

'I do indeed,' Fidelma replied as she got out from the car. 'Have fun, girls, and if you can't be good... well, you know.'

'We'll be careful,' Becky promised, her voice full of laughter. 'Hope you will too, Mam.'

Fidelma waved at Becky. 'I don't have to be. I'm old.'

'That has never stopped you before,' Becky quipped. But Fidelma had disappeared into the restaurant and didn't appear to have heard.

'You two are a gas pair,' Laura said, laughing.

'We do have fun.' Becky turned down a narrow passage and parked in front of a large building with a sign over the door that said 'Brooke's Hotel'. 'Here we are. Let's go and do a quick check-in and then go and join my gang. We're having dinner in a fish restaurant nearby before we go on to the nightclub. It doesn't really get started until around ten, so we have plenty of time. Everything is at walking distance so we don't have to worry about driving. Not that I'm a heavy drinker,' she added. 'But it's nice to be able to have a few glasses of wine without worry.'

Laura agreed. They took their bags, walked into the hotel lobby and got their room keys, Becky and Fidelma sharing a large twin room and Laura in a small double on the same floor. The hotel was busy, and Laura got the impression that a lot of people were here for a night out and to have fun. She put her bag into the room, quickly brushed her hair and touched up her lipstick, then went out again to meet Becky downstairs with butterflies fluttering in her stomach. She hadn't had a night out like this for a long time and felt nervous about meeting new people, wondering what they'd think of her.

Laura needn't have worried. Becky's gang, consisting of three women and four men, were a lively bunch of various ages and they all welcomed Laura into their midst with warm hand-shakes, asking her to tell them about herself, looking as if they were dying to know more about her. Slowly relaxing, Laura began to enjoy the evening that started with dinner at a nice fish restaurant near the hotel. They all sat down at a round table while a waiter poured wine into their glasses. Laura had a bubbly blonde woman called Peggy on her right side, while the chair on her left was empty. 'Adam is being fashionably late again,' Peggy remarked with a twist to her mouth. 'He'll be arriving just in time to make a spectacular entrance. Always so precious, isn't he?'

'Who is Adam?' Laura asked, her curiosity mounting. 'He sounds as if he's a bit full of himself.'

'Ah sure he's just one of those arty-farty types,' Peggy

replied. 'Great fun, very attractive and a real culture-vulture.'
She drank some wine and smiled at Laura. 'I'm pulling your leg.
Adam is a dote, actually. You'll love him. We all do. He runs one
of the art galleries here and he's also an art historian and critic
for *The Irish Times.* I think he's late because he has to close the
gallery after the last visitor, and there was a big buzz there
tonight after the exhibition of the work of a local artist. He'll be
here soon, I'm sure.'

And then, only minutes later as Laura was still talking to
Peggy, someone slid into the seat beside her. She turned her
head and discovered a man smiling at her. He had dark red hair
and blue-green eyes, and wore a red shirt and jeans.

'Hi there,' he said, holding out his hand. 'I'm Adam. Who
are you?'

'My name is Laura,' she said, smiling into the twinkling
eyes. 'I'm a friend of Becky's and I have just arrived in Sandy
Cove.'

'I see,' he said, still holding on to her hand. 'Go on. What do
you do and where did you come from?'

'I'm a nurse.' Laura suddenly felt flustered under his intense
gaze, and wished she could have said she was a brain surgeon or
at least something more exciting than a nurse. 'I used to live in
Dublin, but now I'm here,' she ended lamely.

He let go of her hand. 'You certainly are. And I'm very
happy to meet you, Nurse Laura. Sorry I'm late, but I...'

'Had to close the gallery,' Laura filled in. 'I heard all about
you from Peggy.'

'Did you now?' Adam leaned across Laura and looked at
Peggy. 'What else did you tell your lovely friend?'

'Oh, we just met,' Peggy said. 'But hey, I don't mind being
Laura's friend. Don't worry, Adam, I haven't said anything else
at all. Just that you're an arty-farty culture-vulture. Thought
that might impress.'

Adam laughed heartily. 'Great introduction, I have to say.

I'm sure Laura now thinks I'm some kind of art snob. Which, of course, I am. And a wine snob.' He lifted his glass the waiter had just filled with red wine and swilled it around, sniffed at it before he took a sip. 'Cheeky little red with a hint of liquorice and raspberry,' he said with a wink, his eyes twinkling. 'What do you think, Laura?'

'I'm having a glass of white,' she retorted, breaking into a smile. He was so handsome and charming she couldn't help feeling attracted to him. Those twinkling blue-green eyes with the long dark eyelashes, his wavy dark red hair and the smatter of freckles across his perfect nose were quite irresistible. And his sense of humour was so contagious she felt her spirits rising.

'And what is that like?'

She took a sip from her glass. 'Quite tart with overtones of turpentine. Should go well with oysters.'

Adam nodded, his eyes dancing. 'Oh yeah. I can tell we're kindred spirits when it comes to wine.'

'Oh no,' Laura quipped. 'I don't like spirits at all. Never drink anything stronger than wine.'

Adam waggled his eyebrows. 'But you have a great spirit of the spiritual kind.' He stopped. 'And now we can quit the nonsense, I think, and behave like adults. I'm about to hit the big *five-oh*, you see. So I think it's time to grow up. Not that you'd know this, being years younger, of course.'

'Not at all,' Laura argued. 'I passed that milestone recently,' she said, wondering why on earth she was telling him her age. But she couldn't help being carried away by his charm and lively persona. She felt drawn to his aura, which seemed to glow around him.

Adam's eyes widened in shock. 'What? Are you saying you're older than me? That is not humanly possible. You look at least ten years younger. Honestly. What's the secret?'

'I might ask you the same thing,' she replied, her cheeks hot after the compliment he had paid her. She looked at his smooth, clean-shaven face and marvelled at his youthful looks.

'Maybe it's because we're both single?' he suggested. 'A life free of duties, rows and demands could be the secret.'

'How do you know I'm single?' Laura asked, suddenly annoyed at his assumptions about her.

'Well, no rings on your finger for a start. And then... well, I don't know. You have that carefree air about you. You live alone and you love it. Don't tell me I'm wrong.'

'I'm afraid you are,' Laura replied, trying to keep a straight face. 'I live with a dear old boy called Ken. He's devoted to me and we're very happy together.'

Adam looked taken aback. 'Oh. That's a bit of a blow. I mean, I'm usually very good at reading people. But I suppose one can't be right all the time.'

'Sorry to disappoint you.' She paused and fixed him with her eyes as something suddenly occurred to her. 'Did you say you're an art historian?'

He looked surprised. 'Eh, well... yes. I do have a degree in art history. Why do you ask?'

'Have you ever heard of an artist with the initials P de B?'

'P de B?' He looked mystified. 'As in Patrick de B something?'

'Or Proinsias, maybe? Or Paul or...' Laura stopped.

'Why do you ask?'

'Well,' Laura started. 'I saw a painting recently that intrigued me. It had the initials that looked like P de B at the bottom, but they could be some other similar letters. It was hard to make out. Lovely painting of a girl on a beach. There was something about the woman that caught my interest. She had such a beautiful face, and the whole scene was gorgeous. So I was wondering who the painter was as I had never heard of an artist with those initials.'

'P de... B...' Adam said, looking as if he was thinking hard.

'A Norman name?' Laura suggested.

Adam nodded. 'Could be. Well, de Paor is a Norman name that meant "poverty" and that was often taken by someone who had made a vow of poverty. It was later anglicised to Power. As in Frank Power the sculptor. I believe Becky over there across the table is related to him.'

'Yes, but he didn't paint, did he?' Laura asked.

Adam took a sip of wine. 'No. I think he might just have sketched in preparation for his sculptures. Like drawing the figure before he started the real work, that's all. But he had the wrong initials.' He paused and looked suddenly curious. 'A girl on a beach, you said? What era was this painting from? Did it look like one of the Impressionists?'

Laura tried to conjure up the image in her imagination. She didn't know what era the painting was from, but it seemed more modern than the Impressionist times. In any case, if the woman in the painting was the same person she had spotted in Fidelma's photo, that painting had to be from the early Sixties. So that didn't fit at all. 'It seemed more modern,' she said. 'But then I'm not an expert. I don't know much about art.'

'But you know what you like?' Adam asked with great amusement in his eyes.

'If you want to talk in platitudes.'

Adam laughed. 'Yes, that's a well-known cliché, isn't it? Where did you see this painting? In a museum? Art gallery?'

'In someone's home a while ago,' Laura replied, trying to look bland.

'In Dublin?' he asked, those amazing eyes looking intently at her.

'Eh, yes.' She suddenly felt a little nervous, thinking she might have said too much. Josephine's warning was still fresh in her mind and she didn't want to give away too much, especially to an expert. 'It didn't look valuable,' she added. 'Could have been by an amateur.'

'Maybe the artist was French?' Adam suggested.

'That's possible,' Laura agreed. 'He could have been called Paul de-something.'

'Paul de...' Adam mused. 'Or Pierre? Hmm...'

They were interrupted by a waiter placing plates of food in front of them. 'Steak?' he asked.

'For me,' Adam said. 'And I think that lemon sole is for the lady beside me.'

Laura nodded and the plate was put in front of her. It smelled heavenly of freshly cooked fish, butter and herbs. 'This looks delicious.'

'I'm sure it is.' Adam picked up his knife and fork. 'Bon Appetit.'

Laura took a bite of the lemon sole, which was just as delicious as it looked. Everyone else around the table were now eating and chatting and drinking wine.

Adam seemed to enjoy his steak, but after a few bites, he turned to Laura again. 'So, what else are you interested in, apart from that painting?'

Laura swallowed her mouthful and sipped her wine. 'I love being outdoors, walking and hiking. Swimming in the summer, too. And photography. I love looking at old photographs and, now that I'm in Kerry, I want to take shots of all the beautiful landscapes around here.'

'Really?' He looked suddenly excited. 'I'm actually into that myself as an art form. I love photographing people with interesting faces. Mostly black and white. I'm going to have a photographic exhibition at my gallery soon with work by a number of photographers and also my own work.'

'That sounds really interesting.'

'I'll send you an invitation to the launch if you like.'

'Oh yes, please,' Laura replied. 'My address is Starlight Cottages number two, Sandy Cove.'

Adam smiled. 'What a poetic address. Have you seen the stars there yet?'

'No, it's been cloudy most nights,' Laura replied. 'But I believe the weather is improving next week.'

'So it seems. You'll love the skies on a clear night. The stars look near enough to touch.'

'I can't wait to see that.'

They resumed eating. Eventually Adam turned to the pretty dark-haired woman on his other side while Laura chatted with Peggy, who turned out to be great fun. Laura glanced at Adam from time to time, but he seemed to be listening intently to his neighbour. She wondered if her comments about the painting had made any impression on him and what she would say if he asked any more questions about it. But the look in his eyes while they spoke had been somehow calculating, as if the conversation rang a bell with him and made him remember something. Did he know a painter with those initials? Someone French who might be famous in the art world? The possibilities seemed endless.

But she decided to stop thinking about it and enjoy the evening. Adam was a handsome man with a great sense of humour. Why not relax and enjoy his company, and his admiring glances that she couldn't ignore? But there was something about him that unnerved her. She couldn't quite put her finger on it, but she felt she needed to be on her guard.

10

After dinner they went on to a nightclub in a nearby hotel, where the music was provided by a nine-piece salsa band. Laura had never tried any of these dances, but she soon found her feet and simply followed what everyone else was doing. The pulsating rhythm was infectious; she felt nearly hypnotised as she danced with every man in the group in turn. Then Adam grabbed her and put his arms around her while they danced. She found she liked the feel of his arms, and his warm scent made her a little light-headed.

'So,' he shouted over the loud music, 'you're out on the tiles without your lovely old boy? What does he think of that?'

'Oh, he doesn't mind,' Laura shouted back. 'He likes me to have a good time with friends. And we've just arrived in Kerry, so he thought I should go out and get to know people.'

'So he trusts you?' Adam asked, looking at her quizzically.

'Absolutely,' Laura declared.

'I'd love to meet him.'

'I think he'd like you too,' Laura said, trying not to laugh at the thought of Adam discovering the truth about Ken.

'I asked Becky about him,' Adam told her. 'She said he's lovely with eyes that would melt anyone's heart.'

Laura nodded, nearly exploding with laughter. 'Oh yes, that's very true.' She silently blessed Becky for going along with the lie and not betraying her.

'Interesting relationship, though,' Adam remarked.

'It suits me fine.'

'I bet it does. You have the best of both worlds, I must say. Going out dancing looking like a million bucks and not having to worry about finding love, and then going home to your loyal and trusting partner who only wants you to be happy.'

'I'm very lucky.' Laura laughed and swayed her hips to the music. 'And he knows I love dancing.'

'I can see that.' Adam smiled into her eyes as they continued to dance, the music drumming in their ears.

After a while, Laura started to feel tired and hot and very thirsty. She stopped dancing and smiled apologetically at Adam. 'I think I have to sit down for a bit and have something to drink. It's very hot here and I've been on my feet for a long time.'

'It's quite late too,' Adam remarked, taking her arm and leading her back to the table where the gang had settled, having drinks and laughing.

Laura checked her watch. 'Oh God, it's nearly two o'clock.' She hadn't been out this late for a very long time. But neither had she had so much fun. Time had just disappeared as she danced and talked and joked with everyone.

Adam pulled out her chair. 'I'll get you something to drink. What would you like?'

'Just a glass of water, please.' Laura smoothed her dress and smiled at Becky, who, after having danced several dances with a tall blond man, sat down beside Laura. 'Thanks for not exposing my lie,' she mumbled in Becky's ear when Adam had walked off to get her drink.

'Of course I wouldn't,' Becky protested, 'even if I nearly died laughing when Adam told me you lived with an older man called Ken.'

'Yeah, and we have an open relationship,' Laura said, shaking her hair out of her eyes. 'He just wants me to be happy, you see, so I can go out and have fun without him.'

Becky dabbed her hot face with a paper napkin, breaking into a fit of giggles. 'Sounds like the perfect relationship. Pity he's only a dog. I'd marry him in a heartbeat if he was human.'

'Me too,' Laura agreed with a broad smile. 'But shush, here is Adam with my water.' She smiled sweetly at him when he placed a tall glass with water, ice cubes and a slice of lemon in front of her. 'Thank you, Adam. That's just what I wanted.'

'You're very welcome.' He looked at Becky. 'Can I get you anything?'

'No thanks, pet,' Becky replied. 'I think I'm ready to call it a night, actually. What about you, Laura?'

Laura took a big mouthful of water before she replied. 'Yes, I think I should follow your example. It's been a lot of fun but I think I need to get to bed.'

Becky got up and took her evening bag. 'Great. Let's go then.'

Laura quickly drank the rest of the water, picked up her evening bag and rose. 'Bye, Adam. Thanks for being such great company.'

'The pleasure was all mine,' he said with a teasing smile. 'Are you sure you don't want me to walk you back to the hotel? Just to make sure you're safe.'

'Nah,' Becky said. 'This is Killarney, not New York. We'll be fine. Thanks for the offer, though. Very gallant of you.' She waved at her friends around the table. 'We're off. It was great craic, wasn't it, Laura?'

Laura smiled at the gang. 'It was lovely to meet you all,' she shouted above the loud music. 'Thanks for the welcome and the laughs.'

'Ah sure it was lovely to meet you. Laura. We needed a bit of new blood,' Peggy shouted back. 'Becky, thanks for bringing her. Will we see you next week?'

'Not sure,' Becky replied. 'I'll let you know.'

Adam drew Laura into the lobby while Becky said her good-byes. 'Hey, before you go...'

'Yes?' Laura looked up at him, slightly dazzled by those twinkly blue-green eyes.

'About that painting you mentioned... Do you remember where exactly you saw it?'

'Eh... well, it was at the home of an old woman I was looking after. But she died, so...'

'So you don't know what happened to the painting?' he filled in.

'It must be in someone else's house by now,' Laura suggested, as he helped her put on her coat. 'I mean...'

'I suppose.' Adam looked thoughtful. 'Must have been left to someone in that family, I guess.'

'Possibly. Why do you ask?'

He shook his head. 'Oh, just curious. It seemed to have made an impression on you. And then the initials... I have a faint recollection of seeing those somewhere. I'll look it up in my books.'

'It would be interesting to find out who he is.'

'Or she,' Adam remarked. 'Another thing... I would like to take your picture. You have a very interesting face.'

'Do I?' Laura asked, startled. 'In what way?'

Adam looked at her for a moment. 'Your eyes are very expressive. And you have a great bone structure. I'd love to see that in black and white. Would you mind?'

'No,' Laura said, startled. Nobody had ever said she had an interesting face before. 'That could be fun.'

'Great. If you give me your number, I'll give you a call and we can agree on a day. If Ken doesn't mind, that is.'

Laura smirked, trying not to laugh out loud. 'Of course not. He'd have no objections.' She read out her number and Adam put it into his phone.

'Grand, so. I'll give you a shout when I have a window.' He smiled at her as Becky joined them. 'Well, goodnight, then. Nice to see you both. Sure you don't want me to go with you?'

'Absolutely,' Becky said as she put on her coat and took Laura's arm. 'You go back in and have fun. Peggy said you forgot to dance with her.'

Adam looked taken aback. 'Did I?' He shook his head. 'I must be getting old. But I'll go and remedy the situation. Goodnight and sleep tight.'

'We will,' Becky said as they walked out of the nightclub into the cold wind.

They made their way down the street, turned the corner into the main street, past a pub with a sign that said 'Karaoke all night'.

'Look.' Laura pointed at the sign. 'I didn't know there was karaoke here.'

'Oh God,' Becky exclaimed. 'That would have been fun. But I'm too tired after all the dancing. Maybe next week? I kind of like hearing everyone croak out their favourite tunes.'

'I'd love to do that next week.'

Becky clutched the collar of her coat against the wind. 'Why not?' She slowed her pace and looked curiously at Laura. 'Hey, what happened with Adam? He seemed very interested in you. What was that about pretending to be living with someone? Not that it wasn't a hoot, but...'

Laura stopped walking. 'I don't know... It was just... he was so charming and interested. It scared me. I don't think I'm ready to...'

'To flirt with a handsome man?' Becky filled in.

'Yes. Something like that.' She was about to say that he reminded her of her father, whose charm and good looks had been what destroyed their family in the end. But this was not a good moment to discuss the traumatic events of her childhood. In any case it was unfair to attribute her father's flaws to Adam just because of the way he looked. 'Oh, I know he's probably very nice and great fun and all that,' she soothed. 'But right now, I'm a little fragile and lost.'

Becky gave Laura a tight hug. 'Of course you are. I should have realised. You need to settle in and to heal. It's not a good time to have a fling with someone like Adam. Even if that would be great for your ego, of course. And you'd have the time of your life.'

'And then we'll break up and I'll be sad and lonely again,' Laura cut in. 'I know the type. He doesn't really need anyone except for a bit of fun. I bet he has a big family with lots of brothers and sisters and nieces and nephews and maybe even parents and they all gather in their huge country house for Christmas and they all love Adam as he is the star of the family.' She drew breath. 'Am I right?'

Becky burst out laughing. 'Yes! Oh holy mother, you really have his number. And he's very successful at his job and gets invited everywhere. He only joins the gang when he has nothing much else to do and we're so honoured. A happy-go-lucky lad with the perfect life who has no intention of ever settling down.'

'Thought so. How do you know him?'

'I went to school with him.' Becky pulled Laura along. 'I've had a crush on him ever since. I'm still hoping he'll see the light and want to commit. Pathetic, don't you think?'

'Not really,' Laura replied, noticing an edge in Becky's voice. 'I think he's missing out on being with someone really special.'

Becky shrugged. 'Ah sure that's life, isn't it? But thanks. Come on, I'm freezing and we need to get to bed.'

'You're right.'

They started to half-run down the street and arrived, breathless, at the hotel at the same time as Fidelma, who beamed at them as they nearly fell into the lobby, the wind blowing the door shut behind them.

Becky stared at her mother. 'Mam? What are you doing out so late?'

'Is there an age limit to being out at night?' Fidelma replied in a strangely hoarse voice.

'No but...' Becky stopped. 'Do you have a cold?'

'No,' Fidelma said in a near whisper. 'I was at the karaoke thing and got a bit carried away, maybe.'

'Karaoke?' Becky looked shocked. 'You mean you were in that place, singing?'

'I was,' Fidelma said and let out a laugh. 'You should have heard me belt out "Whiskey in a Jar".'

'Mother!' Becky chided. 'Have you been drinking?'

'Yes,' Fidelma replied. 'Haven't you?'

'Yeah, but...' Beck started.

'But you're young and I'm too old?' Fidelma remarked sourly. 'Well, I'm not dead yet and I had great craic tonight. Except there was this woman from Cork who had the nerve to stand up and sing "My Own Lovely Lee", so we decided to fight back with Kerry songs and then one thing led to another and...' Fidelma coughed.

'And you nearly lost your voice, you silly woman,' Becky said, looking exasperated.

Laura giggled, listening to the two of them. This was ridiculous but at the same time funny. 'I wish I had been there.'

Fidelma smiled and nodded. 'You'd have loved it. We laughed ourselves silly. And we didn't really drink that much. Just a little wine and one glass of champagne, that was all. Dinner was delicious and we had such a great chat about the old days. Oh and...' She stopped suddenly, looking at Laura. 'You know what? I think I have a name for that woman you were asking about. The girl in the back row in that photo, I mean. One of my friends knew her.'

Laura's heart beat faster. 'What was her name?'

'Oonagh,' Fidelma replied. 'Oonagh Nolan.'

'Oonagh,' Laura said, as if to herself, feeling that the young woman was suddenly beginning to seem like a real person with a name.

'Where was she from?' Becky asked.

Fidelma thought for a moment. 'Valentia Island. And she was a teacher, like you said, Becky. She filled in for one of the teachers who was away on leave for a term at the primary school in Sandy Cove. Then she left.'

'To go where?' Becky asked.

Fidelma shrugged. 'No idea.'

'When was this?' Laura asked.

'Not sure. Maybe sometime in the mid-Sixties, during that time I was away in England.' Fidelma started to walk to the lift. 'That's all I know. And now I'm going to bed, girls. And so should you. Come on, Becky,' she ordered.

They all piled into the lift, which swiftly brought them to their floor, where they said goodnight.

Laura opened the door to her room, that name resonating through her mind.

Oonagh Nolan. Now she has a name, she thought. *But what happened to her? And who painted her sitting on the beach in a white dress? Oh, Josephine, what a riddle you gave me; will I ever solve it?*

Laura slowly undressed and got into bed, her mind whirling. It was late and she should try to sleep. But as she lay in the hotel bed and closed her eyes, she couldn't get those twinkly blue-green eyes out of her thoughts. Glamorous, fun and flirty – but someone she would find hard to trust. Even though she had enjoyed his attention, had felt suddenly young and pretty, which had given her a buzz of excitement.

Then Laura's mind drifted to another man, another pair of eyes, grey with a slightly sad look as his gaze met hers. Sad but also amusing and teasing at the same time, with a promise that he'd be her friend if she wanted. A complicated man.

Confused, Laura finally drifted off, dreaming of a sunlit beach and a man and a woman meeting... *In secret?* she wondered fleetingly, before everything disappeared into the oblivion of a deep sleep.

11

Laura got back to Sandy Cove late the following morning, the evening in Killarney still fresh in her mind, like a kaleidoscope of different images of fun and laughs and dancing. Especially with Adam, whose handsome face flitted into her mind from time to time. In other circumstances, she would have been ready to respond to his flirty gaze, but she had felt too raw and too emotionally exhausted to respond. It probably wasn't meant to happen. She was nearly sorry she had agreed to that photoshoot he had talked about, and almost hoped he wouldn't call.

Gino brought Ken back just before lunchtime and they went to the little beach to walk the dogs. Walking with Gino again was lovely, and Laura found herself comparing him to Adam. Gino was calmer, more contemplative and didn't snap out one-liners the way Adam had, expecting her to respond. But maybe that was just his party trick and he might be calmer in other circumstances. Perhaps Gino, on the other hand, just wasn't as eager to impress.

It was a beautiful day with brilliant sunshine and a hint of spring in the air. The sea lay flat and calm, with gentle waves lapping the beach, and Laura felt a surge of pure joy as she gazed out at the horizon, breathing in the salty tang as she felt the balmy breeze gently playing with her hair.

She looked up at the blue sky and let out a sigh. 'Oh, this is wonderful. Such a heavenly day in the middle of winter.'

'Nearly spring, though.' Gino smiled down at her. 'I saw the camellias were in bloom in Fidelma's garden. Spring comes early to Kerry, you know, even if we'll still have the odd storm.'

'I love that. It would still be quite chilly on the east coast.'

'I'm sure it is,' Gino agreed. 'So,' he said after a moment's silence. 'How was your evening?'

'Great fun.' Laura laughed suddenly. 'I had no idea Killarney was hopping on a Saturday night.'

'It certainly is.'

'Fidelma was a hoot,' Laura told him as they walked along. 'She went to a karaoke bar with her friends and sang her heart out so much she could hardly talk. I think she's still hoarse. But she said it was worth it. Isn't it fabulous that she still gets out and has a good time at her age?'

'I don't think age has anything to do with having fun,' Gino remarked. 'But how about you? Did you enjoy your evening with Becky and her gang?'

'Yes, I did. The craic was fantastic. What a great bunch they are.'

'They certainly like to have a good time,' Gino remarked.

'Yes.' Laura looked out at sea, thinking it was exactly the same colour as Adam's eyes. The way he had looked at her had made her feel warm all over. She knew she could have had a great time flirting with him and it would have been quite thrilling. But then she had pretended to be in a relationship and that, of course, had put him off. 'I did something stupid, though,' she started, feeling that Gino would be a good listener.

'Like what?'

'I met this very good-looking man who...' She stopped,

suddenly changing her mind. Why was she telling someone she just met about the silly little fib? What would he think of her?

'Who?' Gino asked as he stopped walking so suddenly Laura nearly fell over.

'Oh, nothing,' she said, trying to steady herself. 'Just something ridiculous. You'd think I was mad if you knew.'

'I won't think you're mad whatever you say.' Gino looked at her with a steady gaze. 'I'm curious now, but don't tell me if you don't want to. Whatever you feel like.'

Laura looked up at the opposite slope, where the dogs were running around, having a lovely time sniffing at things and digging in the soft earth. 'I told this guy that I'm in a relationship and that I live with an old fella called Ken,' she said very quickly.

Gino burst out laughing. 'Sorry, but that was too funny. What made you say that?'

Laura thought for a moment, trying to think of a plausible explanation. She glanced at him, wondering how he felt about her being attracted to someone like Adam. 'I don't know why I said it, but I think it was because he was expecting me to swoon at his good looks and charming ways. I wasn't in the mood to flirt back. I'm not very good at that sort of thing.' She looked at Gino and smiled weakly. 'So now you know. I'm a big chicken when it comes to men like that.'

'Glamorous men, you mean?' he asked, a little smile hovering on his lips. 'Who are very sure of their powers?'

'Something like that,' Laura confessed. 'I did find him very handsome in a film star kind of way. But then could see the whole scenario in front of me. We'd have this lovely flirty time and then crash, bang, it would all end and he'd move on to the next woman and I'd be left with a broken heart. It's happened before and I don't want to go there again.' *And it also happened to my mother*, she thought, but decided not to start up a conversation about her father. She had felt a long time ago that she would never meet the man of her dreams and had given up looking. That had made her both resigned and free in an odd way. She would still go on dates if asked, but as she grew older most men were already taken, and the thought of joining a dating app made her cringe.

'How can you be so sure it would end like that this time?' Gino asked as he sat down on a boulder. He pointed to a rock next to it. 'Sit down and take a break, willya. You look so frantic.'

Laura sat down and gazed out to sea. 'I'm not frantic. Just regretting what I did. He's a nice man. It's not a sin to be a committed bachelor who's just looking for fun.'

'Not that you weren't telling the truth,' Gino said as the dogs ran towards them. 'You do live with an old fella called Ken who you love to bits and he loves you right back.'

Laura patted Ken on the head, which was rewarded with a wagging tail. Then she laughed. 'Yes, that's true. But I should have told him the truth and not insinuated that I was...'

'Not available?' Gino asked with a teasing smile.

'Well, I don't feel available.' Laura sighed and looked at Gino. 'I'm not a teenager looking for a boyfriend. In fact I'm not really looking at all right now. I decided a while back to just go with the flow and stop searching for Mr Right. He's not out there. Or maybe he was and now he's married to someone else. I don't believe in happily ever after anyway.'

'I would agree with that. I don't think there is such a thing as happiness. Only happy moments. The rest of the time we're lucky if we're content.'

'I think that's very true,' Laura said, impressed with his insightfulness.

'What makes you happy?' Gino asked. 'I mean what have been your happy moments?'

Laura thought for a while. 'I have always had happy moments with my family. My sister in particular. And my niece, Rachel. When the three of us are together, I feel really happy.'

'Doing what?'

'Lots of things. Cooking and eating and watching a good movie, listening to music. Going shopping together. And with Josephine it was the same thing. We used to laugh at silly things and she would play the piano so beautifully. We went for walks and then when she was a bit poorly, I'd drive her to the seaside to watch the sunset or just look out at all the sailing boats in Dublin Bay on Sundays.' Laura paused, feeling a pang of sadness, but also feeling so lucky to have had those special times with the people she loved the most. She looked at Gino. 'What about you? What makes you happy?'

'Right now, sitting here, looking at the amazing views and talking to you. And other things that I might tell you about when you come for a visit to my house.' He studied her for a while. 'Would you like to come with me? I could cook something for lunch and show you around. It's another world up there.'

'You mean right now?' Laura asked, startled. He was inviting her to his home, which had sounded like a secret hideaway where he lived alone, away from the world down here. She hadn't expected him to invite her so soon, but perhaps he felt a special bond with her through Josephine.

'No, next time there is a full moon,' he teased, his teeth flashing white against his dark beard. 'Yes, of course right now. It's a perfect day for me to show you my little mud hut in the hills. And I thought we could walk there, so the dogs get a good workout. Unless you have other plans, of course.'

Laura laughed. 'What other plans could I possibly have on a Sunday just a week after I've arrived? Yes, please. I'd love to take a little hike up the hill to see your house.'

Gino jumped up from the boulder. 'Okay, then. Let's go. You already have good shoes for hiking so no need to change.'

He let out a shrill whistle, which resulted in Anne-Marie barking and running down the slope to his side. 'Home,' he said to her. 'And we have visitors, so behave yourself, okay?'

Anne-Marie wagged her tail.

'Off we go,' Gino said, leading the way up the steps.

With a feeling of great anticipation, Laura followed him, with Ken trotting beside her. The invitation had come out of the blue and it had both surprised and delighted her. She looked at his figure walking up the slope with an easy stride and felt a dart of excitement. What did mean by inviting her just like that? Was it just a friendly gesture or was it more than that? They had only just met, and she had thought him to be a loner who didn't want to get close to anyone, but then he had asked her to his house as if he wanted to show her a part of himself and his life that few people knew about. She suddenly felt she couldn't wait to see Gino's home, that cabin he had built with his own hands. She was sure it would be a place like no other.

12

They climbed up the steep hill as the sun warmed their backs, Laura having to take off her jacket when they were halfway up. Gino, who was in shirtsleeves, took it and tied it around his waist, smiling at her. 'It's a little bit of a leg burner if you're not used to climbing. Take your time. There's no rush.'

'I couldn't rush if I tried.' Laura wiped her forehead with the back of her hand. She stopped to catch her breath, and also to look at the view of the bay and the islands, which was breath-taking up here with the dark blue water meeting the sky at the horizon, the old stone walls of the ancient monastery on Skellig Michael clearly visible even at this distance. The slopes were covered in heather with tiny leaves that were beginning to unfold. 'The mountains will soon be green again,' she remarked. 'Much earlier than in the east. There, the slopes are still brown and dry looking.'

'Yup,' Gino replied above her. 'That's Kerry for ya. Spring has sprung all around us.'

Laura laughed and resumed walking up the steep path, wondering how on earth Gino got up here on his quadbike, never mind the van. 'Is there another way up here?' she asked.

'Yes, around the bend up there, you'll see a wider path that I take with the bike and the van. Still steep but smoother. Takes a little longer too. I thought I'd bring you up the scenic route.'

'Gee, thanks,' Laura panted as she made her way up the rough trail. 'But you're right, it is spectacular,' she said, as they finally arrived at the plateau on which stood a log cabin with a deck in front of it. She nearly gasped as she looked out over the blue ocean meeting the horizon far in the distance. The islands shimmered in the bright sunlight, and she could see a flock of seabirds flying around the highest peak of Skellig Michael. Up here she could also see the coastline of this part of the Ring of Kerry and the jagged outline of the MacGillycuddy's Reeks mountain range to the east. 'I can see Carrauntoohil!' she exclaimed. 'How amazing.'

'That's another steep climb,' Gino said.

'Oh yes, it would be,' Laura said, her eyes on the highest peak. 'Not something I'd tackle in a hurry.'

'No, you'd need to be very fit,' Gino agreed. 'And even then, I'd use a guide. Look,' he said, pointing at Ken and Anne-Marie lying stretched out on the deck, fast asleep. 'They're a little tired, too.'

Laura laughed. 'I was wondering where they got to. And here they are, having managed that slope without a problem.' She walked across the deck and sat down on a chair by a round wooden table. 'I need to rest after all of that.'

'I'll get you a glass of water,' Gino said. 'Don't move, I'll be back in a tick.'

'Oh, I'm fine,' Laura argued, getting up again. 'And I want to see your house.'

'In that case, you can have a glass of water inside.' Gino walked to the red door that was split in two parts and held them open. 'After you, ma'am.'

'A half door,' Laura said as she stepped inside. 'That's very quaint.'

'It used to be to stop animals going into the house. But in this instance it's to stop Anne-Marie going outside behind my back when I open the door to air the living room.'

'Oh,' Laura said, but then stopped, speechless, as she came straight into the living room.

She looked around in awe. It was like coming into another world, an Aladdin's cave full of treasures. The wooden floor was covered in an oriental carpet, with colours that glowed like jewels in the light from the large window, where a window seat invited her to sit and gaze at the spectacular view. A telescope stood beside the window that was hung with deep red velvet curtains. Three of the walls were lined with floor-to-ceiling bookcases full of all kinds of books: paperbacks, leather-bound volumes, large coffee-table type books on art and nature, and the back wall was covered in paintings and framed photographs around a fireplace that was stacked with logs.

The furniture consisted of an Eames chair with a reading lamp beside one of the bookcases, a dark blue chesterfield sofa with stacks of cushions in all colours in front of the fireplace and a large round mahogany dining table near the window with four chairs. The room was flooded with light from the window but she could imagine how cosy it would be in the evening when the curtains were drawn and a fire blazed in the fireplace.

'What an amazing room,' Laura said. 'I didn't expect it to look like this.'

'What *did* you expect?' Gino asked, looking quizzically at her.

'I don't know. Something simpler and less... sumptuous.'

Gino laughed. 'I suppose a log cabin should be more basic. But everything I love is here. Through that door is quite a modern kitchen and I even have a bathroom with a power shower, and there's a hot tub on the deck, you might have noticed.'

'No, I didn't,' Laura confessed. 'I didn't take a proper look, really. Do you have electricity up here?'

'Yes. I finally managed to get connected six months ago. But there are solar panels on the roof, too. That helps to run the hot water and a few other things. There's a solid fuel cooker in the kitchen, so if there's a power cut I can keep warm and cook food.'

'How brilliant,' Laura said, walking to the bookcase. 'Do you mind if I take a look at your books? I love reading, too, and a room like this, full of books, is irresistible.'

'Go ahead,' Gino said, walking to the kitchen door. 'I'll throw something together for lunch while you have a browse. We can eat on the deck I think as it's still quite warm.'

'Fabulous,' Laura said, already lost in the books. She was deep into a book about Kerry in the 1930s, with fascinating photos, when Gino came through the room carrying a big platter.

'I made pizza,' he said. 'Could you grab the plates and stuff on a tray in there and carry it outside?'

'Of course.' Laura put away the book and went into the kitchen, which was small and cosy, the woodburning stove radiating warmth. She took the tray laden with cutlery, glasses and a jug of water from the pine table and carried it out through the living room into the warm sunshine. Gino was already cutting the pizza into wedges at the table on the deck.

He smiled as Laura arrived. 'Thanks. I hope you like chorizo and a lot of cheese.'

'Love it.' Laura sat down as Gino put a large wedge on a plate and handed it to her. 'This smells delicious. How did you do the dough for the base so fast?'

'I keep pizza dough in the freezer and thaw it in the microwave. Then all I have to do is roll it out and put on the topping. I thought you might be hungry after the hike up here, so I put on a lot of stuff.'

Laura nodded, her mouth full. Her eyes nearly teared up as the flavours hit her tastebuds. Tomato, mushrooms, olives, chorizo and fresh herbs topped with mozzarella made up a wonderful mix as she wolfed down the wedge. 'Oh my God,' she exclaimed when she could speak. 'That's the best pizza I've ever tasted.'

Gino nodded as he chewed on his own wedge. Then he swallowed and gestured at the platter. 'Have another one. There's plenty, as you can see.'

'Thanks.' Laura took another wedge and ate it more slowly this time, savouring the flavours. Then she poured herself a glass of water from the jug and sipped it slowly, looking around the deck. 'Where's the hot tub you were talking about?'

'Over there, just below the deck, on the gravel.' Gino pointed to an object wrapped in tarpaulin. 'I cover it up so it won't rust.'

'Rust?' Laura asked and got up to investigate. 'Mind if I take off the tarpaulin?'

'Go ahead.'

Laura grabbed the cover and pulled it off, revealing an antique roll-top bathtub. She stared at it and then started to laugh. 'This is your hot tub?'

'Yes.' Gino walked across the deck to join her. 'Works brilliantly. I fill it with the hose and then top it up with a few buckets of hot water from the kitchen. Then I lie back and look at the sunset or the stars at night, depending on the time of day.'

'Wow,' Laura said as she looked out over the rolling green hills that met the sea in the distance. 'The views from here are even more spectacular than from the deck. Must be amazing to lie here and look at it. Especially at sunset. And I love this tub. Beats any modern hot tub I've ever seen.'

'I'm glad you like it. Becky couldn't stop laughing when she saw it. But then she loved it when she got in. Couldn't get her out until the water was freezing.'

'Really?' Laura said, trying not to sound shocked at the thought of Becky and Gino together in the tub that was large enough for two. There was suddenly a tight knot of disappointment in her stomach. He had only invited her to his house as a friend, nothing more, she reminded herself. 'Where did you find it?' she asked to cover her dismay.

'In an architectural salvage yard. I loved it but knew it would never fit in the house, so I decided to use it like this.'

'Brilliant. And it would be easy to empty. You just pull the plug and the water drains away into the gravel, I imagine,' Laura remarked, keeping her tone light.

'Exactly.' Gino went back to the deck. 'How about coffee and something sweet?'

'Sounds lovely,' Laura said with a last look at the tub. 'Do you want me to put the cover back on?'

'No. I'll probably have a soak later this evening.' Gino gathered the plates and went inside, leaving Laura on the deck, feeling suddenly cold. The thought of Becky and Gino together had given her an odd dart of disappointment that she couldn't really explain. Becky had confessed to having a crush on Adam, but maybe she found Gino more dependable. And he might feel the same about Becky.

Laura hadn't felt anything but friendly vibes from Gino, even though she found him madly attractive. His grey eyes and his warm voice combined with his kindness and generosity had touched her deeply. She had felt so at home here in his little house, but now she just wanted to get back to the cottage. The spell of the lovely day had been broken by the suspicion that he was somehow taken.

Then Laura told herself not to be silly. Had she imagined something would happen between her and Gino? They had only just met, and here she was daydreaming about the two of them. He was such a nice man and someone who was fast becoming a friend. He had been generous enough to invite her to his house and cooked a delicious lunch. Why did she have to ruin it by wanting more?

She smiled at him when he came back carrying two steaming cups of coffee and a plate with homemade cookies on a tray. 'This is such a treat. It was so kind of you to invite me here and then serve up that fabulous lunch.'

'I'm glad you enjoyed it.' Gino sat down again, putting a cup in front of her.

'Lovely.' Laura sipped the hot liquid with care. 'And I suppose those chocolate chip cookies are not from a packet.'

'No, from the bakery.' Gino looked at Laura over the rim of his cup. Then he put it down. 'I have a feeling you are full of questions about something. That you're trying to solve a riddle or a problem?'

'Yes.' Laura paused for a moment. There was something she'd been dying to ask him about. 'I was wondering if Josephine ever said anything to you about a painting when she talked to you late at night. The one that led her here.'

'No. But...' He paused as if he was trying to remember. 'She did say that something she saw had made her come to the village. That a beach she had seen somewhere intrigued her and she simply had to find that spot. I thought it might have been a postcard or a tourist ad for Kerry or something similar. I didn't ask what it was.' He looked at her with curiosity. 'So it was a painting?'

'Yes,' Laura said, deciding it would be safe to tell Gino about it. She went on to describe the scene with the woman she was sure had been painted on the beach below Starlight Cottages and how she was now trying to find out her identity. 'I don't even know who painted it,' she said. 'But the message from Josephine says I have to find the rightful owner.'

'Maybe it's you?' he suggested. 'She gave you the cottage and probably wanted you to find out the history of the painting, but maybe that's all?'

'I don't know. That's a possibility. But I think I have to find out who painted it and the woman in it. I'm getting a little closer to the woman, but not the artist.'

'You have plenty of time,' Gino assured her. 'What's the rush? I'm sure you'll get there in the end.'

'I hope so.' Laura smiled at him. He was so comforting to be around and seemed so laid-back and accepting of everything. But what he didn't know was the threat that Michael Monaghan would start court proceedings against her. Then she could lose everything and have to go back to Dublin and try to pick up her life again.

She looked out across the bay again and felt a strange calm come over her. He was right. She would try not to fret and just let things come to her in their own good time. And even if there would never be anything but friendship between them, that was good too.

13

The weeks flew past, and the end of March arrived with blustery winds and rain showers. Laura had thoroughly enjoyed the good weather during her first few weeks and her daily walks with Ken on the beach and on the headland. Gino often joined her when he had the time, and she found herself enjoying his company and their conversations that often became personal, delving into their life experiences. She did her best to push away any thoughts of a romance between them and simply appreciate a very sweet friendship. He had been Josephine's close confidant and maybe that was all Laura could hope for. Having a friend like Gino was also a gift, she decided, and maybe that was all it was meant to be. She had to try to be content with that.

Those first weeks were enjoyable and gave Laura an opportunity to settle in and become accustomed to the village and its inhabitants, including celebrating St Patrick's day on 17 March, which had been fun, with a parade that ended at a party in the community hall. There had been no news about Michael Monaghan and his plans to contest his mother's will, to which her sister Maureen had said, 'No news is good news. Maybe he'll drop it.' Laura hoped she was right and tried her best not to worry about it.

As she now felt truly settled after more than two months in the village, she was beginning to feel at a loose end. Everyone else she met was occupied with work and families, and although they were friendly and ready to chat, there wasn't much going on during the working week. Gino was increasingly busy with the bakery and some catering assignments, but as her feelings for him grew deeper, Laura was quite happy not to spend time with him apart from a short chat from time to time. A little distance was a good thing right now, she decided. Elaine was tied up with the children's exam work and even Becky disappeared into what she called her 'writing cave' to work on a new project: a series of young adult fantasy novels her publisher had commissioned her to write. The library was closed for renovations so Laura couldn't even go there to look into their archives.

After her long walks, and a bit of shopping in the grocery store, she didn't know what to do with herself for the rest of the day. She wasn't used to so much free time, and she wondered if she could put up with it much longer. She simply had to find something useful to do. She was even considering returning to Dublin to look for work when Bridget, the surgery nurse, came to the rescue.

'Hi, Laura,' she said as she stood on the doorstep on a Saturday afternoon, wringing her hands, looking both tired and nervous. 'I was wondering if I could have a word?'

Laura opened the door wider. 'Of course. Come in. I'll put the kettle on. I've just lit the fire, so go and sit down on the sofa and get warm. You look frozen.'

'I am,' Bridget confessed, rubbing her hands as she stepped into the hall. 'It suddenly got colder after that lovely week we had. I ran over here without putting on a coat and it's freezing with that wind.'

'I know. I tried to let Ken out for a bit, but he refused to leave the house.'

'Smart dog,' Bridget said approvingly, giving Ken a pat on the head before she sat down on the sofa.

Laura quickly made a pot of tea and put mugs and a plate of biscuits on a tray and carried it all in, placing it on the coffee table. 'There you go. A hot cuppa and a few ginger snaps.'

'Oh thank you. Just what I need,' Bridget said and grabbed a mug as soon as Laura had poured it.

Laura sat down and helped herself to tea. Then she looked at Bridget. 'So what is it you wanted to talk to me about?'

Bridget took a sip of tea and then put her mug on the table. 'A job,' she said. 'My job, I mean. I need someone to fill in for me for a week or two. I heard Shane talking about you in such glowing terms that I thought I'd ask...'

'If I'd work in the surgery?' Laura filled in. 'I have never done that kind of work, but...'

'Oh, it's not that hard,' Bridget said. 'The paperwork takes a little time but I'll take you through it before I go.'

'Where are you going?'

Bridget sighed. 'Not on a holiday, if that's what you think. My husband hasn't been well for a long time, and now he wants to go to Galway to stay with our daughter who lives there for a bit. He's had treatment for cancer that affected him badly. The cancer is gone but he needs rest and full-time care for a few weeks, maybe even longer.' Bridget drew breath and looked at Laura with worried eyes.

'Of course you want to go with him to look after him,' Laura said, feeling a dart of sympathy. She considered the problem for a moment while Bridget, holding the mug of warm tea in both hands, looked at her expectantly. 'You must go with him.'

'Yes,' Bridget said with a deep sigh. 'He needs me to help him to get back to his full health.'

'I'm sure he does.' Laura nodded.

'I knew you'd understand,' Bridget said, looking hopeful.

'I do, of course.' Laura paused. 'And yes, I'll be happy to fill in for you while you're away.'

Bridget let out a long, relived sigh. 'That's wonderful. Thank you so much, Laura.'

Laura laughed. 'I should thank *you*. I was just thinking I need a job or I'd go crazy. Idleness isn't really my thing, even though I've been told to rest to get over the grief.'

'I don't think idleness is the way to go,' Bridget stated. 'Being busy will help take your mind off painful things for a while. And then you'll be tired and that will help you sleep.'

'Just what I need.' Laure held out the plate of ginger snaps. 'Here, have another. They're from Gino's bakery.'

'Delicious.' Bridget took another biscuit from the plate. 'So buttery.'

'He is an amazing baker.'

'And a very attractive man, too.' Bridget smirked. 'I'm sure you've noticed.'

'Of course.' Laura smiled, even though the mere mention of Gino made her feel strange. 'He's a good friend, too. And he knew Josephine. They used to phone each other often, which I didn't know until he told me.'

Bridget nodded. 'Yes. So I've heard. Kindred spirits and a mutual understanding, I guess.'

'I'm sure that was the case,' Laura agreed. 'Josephine was an unusual woman. Ageless, I think.'

'Very much so.' Bridget paused. 'I met her only once, when she came here to look at the cottage when it was for sale. Edwina and Shane had just moved in next door and I came to bring them a housewarming gift. They were showing Josephine around and that's when I met her. Edwina and her mother owned the whole row of cottages then and they were the developers of the renovations, you see. Edwina is a very successful project leader now. This was her very first renovation.'

Laura looked around the room. 'She did a great job with the houses. This one anyway. I haven't seen the others.'

'They're just as nice but each one is a little different. Josephine picked this one because there was something about it that had to do with a picture she had seen somewhere. A photo or a drawing or something. I forget exactly what she said.' Bridget looked thoughtfully at Laura. 'Do you know anything about that?'

'Eh, well, I think she mentioned something about a young woman and an artist. Something that happened in the Sixties, I think,' Laura said, trying to keep it vague. She looked back at Bridget. 'Did you grow up in this village?'

'No,' Bridget replied. 'I'm from Tralee, but my husband is from here.'

'So he went to school here? Primary school, I mean,' Laura asked, trying to figure out how old Bridget was. She looked to be in her sixties but could be younger. But her husband could be older than her.

'Brendan? Yes he did, of course. Loved that little school. It was so different when he was a child. It was a very simple, quite basic building back then, with an outside toilet and a fireplace in each classroom. Each child had to bring a sod of turf for the fire every day.' Bridget laughed. 'You'd think it was a hundred years ago. But it was actually in the 1960s. He's a bit older than me, of course. I was only a baby then.'

'I didn't think you would be old enough to have gone to school in the Sixties,' Laura assured her. 'But your husband... Would he have been going to the primary school in, say, 1964 or '65?'

Bridget nodded. 'Oh yes. I think that's the year he started in junior infants. But if you're interested in the history of the school, you might ask him yourself. Today is Saturday, and we were hoping to leave for Galway on Tuesday or Wednesday. Why don't you come to the surgery on Monday at lunchtime?

Then I can take you through everything and I'll get my husband to call in so you can ask him yourself. He'd love to meet you.'

'That sounds perfect. What time would suit you?'

'Around this time, just after lunch. Dr Kate and her family will be out so the house will be quiet. Shane shares the surgery with her, you see, and she also lives there. I think you'll love working with both of them, even if the pace is quite hectic at times.'

'I think I can cope with that,' Laura said, laughing. 'I'd welcome something hectic right now.'

'You might be sorry you said that.' Bridget finished her tea and put the mug back on the tray. 'I'd better be off. I'll see you tomorrow. Thank you so much for doing this, Laura. It means a lot to leave the surgery in your capable hands.'

'I'm glad I can help,' Laura said. But when Bridget had left, she wondered what she was getting into. A busy GP surgery in an area like this might mean little time for fun. And what on earth would she do with Ken?

Her concerns were interrupted by her phone ringing. She picked it up from the coffee table and answered after the third ring.

'Laura?' a deep voice said in her ear. A voice that belonged to a very handsome man, and it made her heart beat faster, despite having only met its owner once a few weeks ago. She had thought she'd never hear from Adam again, but here he was, calling her. Even before she said a word, she had an eerie feeling something was about to happen that she wouldn't be able to stop.

14

'Yes?' she said, trying to sound cool even though her heart was beating like a drum in her chest. 'Who's this?' she said, pretending to have forgotten.

'It's Adam,' he said, laughing. 'Sorry if I sound stressed. I just came back from a long trek up MacGillycuddy's. Didn't quite make it to the top of Carrauntoohil though.' He paused. 'I hope you remember me? We met in Killarney a few weeks ago.'

'Yes, of course I remember you,' Laura replied, his handsome face with the flirty eyes popping into her mind.

'Oh, good. I thought you might have forgotten all about me. Anyway,' he continued. 'I was wondering if... well, forgive me if I'm intruding, but I'm on my way to Ballinskelligs and thought I'd pop in to see you and discuss that photo session I was talking about? You didn't seem to mind me taking a few shots of you. And I'd like to meet your partner to make sure he doesn't mind. I don't want to make any trouble between you.'

'Oh,' Laura said, taken aback. 'Well... That would be... I mean...' She looked at Ken asleep at her feet and suddenly laughed. This was ridiculous. 'Okay,' she said. 'We're at home so that would be fine. Where are you right now?'

'I'm just leaving Killorglin. Could be there in half an hour. I know where the cottages are. Which one is yours?'

'Number two,' she said, her voice shaking just a little.

'Great. See you soon,' Adam said, and hung up.

'Oh God, what am I doing?' Laura asked out loud. She patted Ken on the head. 'You'd better be on your best behaviour when Adam comes. He thinks you and I are...' She stopped and buried her face in her hands. 'What is he going to think when he hears the truth? He'll probably be as annoyed as hell and there goes my career as a model. But it's probably for the best. I'd say he takes these candid shots where his subject looks awful, all the wrinkles and pores clearly visible and that look in the eyes that reveals some bitter feelings and a whole load of sadness and anger.' Then she laughed and jumped up from the sofa. 'And here I am talking to a dog instead of running into the bedroom to put on a shedload of make-up. I'd better get a move on. He'll be here soon.'

Laura ran into the bedroom, grabbed her make-up bag and continued into the bathroom, Ken at her heels. He sat down at her feet and looked on while she applied foundation, blusher, eyeliner and lashings of mascara. She decided to skip the lipstick, which would look more natural. She considered changing into something dressier than her jeans and red sweat-shirt, but changed her mind. Why look as if she had made a huge effort? She suddenly knew that while she had been nervous when they first met, and had still wanted to hide behind the wall she had built up ever since Josephine's death, she was ready to peep through that wall and have a little fun with an attractive man. Even if it carried certain risks.

On her way from the bathroom, Laura caught sight of the painting and started to panic. She didn't want Adam to see it. Not that he would have any reason to go into her bedroom, but... *Just in case*, she thought and draped a throw from the bed over it. There. Now the whole canvas was completely hidden from view, which made her feel calmer. She looked at her reflection again and tried a cool smile that would hide her nervousness. And then, while she was dithering in front of the mirror, the doorbell rang.

'Here we go,' she said to Ken. 'Try to make a good impression.'

Her stomach churning, Laura walked to the door on weak legs, trying to pull herself together. Then she was at the door and smiled cheerfully while she opened it. 'Hi!' she chortled. 'Welcome to my humble abode.'

Adam, dressed in jeans and a green hoodie, stared at her and then returned her smile. 'Not so humble at all. And hi there. Lovely to see you again.'

Ken pushed forward and sniffed at Adam, wagging his tail.

He patted the dog on the head. 'And who is this lovely fella?'

Laura swallowed and cleared her throat. 'Well,' she said. 'This is... eh, Ken.'

Adam blinked and stared at her. 'Ken? You mean you named your dog after your partner? How does that work?'

'Eh, no.' Laura's smiled died on her lips as she saw the confusion in his eyes. 'This the Ken I was talking about.'

'And the lovely older man you live with? What's his name, then?'

'He doesn't exist.' Laura smiled apologetically, feeling a dart of guilt. 'I told you a dirty lie when we met.'

'Why?' Adam laughed gently but still looked confused.

'Because, well...' She shifted from foot to foot.

'You wanted to put me off?' he asked incredulously.

'Something like that, I suppose,' she continued. She cleared her throat. 'This is where you say, "Weird to meet you," and run for your life.'

He stared at her for a long time and then laughed. 'Of course not. Had there been an old gentleman here in a cardie sitting by the fire drinking hot milk, I might have.' His eyes narrowed as he looked at her. 'I knew there was something strange about that story. You didn't look quite the type.' He smiled at her.

'What type is that?' Laura asked, cheered by his reaction. He wasn't a bit cross but seemed to find the situation funny.

'The type to...' He stopped and shrugged. 'Well, whatever. Can we move on now?'

'Absolutely.' With a huge sigh of relief, Laura stepped back into the hall. 'Come in. I'm sure you want to see the house.'

Adam followed her into the hall. 'Yes, but the back garden is what I really wanted to see. I bet the views from there are spectacular. These cottages are built right at the edge of the cliffs, so it has to be amazing. I saw you against that backdrop in my imagination.' He gestured at the camera hanging by a strap from his shoulder. 'I thought as the light right now is fantastic, we could try a few shots, if that's okay with...' He laughed. 'I was going to say Ken, but as I can see he doesn't seem to mind.'

Laura glanced at Ken, who was trotting behind them, still wagging his tail. 'No, he doesn't mind at all. In fact, he seems to like you a lot.'

'I have that effect on dogs, it seems.'

'Some people do.' Laura walked across the living room, opened the door to the sunroom and then led the way onto the deck, where she stopped. 'Well, here we are.' She made a sweeping gesture in the direction of the ocean, its water a dark blue-grey reflecting the clouds, the cliffs and the beach below. 'The view, as you predicted, is spectacular all right. Even now when it's cloudy.' She turned around. 'Why do you say the light is good? Wouldn't it be better in bright sunlight?'

Adam lifted his camera and started to take shots of the view. 'This is great for black and white with you in focus and the background a little misty.' He turned to Laura, still looking into the camera. 'Stand over there, against the view of the islands and look out. I love your profile and the strands of your hair across your face, the slightly wistful expression in your eyes...'

'Oh,' Laura said, suddenly stuck for words. Turning slightly, she looked at the coastline to the east, where the side of the mountain met the sea, the waves crashing in. The tide was coming in and the light was fading, but then the sun suddenly shone through a hole in the clouds, casting an eerie glow over the water. She felt as if she could drift away across the ocean, to the islands behind which the sun was slowly sinking.

'Amazing,' Adam said as he kept clicking the shutter and then, very quickly, darkness fell, and the views were no longer visible.

Laura relaxed and turned to Adam, whose shadowy figure was outlined against the darkening sky. 'There. Too dark to take pictures.'

Adam hung his camera on his shoulder. 'Yes. I got some great shots, though. Thank you for being such a great subject. How about dinner somewhere nice to thank you for posing for me?'

'Dinner?' Laura hesitated. 'That sounds nice, but...'

'But what?' He looked at her for a moment through the gloom. 'Now that I know you're single, I don't see any obstacle. Except if you have other plans, of course. Or you're not hungry. Or you actually don't like me.'

Laura laughed. 'How could anyone not like you?' She mentally chided herself for being silly. So he was very handsome but every handsome man wasn't a bounder like her father. She just had to get that notion out of her head. He was only asking her to have dinner with him in what seemed a very friendly way. Why was she suspecting him to have other motives? She was behaving like a simpering teenager, not a mature woman. She had to stop jumping to conclusions, she told herself sternly. A nice man was asking her out; what was so scary about that? 'Dinner sounds lovely,' she said. 'But I don't know anything about the restaurants around here as I've only just arrived.'

'But I do,' Adam replied. 'And I know one that can serve up a truly decadent meal. It's a new place in Waterville. We can go in my car and then I'll bring you back. That way you can have a glass of wine or two while I stay sober.' He winked. 'I know how much you love a glass of turpentine.'

Laura had to laugh. He was so funny and such a charming man with no obvious sides to him at all. She suddenly decided to let go of all her inhibitions and forebodings and simply enjoy his company. Life was too short to be careful and gloomy. 'Sounds fabulous,' she said. 'I'll just change into something dressier.'

'No need,' Adam argued. 'I'm not going to change either. It's quite a casual place where golfers hang out and they don't dress up that much. They just arrive straight from the golf course, wearing those silly golfing outfits. So we'll have to try not to laugh at them.'

'I'll do my best.' Laura looked around for Ken but saw that he was already lying on his cushion in the living room. 'I'll just say goodbye to Ken and put out the lights.'

Adam went to the door. 'Great. I'll wait for you in the car. It's the slightly wrecked thing outside the house.'

'Won't be a moment,' Laura said and went to put out the lights, except the one beside the window. It would be nice to have a light on when she came back. And Ken wouldn't want to be in the dark. She patted him on the head and promised to be back soon, picked up her denim jacket from the hall stand and closed the door behind her. Adam's car turned out to be a red vintage MG sportscar with leather seats, which made her laugh. So typical that he would have a sexy car like that. It fitted his image perfectly. 'Love this wrecked thing,' she said as she got into the passenger seat.

'Oh, it's an old love of mine.' Adam started the car and

slowly drove it up the lane. 'A bit bumpy here so I have to be careful. But once we're on the road I can let her go.'

'Wow,' Laura said, as the car gathered speed once they were out of the village and driving along the coast towards Waterville. 'How old is this car?'

'About forty,' Adam replied. 'Doesn't she go well for such an old thing?'

'Amazing.' Laura glanced at the coastline, where she could see the jagged edges of the cliffs and the steep slopes down to the sea lit up by the headlights as they went along. 'How long have you had her?'

'About three years.' Adam changed gears as they rounded a bend. 'I've had her resprayed and redone a bit since then. Cost me more than the actual car but she was worth it, don't you think?'

'Absolutely,' Laura agreed. 'Does she have a name?'

'No. Couldn't think of one.' He gave her a quick look. 'Maybe I should call her Laura? That would fit. Mature yet lively and in great nick.'

'Well, thank you,' Laura said with a giggle. 'Never thought of myself as a car. I'm honoured.'

'Fits you like a glove,' Adam quipped. Then they arrived in Waterville, and he drove up the main street and parked in front of a brightly lit restaurant with a sign that said 'Bernie's Bistro' in blue letters. 'Here we are,' Adam said, and turned off the engine. 'Brand new place with a view of the sea in daylight. But also wonderful inside.'

'Looks nice.' Laura started to get out of the car, but Adam stopped her.

'Just a moment.' He jumped out of the driver's seat and ran around the car to open the door for Laura. 'Can't forget my manners, even if I'm hungry.'

'I'm impressed,' Laura said as she got out. She breathed in the air that was cool and fresh with a hint of garlic and herbs coming from the restaurant. 'And hungry. Something smells amazing.'

'Everything they serve is amazing.' Adam held the entrance door open. 'I gave them a quick call and ordered our meal in advance. Hope you don't mind.'

'Not at all. Can't wait to see what you ordered.'

They entered the warmly lit restaurant where logs blazing in the fireplace spread a warming glow around the dining room, which had round tables with groups of people chatting and enjoying what looked like delicious food and wine. But the head waiter who welcomed them led the way to a table in a cubicle at the far side. 'I reserved this table for you,' he said as he pulled out a chair for Laura. 'I hope it's all right.'

'It's perfect,' Laura said, as Adam sat down opposite Laura. 'Let the fun begin.'

And it was indeed a fun evening. Laura thought she would never forget it. She thought fleetingly of Gino, but pushed the image away. He wasn't on the menu tonight, she said to herself, smiling at the notion. She was here with Adam and he deserved her undivided attention. The food Adam had ordered was a four-course meal of light and delicious dishes: a seafood salad, followed by a slice of grilled lamb in a garlic and rosemary gravy, fluffy mashed potatoes and grilled tomatoes, followed by a light-as-air cheese soufflé, and finally a strawberry sorbet with tiny meringues, and then a few chocolate pralines with coffee. Adam had ordered two glasses of a wonderful Bordeaux that was as smooth as velvet, but he only drank half a glass as he was driving.

They talked all through the meal, sharing their life stories. Adam lamented the lack of drama in his life. 'I had a happy childhood with no major upsets, which is both a blessing and a curse.'

'Why would it be a curse?' Laura asked, startled.

'Because if I had suffered, I could have been a great artist or a writer, pouring all my angst and traumas into my art. But as it is, I can only admire those who did.'

Laura shook her head. 'I think you're very lucky. Not many people can say that.'

Adam sighed and finished his wine. 'Yeah, I know. How about you? Happy childhood?'

'It had its ups and downs,' Laura replied, images of her own childhood flicking through her mind. 'My parents split up when I was four. My mother brought my sister and me up on her own. We didn't have much money and my mum had two jobs, working in an office during the day and doing translations at night. She speaks German fluently as she spent a few years there, so it came in handy.'

'And your father?' Adam asked.

Laura scraped the plate with the last of the sorbet and licked her spoon. Then she looked at Adam. 'My father? Well, he was around for a bit and we saw him at weekends. But then it became every second weekend, and then more and more seldom. And then he went to England to work and that's when we lost touch completely. I haven't seen him since I was about twelve.'

'That must have been hard for you all.'

Laura shrugged. 'It didn't cause me that much trauma. We got used to not seeing him and then he just faded away. I remember him as a very good-looking man who bought us presents and seemed a little bored with us. And when he wasn't part of our lives any more, I felt kind of relieved, to be honest. I think Mum felt the same. So we were this cosy little team with Maureen – my sister – Mum and me. She managed to give us a safe and secure home, food on the table and a good education.'

'What a strong, loving woman she must be. Where is she now?'

'She met a really nice American and married him about twenty years ago. They moved to Florida when they both retired. So now Maureen and Rachel and I can go and get a bit of sunshine there from time to time. And we're so pleased to see Mum so happy, even if we miss her.'

'Who's Rachel?'

'My niece.' Laura smiled. 'She's a little like a daughter to me. Maureen and her husband needed lots of help when she was a baby, so I stepped in and helped out with childcare. We really bonded during her baby years.'

'The best kind of bonding.' Adam smiled as he seemed to remember something. 'I was the baby of the family. The youngest of five children. In my case I bonded with my granny who minded me a lot while my mother went back to work. I was very close to her until she died at the age of ninety. She was a lovely woman. So wise and fun. I miss her so much.'

'I'm sure you do,' Laura said, touched by the glint of sadness in Adam's eyes. 'I miss my granny very much too.'

'And you miss that lovely old woman you cared for,' he said softly, touching her hand.

Laura nodded. 'Yes. We became very close. She often said I was the granddaughter she wished she had. But now I'm trying to move on.'

Adam sighed. 'Yeah, well, we have to be happy we have had such wonderful people in our lives, even if the loss is very hard to bear. That's the price we pay for loving someone.'

'It's worth it,' Laura said after a moment's reflection.

'Most of the time.' Adam straightened up as the waiter arrived with coffee and chocolates on a saucer. 'The perfect end to a perfect meal. I hope you thought so too.'

'It was truly exquisite,' Laura replied. She meant it. The food had been wonderful and she had savoured every bite. But it wasn't the food that had delighted her the most. It was being with Adam. Once she forgot about her distrust in all handsome men, she had felt herself being drawn into a bright, warm circle as he talked to her. His twinkly blue-green eyes, his thick dark

red hair, face full of freckles and warm smile made up a kind of
magnetism she couldn't resist. She had basked in his admiring
glances all evening and now she found herself, if not in love,
truly dazzled by this charming man. The fear of having her
heart broken was still there, but now she began to wonder if it
wouldn't be worth it just to experience the thrill of being
with him.

'Here, have one of these,' Adam said, interrupting her
thoughts as he handed her the plate with the chocolates.
'They're from the chocolate factory in Ballinskelligs.'

Laura nibbled on a chocolate while she looked around the
restaurant. She supressed a giggle as she spotted a group of
women at a nearby table wearing checked trousers in loud
colours and bright sweaters. 'I see what you mean about the
golfers,' she said in a hushed tone to Adam. 'But they must have
stopped playing hours ago. It gets dark at around five this time
of year.'

'Yeah, but they don't want to get out of the clothes,' he whispered back. 'It's a badge of honour to them. And the clothes are
very expensive; it's also a status symbol.' He turned back to
Laura. 'I have to get back to Killarney, so I'll drive you home
and then I'll be on my way.'

'Great. Thank you for dinner. It was a real treat.'

'Yeah, this place always delivers.' Adam got up to pull out
Laura's chair. 'We should come back another time. Would you
like to?' he asked, looking almost shy. 'Or we could do something else, maybe? You could come to Killarney to see my
gallery. I know you're interested in art.'

'That would be lovely,' Laura replied as she got her handbag
from the back of her chair, feeling a dart of happiness. He
wanted to see her again. She had to admit that she would love
it too.

A waiter arrived with Laura's jacket as Adam paid the bill,
and then they walked out into the cold, crisp night. Laura

looked up at the glimmering stars and took a deep breath, feeling a surge of joy at being here, right now in this beautiful place with this charming man who had made her feel so good. Could life be better?

When they reached the car, Adam turned to Laura. 'I have a better idea.'

'What's that?'

'Come and meet my family. My parents, my siblings, my nieces and nephews, I mean. They're a fun bunch and they'll love you.'

'Meet your family?' Laura asked, confused. What did this mean? They didn't know each other that well, and she had felt the flirty banter between them had been just for fun.

He laughed. 'Yes. That's what we do in Kerry, invite friends and acquaintances to our homes just to liven things up a bit. No ulterior motives at all. My parents just love to entertain and the more guests the merrier.'

'Oh,' Laura said, realising that what he said was true. People in Kerry were known for their hospitality, so this invitation didn't mean he felt their friendship was becoming more serious or even romantic. This was just an invitation he might have issued to a lot of people the same way. She had been jumping to conclusions. Or maybe it was wishful thinking? It wasn't as if he was proposing marriage; it was just a friendly gesture and a very sweet one at that. She looked at Adam's smiling face and couldn't help smiling back. She wondered briefly if Josephine would have approved of Adam. She liked handsome, charming men, so maybe she would have. Or she might have felt he was a little shallow? 'I'd love to meet them,' she replied, deciding to stop analysing everyone she met through Josephine's eyes.

'We usually do a mad dinner on Friday nights in my parents' house outside Killarney. Anyone who's free comes around so I can't promise everyone will be there, except my parents. I'll give you the Eircode and then you'll find it easily by putting it into Google Maps.'

'What would we do without the Eircode?' Laura asked. 'The best invention since sliced bread.'

'Yes, it's truly genius. I'll text it to you so you'll have it in your phone.'

'Great.' Laura got into the car and closed the door while Adam ran around to the other side. He smiled at her as he started the car, but then they didn't speak until they arrived back at the cottages and Adam pulled up outside number two. Then he turned to her, the engine still running.

'I won't turn her off. She might stall if I do. So I'll say good-night here. Thank you for allowing me to take those photographs. I won't show them to you until I've developed them in my darkroom. Then I'll let you take a look at the ones I want for the exhibition. Is that okay?'

'Of course,' Laura replied. 'I'll be dying to see them.'

'I use a special technique when I develop my photos. Quite old-fashioned but I love to see the image appear slowly on the paper while I work with the chemicals. It's quite magical. I'll let you know when they're ready.' He sat back. 'But I'm looking forward to seeing you next Friday. Text me when you're nearly there so I can meet you at the door. That way you won't come into a room full of strangers on your own.'

'That's perfect,' Laura said and started to open the door. 'Don't get out. I can manage.'

'Thanks.' He looked at her for a moment, then leaned forward and kissed her lightly on the cheek. 'Goodnight, Laura.'

'Goodnight, Adam,' she whispered back, and managed to get out despite her knees having suddenly turned to jelly.

She watched him drive off, the kiss still burning on her cheek, his aftershave still in her nostrils and her heart beating so fast she thought she was going to faint.

15

Laura ran to the surgery on Monday. The heavy showers were fast and furious, so she was trying to get there while there was a break in the clouds. She laughed as she was hit with yet another curtain of rain. She rang the doorbell, cowering against the downpour in the porch while she waited for Bridget to open the door. So, this was it, she was back to nursing again after the break of several years looking after old people. She hadn't hesitated when Bridget asked her to fill in while she looked after her husband. But now Laura felt a little nervous at the thought of working in a busy surgery. Would she remember the drill of nursing and what to do in an emergency? But then she realised she'd be assisting Shane, the best doctor she had ever worked with. It would be fine. It would all come back to her in no time.

'Holy mother,' Bridget exclaimed as the door swung open, 'you'll need a boat to get back home.' She pulled Laura into a brightly lit hall and slammed the door shut. 'Phew. You made it. Take off the wet jacket and come into my office and we'll go through everything. Both doctors are out on calls and the waiting room is empty for the moment, so we have a little while before the post-lunch stampede.'

'On call?' Laura asked as she hung up her dripping rain jacket and followed Bridget, dressed in blue scrubs, into her small office just off the waiting room. 'Isn't that unusual these days?'

Bridget pulled out a chair by the desk. 'Yes, I suppose. But so many older people live far up the mountain roads, and if they're too poorly to drive the doctor comes to them instead. It works here because we have two doctors. But, in any case, not to worry. The nurse stays here and you'll have normal working hours. Nine to five with half an hour for lunch and the weekend off. A coffee break might be possible here and there but you'll have to grab it when you can. You'll find scrubs in the wardrobe just outside my office, so pick a set and then put it on before you come in every morning. I hope that's okay. Please sit down and we'll get started.'

'That sounds fine.' Laura sat down on the chair while Bridget settled opposite her.

They went through the paperwork and how the patient details were recorded into the computer with a system Bridget had designed, which looked very simple and easy to work. Then they walked through the surgery with its two treatment rooms and storeroom where the medical supplies were kept. After that, Laura signed a contract that both doctors would counter-sign on their return.

Just as they finished their tour, the entrance door opened to admit a thin, balding man with kind brown eyes behind steel-rimmed glasses. 'Hello,' he said. 'Am I on time?'

'Perfectly,' Bridget said with a warm smile. 'I hope you didn't get too wet.'

The man put a dripping umbrella in the umbrella stand. 'No, thanks to this excellent umbrella.'

'Laura,' Bridget interrupted. 'This is Brendan, my husband.'

The man, who on closer inspection looked pale and tired, held out his hand. 'Hello, Laura. So nice to meet you. And many thanks for agreeing to stand in for Bridget when we're away.'

Laura smiled and shook his hand. 'Hi, Brendan. Nice to meet you. I'm actually looking forward to working here for a bit. I was getting a little bored with doing nothing.'

The doorbell suddenly rang, which made Bridget laugh. 'Here we go. The post-lunch patients are arriving and the doctors will be here in a minute. Brendan, take Laura into the sitting room and make yourself a cup of tea or coffee. Then you can chat away as long as you want.'

'Yes, sir,' Brendan said and saluted. 'This way, Laura. We have to get out of the way for the post-lunch rush.' His words were confirmed by another chime from the doorbell, and Bridget went to let everyone in.

Brendan led the way through the corridor and into a cosy sitting room where the walls were lined with books. A sofa with an array of cushions stood in front of the fireplace, where a glowing fire of logs and sods of turf spread a welcome warmth. 'Sit down and I'll get you... did you say tea or coffee?'

Laura laughed. 'Neither. I'm grand. Don't bother with anything except if you want something yourself.'

'Not at all.' Brendan gestured towards the sofa. 'Let's sit down and get warm. That rain makes everywhere feel chilly.'

'That's true.' Laura sat down on the sofa and enjoyed the warmth of the fire, the slight smell of turf and the cosy feeling of the room while the rain smattered against the windowpanes. It reminded her of her grandmother's sitting room, where, as a child, she had been fed milk and cookies while her granny read her stories.

'So,' Brendan said, when he had settled beside Laura, 'Bridget told me you wanted to ask me about the school? You're doing some kind of research?'

'Not really.' Laura paused. 'I'm trying to find out more about a young woman who used to teach in the primary school in the Sixties. I saw her face in a photo and it captured me in a strange way. You know how sometimes you see someone in a photo or painting and they stick out in a special way...'

Brendan nodded. 'Oh yes, I see what you mean. I do that myself sometimes. Especially in a photo from long ago. A face, a look or expression in someone's eyes hits you and you want to find out what happened to them afterwards. Who were they, what did they do, are they still alive – things like that.'

Laura nodded, pleased that he seemed to understand. 'So,' she continued, 'I have found out that her name was Oonagh Nolan and that she was a teacher here in Sandy Cove. Maybe you remember her?'

Brendan's eyes lit up. 'Oh, you mean Miss Nolan? Yes, I do remember her. She was my very first teacher in primary school. I know it seems strange to remember someone from when I was only five years old, but the very first year in school always sticks in one's mind, don't you think?'

'That's very true,' Laura said. 'My first teacher was called Mrs Murphy. She was strict but kind behind it all. I had her for the first two years and then we changed teachers. Can't remember much about the other ones though.' She looked at Brendan, feeling excited. 'What can you tell me about Miss Nolan?'

Brendan thought for a moment. 'She was pretty and kind. She had a beautiful singing voice. And she taught us to play the tin whistle. But most of all, it was how she taught us to draw and paint that stuck in my mind. I loved that. And she took us on nature walks on the beach. And there, when we were on the beach, we used to meet this man who was a painter. Or maybe he just did it for a hobby? Not sure. In any case he came to the school once and talked about painting. He drew animals on the blackboard and he gave me this...' Brendan stopped and groped in his pocket. 'I found this in my cupboard with the class photo, so I thought I'd show it to you.' He handed Laura a folded piece of paper.

She opened it and stared at a tiny sketch of a sailing boat against the backdrop of the Skellig Islands. The water was choppy and the boat was leaning over. It was just a rough sketch but brilliantly drawn and Laura felt a shiver as she thought that this had to be by the same artist who had painted Oonagh on the beach. 'Nice drawing,' she said. 'But no signature. Do you have any idea who he was?'

'No. I just remember that he was Miss Nolan's friend. Can't remember hearing his name at all. I saw them walking on the little beach below Starlight Cottages once, but I had to hide because I wasn't allowed to go down there. My dad said it was dangerous, which it was. For a small boy anyway. The slope is very steep and in those days the steps were quite rough and broken in places. Much better now. Anyway, I have this to show you as well.' Brendan handed Laura a photo. 'This is the class photo taken that first year. Miss Nolan is standing at the back, as you can see.'

Her heart beating, Laura studied the black and white photo of a class of children lined up, their teacher at the side of the back row. She was indeed very pretty with dark hair and eyes, looking into the camera with a little smile hovering on her lips. Her face was heart-shaped and her hair tied back in what looked like a plait down her back. Laura felt a strange connection as those eyes seemed to look straight at her. 'Pretty young woman,' she mumbled.

'Indeed,' Brendan agreed. 'She was gentle and kind. Just a girl, really, when I think back. Can't have been more than around twenty-one or so. Just out of teacher training school, I guess.'

'Was she at the school during the whole school year?' Laura asked, still looking at the photo.

'No,' Brendan replied. 'She didn't come back after the

summer holidays. We got another teacher whose name I can't even remember.' He smiled and shook his head. 'It was nearly sixty years ago, so not exactly yesterday.'

'I know. But amazing that you remember that much, I have to say.' Laura handed him back the photo. 'Thank you so much for showing me this.'

'Do you want to copy the photo with your phone?' Brendan asked.

'Oh, yes,' Laura said, touched by his consideration. 'And the little drawing, too, if you don't mind.'

'Not at all,' Brendan said, while Laura took a photo of both items with her phone. 'Glad to help with the research. I used to be a history teacher, you know. I love any kind of history, especially of this area. So many ancient sites around here and all up the coast.'

'I know.' Laura nodded while Brendan put the photo and drawing back into the pocket of his jacket. 'I'm looking forward to touring around Kerry when I have a chance. But right now I can't wait to work here for a bit.'

'We're so happy you agreed to do it.' Brendan sat back, looking suddenly drained. 'I do need a little rest and recuperation.'

'Of course you do.' Laura got up. 'If you tell me where the kitchen is, I'll make you a cup of tea.'

'I should have done that,' Brendan protested.

'Of course not. I can see you're very tired.' Laura walked to the door. 'Is the kitchen through here, down the corridor?'

'Yes. First door on the left,' Brendan said. 'Bridget keeps tea and biscuits near the kettle. You'll find mugs on the shelf just above it.'

The bright kitchen was modern with a country feel. Shaker cupboards lined the walls and an AGA stove emitted a cosy warmth. The fridge was covered in drawings by children. The flagstones and the old scrubbed pine table were the only remnants of the old kitchen, but it all went seamlessly with the modernisation. The back window overlooked the garden with shrubs and flowerbeds, which must be lovely in the summer. Laura found the kettle and all the tea things on a shelf and started to make tea for herself and Brendan. It had been so kind of him to take the trouble to come and share his memories of his very first teacher. What he had said about her confirmed Laura's image of what she had been like. That pretty face with the expressive eyes in the photo stuck in her mind, and she was even more anxious to find out the story behind the painting.

Oonagh and the painter had been friends, Brendan said, but maybe there was more to it than just friendship? She had a few clues, but she needed more... Could that rough little sketch lead anywhere?

When Laura arrived back home, she spotted someone at the door of the cottage next to hers. It had been empty until now, the owner having closed the house for the winter, she had been told. But now a woman with pink and green streaks in her blonde hair, dressed in a green wool dress and bright blue wellies, was sticking a key in the lock and opening the door while Ken barked furiously in the hall of Laura's cottage.

The woman turned around when Laura approached. 'Oh, hi. Your dog seems a bit upset. I hope it's not dangerous.'

Laura laughed. 'Not a bit. He gets nervous when he hears noises, that's all.' She held out her hand. 'I'm Laura Keane. I moved in six weeks ago.'

The woman shook Laura's hand. 'Hello there. I'm Vicky Burke. I usually only come here in the summer. But I took some time off from work just for a rest. It'll be freezing in there but I'll get the heating started and try to keep warm until then.' Her smile was wide and her heavily lined green eyes twinkled as she spoke. She looked to be in her late fifties, and her clothes, make-up and green and pink streaked hair gave a slightly whacky impression.

'You could come into my place while you wait,' Laura offered, surprising herself with how Sandy Cove-ish she had become. But that was the spirit of the village, and it seemed quite natural to help a neighbour this way, even if they didn't know each other. 'Ken is a nice old boy really,' she assured Vicky. 'Not aggressive at all.'

'Oh, I'm not afraid of dogs,' Vicky said as she pushed her damp shoulder-length hair out of her eyes. 'Thanks for the offer, though. Very kind of you. I'll be in as soon as I've turned on the heating and got my stuff in the door.'

'Great. I'll put the kettle on.' Laura smiled and went into her house, taking off her jacket and kicking off her shoes to put on her slippers. She patted Ken on the head. 'That was not a burglar. It was our new neighbour. Her name is Vicky and she seems very nice and fun.'

Ken wagged his tail and trotted back to his bed where he settled with a contented grunt. Laura laughed and went to the kitchen to make tea, switching on lamps on her way. She had just poured hot water into the mugs when the doorbell rang, making Ken bark again.

'Shut up,' Laura called as she swung the door open.

'I will,' Vicky said. 'Except I haven't said anything yet.'

'I meant Ken.' Laura stepped aside to let Vicky in, nearly falling over Ken, who had run to her side. 'And here he is. Ken, say a proper hello to Vicky. She's a friend.'

Vicky fell to her knees and held her hands out to Ken. 'Hello, you handsome lad.'

Ken immediately stopped barking and went to Vicky, who wrapped her arms around him. 'You lovely, furry wonderful creature,' she mumbled into his ear. 'You're really very cuddly, aren't you?'

Ken started licking Vicky's face, wagging his tail furiously.

Vicky laughed and got up. 'I knew he couldn't resist that. Telling a male he's handsome works every time. Even with dogs.'

'I can see that,' Laura said, laughing. 'He seems besotted with you. Go inside and I'll get the tea.'

Ken looked adoringly at Vicky and followed her into the living room, while Laura fetched the tea and a packet of ginger snaps from the kitchen.

Once settled on the sofa, Vicky drank tea and nibbled on a ginger snap while she told Laura all about herself. 'I'm just here for a week or two,' she said. 'I'm a textile designer, you see, and my husband is a writer.'

'Oh.' Laura looked at Vicky with interest. 'What does he write?'

'He writes non-fiction,' Vicky explained. 'Right now he's working on a biography of someone in his family who was a bit of a mystery man. A well-known politician of his day who spent some time here in his youth. But apart from that, my lips are sealed.' She looked at Laura with interest. 'But what about you? Are you an artist? This place seems to attract them, me included. The ocean, the coastline, the birds, the air... Oh, it's so inspirational.'

'I can imagine that it would be,' Laura replied. 'But no, I'm not an artist. I'm a nurse. I inherited this cottage from an old lady I was very close to.'

'Did you?' Vicky looked impressed. She paused and frowned. 'That must be Josephine Clarke, the opera singer?'

Laura nodded. 'Yes, it was. Did you meet her when she was here?'

'Only briefly,' Vicky replied. 'But oh what a woman.'

'Yes,' Laura replied. 'Josephine was such a wonderful person to look after.'

'I can imagine. And then she left you this cottage. What a wonderful gift.'

'Oh yes, it was. But tell me about your work,' Laura said, not in the mood to talk about Josephine. 'You're a textile designer, you said?'

'That's right.' Vicky reached for another biscuit. 'I have my own company. Vicky James Designs.'

'I thought you said your name was Vicky Burke?' Laura asked.

Vicky laughed and waved her hand. 'No, my husband is the Burke. I use my own name for work.'

The Burke? Something suddenly clicked in Laura's head as she heard that name; the memory of her very first conversation with Adam popped into her mind. 'The Burke?' she asked. 'Or do you mean de Burgh?'

Vicky blinked. 'What did you say?'

'Eh, de Burgh?' Laura repeated, her heart beating. 'The old Norman form of the name. Was there someone in your husband's family who used de Burgh instead of Burke? The one he's writing about?'

'I can't tell you,' Vicky said and winked. 'I don't want anyone to think I spilled the beans before they're cooked, so to speak.'

'I see,' Laura agreed, even though that name kept spinning in her head. *'The' Burke... Or de Burgh?* she thought. *P de B...* She desperately wanted to ask if that was the man's initial, but Vicky looked as if she was determined not to answer any more questions. *But could it be?* Laura wondered. *Someone famous, who might have come here to paint as a hobby?* No, that wasn't possible. Laura dismissed the idea as soon as it entered her head. That painting was by a real artist, not an amateur. The conversation turned to the area and the people in the village they both knew.

When Vicky had finished her tea and devoured most of the ginger snaps, she got up to leave. 'Thank you so much for the tea and sympathy. I'm sure my place will be warm enough by now, so I will go and unpack and settle in. I want to be all organised before my husband comes and get some time to work on a few designs. You won't see much of me for the next few days.'

'I won't disturb you,' Laura promised as she saw Vicky out. They said goodbye and agreed to get together once Vicky's husband had arrived.

Laura's mind was full of questions, and that name kept popping into her mind all evening, amazed at the lucky break of stumbling upon it. If that was the man who had painted Oonagh Nolan on the beach. But it might not have been, of course, and the name could just be a coincidence. Then she told herself to push the problem away and concentrate on her new job. No need to worry about anything else for the moment.

But when she went to bed, she looked at the girl in the painting again and then turned it around to face the wall. Oonagh Nolan and her artist friend would have to take a back seat for a while. At least until there was another clue. She had a feeling she knew where she might find it...

16

Laura quickly fell into the routine of the surgery, finding out the very first morning that her little office was the hub of the practice, and that she would hold all the strings when it came to organising patients and various medical procedures such as blood and other tests to be sent to the lab in Killarney. The administrative side took a while to get used to, as she was more familiar with emergency situations. The actual nursing she found came back in a flash, and she quickly managed to assess each patient and sort out what they needed. She realised that she had missed the medical environment. Working in a practice was less stressful than a hospital, and this job was ideal as she had plenty of free time as well.

She made sure she was available each morning on the phone to give out results and then discuss various tests with Shane or Kate, who turned out to be a sweet woman with short brown hair and lovely hazel eyes. Shane could be snappy if things were a bit hectic, but Laura knew how to deal with him, just as she had when they were working together at the A&E in Limerick.

Kate was unflappable, and they quickly bonded in a silent

agreement that women were more practical and better at dealing with stressful situations than most men. But Shane was a brilliant doctor who could suture a wound in such a way that the resulting scar was nearly invisible. And in a real emergency he was brilliant.

Laura felt at home at once in the busy surgery and her nursing skills came back to her in a very short time. But it was quite tiring all the same, she realised, and she gratefully sank into a hot bath every evening with Ken on the bathmat and the radio tuned to classical music. Not much time to think or worry, which was a great change from the idle days when her thoughts had been full of grief. Now, the days were too busy for much thinking, except to do her best at the surgery, running home at lunchtime to walk Ken and then a quick bite before going back to work again. She had still not heard anything from Michael Monaghan, but her solicitor told her it looked like they were putting together some evidence. 'Not that I believe for a second they have a case,' he said. 'But it wouldn't do any harm for us to get some witnesses together who'd be able to confirm that Josephine's mental health was good when that will was drawn up. I have contacted her doctor and her solicitor and they have both agreed to sign a statement to that effect.' He told her not to worry and Laura tried her best not to, even if there was a constant niggle in her mind from time to time.

Gino called late on Thursday when Laura had just gone to bed. 'Hi,' she said. 'I've had quite a hectic day, so I'm in bed already.'

'You must be tired,' Gino said. 'It's only nine o'clock. But I'll hang up if you don't want to talk.'

'No,' Laura protested, his warm voice making her feel good. 'I'm not too tired to chat. But don't ask me to go for a run or hoover the house.'

Gino laughed. 'I wouldn't dream of it.'

'What did you want to talk to me about?'

'Becky's birthday,' he replied. 'It's on Sunday and I'm planning a fun lunch for her as a surprise. I've invited Fidelma and Elaine and her husband and their kids and a few other people that you might like to meet. The weather is set to improve so we can be outside, and I'll grill some meat and cook something special.'

'That sounds great. Sunday will be good because I'll have had a rest from a dinner in Killarney tomorrow.'

'Dinner in Killarney again?' Gino asked, laughing. 'You're a real party princess.'

'The last party was a long time ago. And it's just a family thing, nothing fancy,' Laura said, in an attempt to downplay the dinner at Adam's parents' house. In any case, it was probably true. She imagined that Adam's family would be fairly down to earth and ordinary. 'How are you anyway?' she continued. 'It seems ages since the last time I saw you.'

'I know. I kind of miss you on my morning walk.' He paused. 'I became so used to meeting you that now I'm constantly looking around for you.'

'Oh,' Laura said, his deep voice making her feel warm all over. She imagined his grey eyes looking at her with that glint of affection that she had hoped would mean something more. 'I miss you too,' she said in a near whisper. 'And those morning walks with the dogs,' she added, not to seem too eager. She didn't want to give the wrong signals if he and Becky were getting close.

'It was great to have someone to talk to. But I'm guessing you don't have the time for that now that you're working at the surgery.'

'No. It's difficult to fit dog walking into my day at the moment. But I manage to take Ken out at lunchtime and I let him out for a bit of a wander when I come home in the evening. He doesn't seem to mind.'

'I'm sure he doesn't. Old dogs don't need to race around.'

'Neither do I at the moment. I just had a bath after work and got into my pyjamas and had some dinner. Would have had tea and biscuits before bed but my neighbour ate all my ginger snaps the other day and I haven't had a chance to go to the shop yet.'

'Edwina ate all your ginger snaps?'

'Not her. The other one. Vicky Burke.'

'I thought she was only here in the summer,' Gino remarked.

'So she said. But she came for a few weeks' break to work. And her husband will be arriving soon too.'

'Unusual couple.'

'She was a little weird but nice,' Laura said and laughed. 'Green and pink hair, bright green dress and blue wellies. Is she colour blind?'

'She's a textile designer, so she couldn't be,' Gino argued.

'I suppose not. She's just an eccentric. Very nice if a bit unusual. You couldn't help liking her.'

'I know. She always makes me laugh,' Gino replied. 'Hey, why don't I invite them too? Becky likes them a lot.'

'Good idea,' Laura agreed.

'So,' Gino continued after a brief pause. 'How are you doing really? Are you coping better with the loss of Josephine?'

'Yes and no,' Laura replied, happy to talk about it with someone who knew Josephine so well. 'I feel her presence here very strongly. And it's as if she's waiting for me to find out about that woman and who the artist was.' Laura stopped suddenly, remembering that warning. But she had told him a lot already. And this was Gino, not some stranger who would gossip about what she shared.

'Have you found out anything? Josephine seems to have set you a difficult task,' Gino asked, his voice so soft it nearly made Laura's eyes well up. As always, when something or someone conjured up images of Josephine, all the pent-up emotions floated to the surface.

'Yes, a few things,' she whispered. 'Oh, Gino, I shouldn't tell you about it. Josephine warned me not to, but I'll go crazy if I don't tell *someone*.'

'Your secret is safe with me,' he murmured. 'I might tell Anne-Marie, but she doesn't like to gossip.'

Laura laughed softly, relieved to have him at least as a friend she could confide in. 'Oh, I know I can trust both of you.' She paused and sighed. 'Okay, here's what I know so far.'

'Go on.'

Laura shifted in the bed and fluffed up the pillow under her head. 'You know how Josephine left the cottage to me in her will? And I told you she also left me a painting of a woman on the beach below the cottages.'

'Yes, you did.'

'And I have to somehow find the rightful owner, which seems an impossible task. But so far, I have managed to find out who the woman is.'

'Oh really?' Gino's voice brightened. 'Who was it?'

'A young woman called Oonagh Nolan. She was a teacher here for a while in the mid-1960s. I've seen her in a class photo Bridget's husband showed me.'

'Are you sure it was her?'

'Yes,' Laura said. 'It's unmistakable. They're one and the same. Couldn't be anyone else. But I haven't a clue who the artist was, which is very frustrating.'

'That might be the most difficult part of the puzzle.'

'That's for sure. I seem to be stuck now.' Laura sighed. 'Anyway, Vicky's husband is some kind of historian and he's writing a book about one of his relatives. Some politician who was here around that time, so maybe he can help.'

'Could be that he is the one who has the rest of the story. It sounds like you're on the right track.'

'Do you have any idea who his relative might be?' Laura asked. 'Someone called de Burgh.'

'No, but then I'm not really that clued in about history. Or art. Music and cooking are my first loves.'

'And Becky?' Laura asked, her voice light despite the tiny dart of pain in her heart. Then she was sorry she had said it. 'Forget that last bit.'

'Okay.' Gino laughed.

'It was just a little joke,' Laura said, regretting that last comment. But he didn't seem to have noticed. Was he pretending Becky and he were not involved? Or did they have one of those on-off relationships? Whatever it was, she didn't want to ask questions. Suddenly sleepy, she stifled a yawn. 'I think I'm beginning to drift off. I'd better hang up or I'll snore in your ear.'

Gino laughed softly. 'Okay. Nice to chat with you. Have fun tomorrow. Are you staying the night in Killarney?'

'I haven't decided yet.'

'Well, if you do, I'll mind Ken for you. Let me know.'

'Thanks, Gino. That's very kind of you.'

'No problems. Sweet dreams. Talk soon.' He hung up before she had a chance to reply. Laura went over the conversation before she drifted off. But she couldn't really get a grip on her feelings or figure out how Gino felt about her. Was she becoming a friend – or just a new arrival he was being kind to? Like most people in Sandy Cove, he was extraordinarily helpful and friendly. But was his kindness to her simply courtesy or did it spring from a deeper feeling? Then she realised that she had to stop trying to figure out how he felt about her. He and Becky were together, so a romantic involvement with Gino was not on the cards for Laura, even if he was slightly attracted to her.

She had no answer to these questions and decided to stop asking. If it was meant to happen, it would, whatever 'it' was. She would look forward to the dinner at Adam's house and enjoy herself without worrying about other people's motives or feelings. *Que sera, sera*, she thought, and drifted off to sleep.

As luck would have it, Laura was able to leave the surgery at four o'clock on Friday afternoon, as Kate offered to 'mind the shop' when she heard that Laura had to go to a dinner in Killarney. 'Stay the night there in a nice hotel,' she advised, 'and get a rest and treat yourself to a leisurely breakfast in bed. You've earned it. This week was quite hectic and you managed beautifully.'

Laura thanked her and walked home, her thoughts on the evening ahead. She would book a room in Brooke's Hotel and make her way there as soon as she could. Hopefully Gino would pick Ken up and take care of him for the night.

But when she got home, another lucky break awaited her. Vicky stuck her head out the door. 'Hi there. You're home early. Just to say that Gino called and invited me and Peter to his lunch party on Sunday. Peter is my husband, by the way, and he's arriving tomorrow.'

Laura nodded. 'Oh great. I'm looking forward to meeting him.'

Vicky opened her door wider. 'You want to come in for a cup of tea?'

'Thanks,' Laura said as she took out her key. 'But I'm going to Killarney tonight and I have to get organised. I must call Gino and ask if he'll take Ken for the night.'

'Oh but I'll take him if you like,' Vicky offered. 'That way you don't have to bother Gino and I'll have some company. I can walk him on the beach before it gets dark, if you like, so you can get ready in peace.'

Laura smiled. 'That's so kind of you, Vicky. And I'll take you up on that. Much easier than having to lug him up to Gino's place. And I know Ken adores you.'

'I adore him right back,' Vicky said with a tender smile.

'Wonderful. If you don't mind, I'll give him to you now. I'll give you his bed and his bowls as well.'

'Perfect. I was just going for a stroll on the beach, so it'll be lovely to take him with me.'

When she had organised Ken and seen him and Vicky off down the steps to the beach, Laura went inside to book her room and pack a small overnight bag, wondering idly what to wear.

She had understood from Adam that it was a fairly casual event, so she picked out a white cashmere sweater, her best jeans and high heel boots. A pair of dangly earrings with blue stones completed the outfit perfectly, and Laura felt pleased with her choice. *Casual and trendy*, she thought, *with just a little bit of make-up, the perfect look for a family party*. She began to look forward to the dinner and to meeting Adam's parents and siblings. She imagined it would be a fun gathering with people of all ages from old to very young. Just the kind of lively Irish party she enjoyed.

Added to that, she had sent Adam the little drawing from Brendan she had saved on her phone. Just to see if he recognised the artistic style, which she felt was quite recognisable, even in that rough little sketch. He hadn't replied yet, but she would ask him if he had looked at it. Maybe he could give her a clue that would lead her to the identity of the artist and perhaps even more clues to the relationship between him and Oonagh Nolan...

17

Laura's heart sang as she drove through the beautiful countryside, down winding roads, across bridges and fields dotted with sheep. Large rhododendron bushes already in bloom lined some of the way and, with the setting sun and the slight whiff of grass and woodsmoke, it made her feel like she was in some kind of heaven.

She tuned the car radio to the Irish speaking station and soon the sound of a beautiful ballad played on the tin whistle filled the air. She suddenly felt free of her sorrow and sent a thank you to Josephine for the gift she had left. Life had taken a turn for the better when she came to Kerry, and now, with the job at the surgery that she was sure might last longer than a few weeks, her life was complete. A home in a beautiful village, new friends and a handsome man inviting her out – what more could a woman her age desire? She looked forward to the evening with great anticipation, and especially to seeing Adam's happy face again. Nothing could ruin this evening and the way she felt at this moment.

It didn't take Laura long to get ready once she had checked in at the hotel. She had a quick shower, put on the jeans and sweater, combed through her now shoulder-length curls, pushing them behind her ears, and attached the dangly earrings. Foundation, blusher and several coats of mascara was all she needed. Her glowing cheeks and sparkly blue eyes matched her mood perfectly. She smiled at herself, remembering what Josephine had said about Laura's looks in her letter that she hadn't believed then. But now she did. Her smile widened and she winked at herself in the mirror, then grabbed her handbag and pulled on her jacket. She was ready to meet Adam and his family. She knew she'd like them and hoped they would like her too. *Of course they will*, she told herself as she ran downstairs and got into her car.

It was already dark when Laura set off from the hotel, but Adam had given her a detailed description of the way to his parents' house that was only about ten minutes' drive away. With the added help of the Eircode and Google Maps, she arrived at the surprisingly fancy front gates just after seven o'clock. After they opened, Laura drove up the short drive and stopped in front of the house, staring at it in shock.

This was not the modest four-bedroom house she had imagined; it was a huge modern mock-Georgian house with steps leading up to a pillared portico. Laura looked up in awe at the façade with a multitude of windows, the larger ones on the ground floor all lit up, through which she spotted heavy curtains and a chandelier in the ceiling. She realised that Adam's parents had to be very well off. She could hear music and chatting and realised the party was already in full swing. She parked the car beside a brand new Mercedes, noting its sleek shape and cream leather upholstery. She got out of her car and walked across to the house, the gravel crunching under the high heels of her boots. Just as she was walking up the steps, the massive front door opened and Adam ran to her side, kissing her cheek.

'Hi, gorgeous. Thought I'd come to escort you inside and introduce you to everyone so you don't have to face a bunch of strangers all on your own.'

'Thanks,' Laura replied, basking in his admiring glances. She wondered briefly how he really felt about her but what the hell, why should she try to analyse a good-looking man making her feel good? 'That makes it a lot easier.'

'Thought so.' Adam took her arm and walked up the steps with her as he kept chatting. 'Loads of people here tonight. Mostly family but my older brother brought a guest from the golf club. Having some sort of issue with his mother apparently. But let's hope we can cheer him up, eh?'

'I'll do my best,' Laura promised.

'Your lovely smile is a good start,' Adam remarked, making Laura's face turn pink with pleasure.

When they got into the big, brightly lit hall, Laura noticed that Adam was dressed in a navy velvet blazer, a light blue shirt and a dicky bow, jeans and Gucci loafers. Gone was the artist look, and now he was the picture of style and money. 'You're very elegant tonight,' she said as he helped her take off her jacket.

'Well, we dress up a little bit on Friday nights,' he replied, eyeing her sweater and jeans.

'You do?' Laura asked, suddenly cold, knowing in an instant she was dressed completely wrong. 'You didn't tell me that.'

'I forgot. But hey, who cares? You look lovely in anything.' Before she could protest, he had put his arm around her and ushered her into a huge living room with a cream carpet and what looked like very expensive furniture. A group of people were gathered around the marble fireplace where logs blazed. Laura noticed instantly that everyone was dressed up to the nines, the men in similar outfits to Adam's, some even in full black tie. The women were in strappy dresses and full-on bling.

But that wasn't what startled Laura the most. It was the

person holding court among them. Someone talking loudly in a voice that was horribly familiar. When there was a sudden hush, Laura could hear the man's loud voice saying something that made her freeze. She thought she knew that voice, but couldn't believe he was really here. But when the group shifted, she could see that she had been right. It was him all right. What he said next shocked her to the core.

18

'My mother was old and confused,' Laura heard the man say. 'And the woman caring for her was clever enough to manipulate her to include her in the will.' He paused. 'I didn't mind the money or the painting, but the house...'

'Her house?' someone asked. 'That gorgeous Georgian house in Dublin?'

'No. That was left to me,' he replied. 'It was a sweet little cottage in Sandy Cove my wife had her eye on. Didn't you, darling?' he asked, looking at the woman with platinum blonde hair in a too-tight lamé dress standing beside him.

She nodded. 'Oh yes. I thought it would be the perfect place to stay for a few weeks in the summer. Such a gorgeous cottage for a short break. You know, when it gets too hot in Marbella. The perfect place to cool off.'

'But now this woman is living there,' the man continued, 'and pretends that my mother wanted her to have it. Well, that won't last long. I'm in the process of contesting the will. My solicitor is drawing it up at the moment and we'll be in court soon.'

Feeling suddenly dizzy, Laura gripped Adam's arm as the

group shifted and she could see the man clearly. Her fears were confirmed. It was Michael Monaghan, Josephine's son. As their eyes met across the room, she backed away, knowing instantly that she had to leave.

Adam looked at her. 'What's the matter? You're as white as a sheet.'

'Not feeling well,' Laura muttered. 'Excuse me...' Her hand over her mouth, she stifled a sob and ran out of the room, across the hall, nearly slipping on the tiles and out through the door without stopping to get her jacket.

Adam caught up with her when she reached her car. 'Hey, wait a minute,' he called. 'What happened there? One minute you were all smiles and then you—'

'He was talking about me,' Laura sobbed.

Adam blinked. 'You? Why...?' Then he stopped. 'Okay. I think I see what's going on. That man – Mick, my brother's friend... is Josephine Clarke's son as far as I know. Was she the old woman you cared for? The one you were so sad about?'

With her back to him, fumbling for the key in her bag, Laura nodded. 'Yes.' She turned around and stared at Adam. 'But it's *not* true what he said.' Her voice shook as she fought back tears. 'I didn't manipulate her or do anything to make her leave me anything in her will. I didn't even know she had a will or that she was planning anything of the sort. I spent the last two years of her life trying to make her happy and comfort her because she was so sad and lonely. You probably don't believe me, but that's the way it was.' She finally found the key and pressed it to open the car. 'I'm sorry, Adam, I can't stay under the circumstances. I'm sorry if I'm rude to your parents but I hope you understand.'

He took her hand. 'I do. Of course. But this is all news to me. You didn't tell me the old lady you were caring for was Josephine Clarke. I only just found out that my brother's friend was her son. But now I begin to see the picture. I don't know

that guy at all, but I do know you. So of course I believe you.'
He paused. 'So the cottage you live in...?'

'Yes,' Laura whispered. 'That's the one he was talking about.'

'And... the painting? Is that the one you were asking me about?'

Laura nodded. 'Yes. I'm sorry I didn't tell the truth about it but I couldn't because—'

'Okay,' Adam interrupted. 'I get it. Wait here a minute. I'll go and make some excuse to my parents and get your jacket. And then we'll go somewhere nice and talk. I'm not in the mood for a party either as you're so upset. And my brother's golfing friend and his wife put me off ever meeting either of them again. Don't go, Laura. We'll sort this out. I won't be long.'

'I'm sorry if I ruined the party,' Laura said as he moved off. 'Your mother must have cooked all day for all those people.'

Adam laughed. 'Cook? My mother? No, they have staff. Don't worry, they won't even notice.'

Laura got in the car while she waited and tried to calm down. She had felt so good earlier; her life had seemed so perfect for just an instant. She had looked forward so much to the party and to meeting Adam's family. But now, after seeing Michael Monaghan and hearing that he was going to make a court case against her, she felt that her happy little world was crumbling. She would lose the cottage for sure. He had so much money and could afford the best lawyers... Laura put her hands over her face. What was she going to do?

Adam got in beside her and gently put her jacket over her shoulders. 'There,' he said. 'Let's get out of here.'

She turned to look at him. 'Are you coming in my car? How are you getting back?'

'I'll get a taxi or something. Now, drive. We'll go to a little pub I know on the way to Killarney. Cosy and quiet and they do a great fish and chips.'

Laura started the car and slowly backed across the driveway. Then she turned the car and made her way down the drive and through the gate. 'You didn't have to leave the party,' she said. 'I'd have been fine on my own.'

'No, you wouldn't,' he argued. 'You need a little cheering up and some food. The pub is within walking distance to your hotel, so if you want a glass of wine or two, you can leave the car outside and I'll walk with you and take a taxi back to my parents',' he added. 'Or I can just as easily go home to my flat over the gallery. Not really in the mood for a party.'

'I've ruined your evening,' Laura said miserably.

'Stop it,' he ordered. 'No need to beat yourself up. What happened wasn't your fault. And you couldn't possibly stay after what that moron said about you.'

'That's true.' Laura looked ahead as they neared Killarney. 'Where is this little pub, then?'

'We're nearly there. It's that little thatched cottage just before the crossroads. One of those tiny places that most people miss.'

'Oh. I see it now.' Laura slowed the car and pulled up outside a whitewashed cottage with a thatched roof and a red door, over which there was a sign that said, 'Murphy's Snug and Eatery'. The little windows were all lit up and Laura could smell a mixture of turf smoke and good food as she got out of the car. She was suddenly hungry and looked forward to something to eat and a glass of wine. She was very grateful to Adam for coming with her. 'It looks very nice,' she said as he held the door open for her.

'A home away from home,' he replied, as he helped her off with her coat, shrugged out of his leather jacket and hung both on a peg inside the door.

'It's really welcoming and cosy.' Laura looked around the small pub that had a bar counter at one end and four small tables dotted around the sawdust-strewn tiled floor. Sods of turf glowed in the old-fashioned fireplace, and she felt as if she had stepped back in time.

The pub was empty, but voices could be heard through the open door behind the bar. 'Hello?' Adam shouted. 'Anyone in?'

A bearded man with curly grey hair stuck his head through the door. 'Oh, hello there, Adam. Didn't know you were coming tonight.'

'Neither did I until a little while ago,' Adam said. 'But the evening took a different turn and here we are, starving and thirsty. Anything you can do about that, do you think, John?'

'Absolutely,' John replied with a grin. 'What would you and your pretty friend like?'

'Fish and chips and some of your best white, please.' Adam pulled out a chair at a table near the fireplace. 'And we'll sit here if that's okay.'

'It is,' John said. 'Wine coming right up. And I'll rustle up some bread and olive oil to nibble on while you wait for the food.'

Laura and Adam sat down and John arrived within seconds, loaded with cutlery, napkins, a basket of bread and a bowl of olive oil. 'Two glasses of Pinot Grigio and plates coming up,' he said. Then he turned to Laura and grabbed her hand. 'Hello there. I'm John Murphy. And you are...?'

'Laura Keane.' She returned his warm smile as they shook hands and felt instantly better. He seemed such a nice man and his little pub was gorgeous. 'What a wonderful place you have here,' she said.

'Thank you.' John beamed at her. 'It's my folly really. Run at a loss but I love cooking for people who become friends after eating here. Anyway, must go and see to your dinner.' He bowed theatrically and left.

Laura looked at Adam and laughed. 'I feel like I'm in some kind of twilight zone or parallel universe. As if this place only exists in a dream and that it will be gone tomorrow.'

'I know what you mean. It is rather special. A bit old school.' Adam nodded and pushed the bread basket towards her. 'Here, try some bread. That'll make you feel more real.'

Laura took a slice of bread, broke it in half and dipped it in the olive oil. 'Delicious,' she mumbled through her bite. 'Just what I needed. I'm starving.'

'Me too.' Adam helped himself to bread and olive oil and smiled at John as he arrived at their table with two glasses of white wine. 'Thanks, John.'

'You're welcome,' John replied. 'Can't stay and chat. The fish and chips need minding. Won't be a tick.' He ran back to the kitchen.

Adam raised his glass. 'Cheers to John and his pub. I think the evening just took a turn for the better, don't you?'

'Oh yes,' Laura agreed, dipping more bread in olive oil and then drinking some wine. 'I'm feeling a little more cheerful now. Even though I know I'll have to face something horrible very soon.'

'Let's forget about that for tonight,' Adam suggested. 'Don't let that awful man spoil our evening.' He paused for a moment. Then he drank some wine and looked at Laura. 'Just one thing... That painting? You actually have it in your cottage?' His eyes on her had an odd glint she couldn't quite decipher.

Laura felt suddenly awkward. 'Yes. I'm sorry I didn't tell you the truth, but I was sworn to secrecy about it. I wasn't to tell anyone I had it. It could be valuable.'

'I see.' Adam frowned. 'So you have no idea who painted it?'

'That bit is true, I really have no clue,' Laura replied.

'You sent me a little drawing earlier. What was that about?'

'I... Well, it was...' Laura paused, trying to find the right words to explain. She wasn't sure what she should reveal, but Adam had left the party with her and she felt like she owed him something. He'd been so kind. So she told Adam about Brendan and what he had told her about Oonagh Nolan and her artist friend, and how he had been given the drawing when he was a small child.

Adam looked at her when she had finished. 'Okay. I'm beginning to get the picture. I haven't actually looked at the drawing, but I will in a minute. I'm getting some strange vibes here. Something is drifting into my memory bank...'

They were interrupted by John arriving at their table with two plates of fish and chips. 'There you go, me darlins,' he said and put a plate in front of each of them. 'I see you're deep in something important, so I'll tiptoe away. Give me a shout if you need anything. Like wine, as I see you've finished the glasses. Will I bring you the rest of the bottle?'

'Yes please,' Adam said, his eyes still on Laura. 'That painting... You think it's valuable?'

She nodded. 'Yes, I do.'

'May I see it?'

Laura squirmed. 'I'll think about it.'

Adam's eyes turned suddenly cold for a moment. 'Don't think too long. You've been asking me about it for a while now. How can I help you find the artist if I can't see it?'

'Okay. Fair enough,' Laura replied, realising how annoying she must have been. She'd been teasing him about this mysterious painting long enough. 'Of course you can come and take a look at it. But call me first and we'll fix a time.'

Adam nodded. 'Of course. I'll let you know when I'm nearby.'

'Great. I need to talk about it, though,' she said. 'Just to explain that I'm worried Michael will want the painting as well as the cottage if he finds out that it's valuable. Not that it means that much to me, except Josephine somehow gave me the task of finding what she called "the rightful owner", whoever that might be. It seems to have meant a lot to her.' Laura drew breath and took a sip of wine from the glass that Adam had filled.

'The rightful owner?' Adam asked and took his phone from

his pocket. 'I'm just going to take a look at the little drawing you sent...' He looked at the photo for a while, studying it with interest. 'It's a rough sketch but whoever drew it has great talent. To get the feel of the wind and the waves like that in just a few lines...' He looked at Laura with excitement. 'This is someone whose work I think I know well. But I can't be sure until I see that painting.'

'I know. And you'll see it next time you come over,' Laura promised.

Adam nodded and put away the phone. 'Great. I won't be able to tell you who I think the artist is until I've seen it.' He smiled apologetically. 'Sorry to be pushy but I'm dying to see it. Art mysteries always excite me. This one is particularly intriguing.'

'But you have an idea who the artist might be?' Laura asked. She wanted to know, even if it was just a hint, so she could do her own research once she had a name to work on. 'Tell me what you're thinking.'

'I might have a clue or two. But can we leave this alone now? I don't like guesswork.'

Laura looked down at the plate with fish and chips that looked and smelled so inviting. She picked up her knife and fork. 'You're right. This looks too good to waste.'

Adam laughed and grabbed his cutlery. 'Yes. Let's dig in and talk about other things, if you like.'

'Oh, yes.' Laura attacked the food with gusto, enjoying the crisp batter of the freshly cooked fish and the chips that were cooked to perfection. She dipped bits of fish into the tartar sauce and gave herself up to the wonderful flavours. 'This is amazing,' she said between bites.

'I'm glad you're enjoying it. In any case, I think we should enjoy the rest of the evening and get to know each other better.' He leaned forward and looked into her eyes. 'I want to make you smile again.'

Laura sighed. 'Oh, I don't think I can smile until the problem with Michael Monaghan is sorted.'

'Who is he really?' Adam asked, sitting back. 'I mean why is he called Monaghan and not Clarke?'

'Clarke was Josephine's maiden name,' Laura replied after a brief pause. 'She was only married to Michael's father for a few years. He wanted her to stop singing and be a housewife and she refused.'

'Josephine Clarke a housewife?' Adam asked incredulously. 'With that voice? She was a world-famous opera singer. Was he out of his mind?'

Laura shrugged. 'No idea. So they split up and I think her ex-husband got custody of Michael. And, later on, she met a man called Edward, who was the love of her life. He was her manager or financial adviser or something like that. They lived together for years until Edward died of cancer. After that, she was on her own. She never stopped loving him.'

'So that would have made her relationship with her son a little strained?' Adam suggested.

Laura nodded. 'Well, yes, it would have, I suppose. She did try to mend things and say sorry for what happened, but he couldn't forgive her, is my guess. I think they made some kind of peace later, but they were never close.'

Adam pushed his empty plate away and picked up his glass. 'So then he didn't feel under any obligation to look after her in her old age, I suppose.'

'Possibly. He just organised someone to care for her through the agency I worked for. So that's how I came to care for her. He didn't come to see her other than once a year or so and the odd phone call. But, I mean, she was his mother. Why couldn't he try to understand her and at least come and see her more often?'

'Looks like he held a grudge,' Adam mused. 'You never know what goes on behind closed doors.'

'I don't know what to do,' Laura said, her heart contracting at the thought of the court case she felt she would be dragged into.

'Do you have a good lawyer?' Adam asked.

'Yes. I have a solicitor who has been helping me. My sister recommended him.' She paused for a moment. 'But now that I think about it, I am hoping that both Josephine's solicitor and her doctor will testify that she was of sound mind when she made that will. Also, my friend Gino promised to help out if this kind of thing happened. Josephine was in constant contact with him by phone all through her final year.'

'Gino, the baker?' Adam asked. 'Becky's Gino?'

Laura flinched at the way Adam described him. She didn't quite know why the idea of Becky and Gino in a relationship disturbed her so much. 'Yeah, well, I'm not sure what their relationship is,' she said. 'But that's the Gino I meant.'

As she looked at Adam's handsome face, his polished appearance down to his Gucci loafers, Gino's windblown hair, dark beard and luminous grey eyes drifted into her mind's eye. Then she chided herself. What was she doing? Was she not happy to have a kind, good-looking man like Adam who was obviously very interested in her? Was all that not enough? He had been very kind tonight and helped her through an upsetting moment, listening to her story sympathetically.

But why was she constantly thinking about Gino? He was obviously taken and had been a good friend, nothing more. He belonged to Becky, even if they hadn't officially declared their relationship status and she had said she had a crush on Adam. But now Laura began to realise that it had been a joke. Gino was off-limits, and she needed to put her feelings for him on hold. Adam was here and offering her both help and sympathy.

Get a grip, she told herself sternly. *Don't get carried away by romantic notions about a man just because he looks like something out of* Wuthering Heights. *You are no Cathy and Gino is no Heathcliff, even if he lives in the wilderness and walks in the hills with his dog in stormy weather.* Then she suddenly laughed at herself, which made Adam raise an eyebrow.

'What was that all about?' he asked. 'You look as if you've been having some kind of conversation in your head.'

'I did,' Laura replied with a laugh. 'With myself. Told myself off for being silly and that I'll get through this. Michael Monaghan is *not* going to get away with it.'

'That's the spirit,' Adam said with a wide grin. 'In any case, he might just be hoping he can scare you to give up the cottage. If you get your solicitor on board and all those other people you mentioned, I'd say he'll back off.'

'Cheers to that,' Laura said and held up her glass.

Adam clinked his glass to hers and they drained them. 'I'm glad that's all sorted, then. But maybe we should get going?' he suggested. 'Unless you want dessert or coffee?'

Laura shook her head. 'No thanks, I'm fine. It was a delicious meal but I don't think I could manage more food.'

Adam nodded and got up. 'Okay. I'll walk you to your hotel and then I'll take a taxi back to the party. Could be an idea to do a little spying on that Monaghan guy and his wife. I might be able to suss out what they're actually up to. And I should really explain properly to my parents what happened.'

'Please apologise to them on my behalf,' Laura said, and rose as Adam pulled out her chair. 'I would have loved to have met them.'

'You will another time,' Adam promised. 'Hang on, I'll just go and say goodbye to John and pay the bill.'

But there was no need; John had already arrived at their table with their coats. 'I'll put it on your tab, Adam,' he said, holding out Laura's coat to her. 'Lovely to meet you, Laura.'

'And you,' she said as she shrugged on her coat. 'The fish and chips were the best I've ever eaten.'

'That's a huge compliment.' John smiled warmly. 'Do come

back soon and then I could cook you up a storm with my famous beef ragu.'

'I will,' Laura promised.

They left the little pub and walked slowly home through the dark and silent streets until they reached the hotel. 'Whatever you do,' he warned before he walked away. 'Don't tell that Monaghan guy that the painting might be valuable. I'll help you with it if it turns out to be something important.' Then he said goodnight and kissed Laura on the cheek, promising to call her soon to arrange a date for him to come and see the painting.

The kiss on the cheek didn't affect Laura the way it had before. She didn't float up the stairs or go to sleep dreaming of Adam. As she lay in her bed in the hotel, the memory of Michael Monaghan's cold eyes made her momentarily freeze, before she conjured up a more pleasant memory to help her finally drift off.

She couldn't help it. What drifted into her tired brain was a pair of grey eyes looking at her over a pizza, on a beautiful afternoon in the hills above Sandy Cove...

19

The following day, Laura didn't linger in the hotel but prepared to leave after breakfast. She didn't want to hang around after last night, even if it had ended in a very nice way. Adam had been extraordinarily kind, and the evening had taken a more pleasant turn after the shock of hearing Michael Monaghan's accusations. Now she just wanted to get home to her house and Ken and to plan what she would do next. She would call the solicitor as soon as she could after the weekend, and he would hopefully advise her on what to do.

Just as she was paying the bill, her phone rang. She excused herself to the receptionist and pulled her phone from her bag; she was surprised to hear Rachel's voice.

'Hi, Auntie Laura, hope I'm not disturbing you,' Rachel said, sounding a little out of breath.

'Not really. But hold on a second.' Laura completed the payment of her hotel bill, thanked the receptionist and picked up her phone again, wandering out of the hotel as she spoke. 'Okay, I'm free to talk. I'm in Killarney and have to walk to get my car that I parked outside a pub last night.'

Rachel laughed. 'Out on the town, were you? Great stuff,

Auntie. But before you go on, I should tell you that I'm not far away, actually. I'm on my way to visit you and I was hoping you could pick me up.'

'Where are you?' Laura asked, not at all surprised by the sudden arrival of her niece. It was typical of Rachel, who always acted on impulse and never asked for permission to do anything.

'I'm at the train station in Killarney,' Rachel replied. 'Just arrived. Took the very early train from Dublin and here I am. I have a few days off lectures and exams, so I thought I'd come and see you.'

'Does Maureen know you're here?' Laura asked.

'Yes. It was her idea. She told me to come when I said I needed a bit of a holiday. Can't wait to see the cottage and the village, not to mention that dishy man you were talking about.'

'Is that the real reason you're here?' Laura asked, always worried about Rachel like a mother hen. 'There's nothing wrong, is there?'

Rachel laughed. 'No, you fuss-pot. Nothing wrong other than I needed a break before the exams start and that I missed you. And I saw that the weather in Kerry is glorious right now.'

'Oh... Okay,' Laura said, feeling both shocked and happy that Rachel was here. She would be good company and cheer Laura up if nothing else. 'Stay where you are. I'll be at the station in about twenty minutes or so.'

'Brilliant,' Rachel said and hung up without saying goodbye.

Laura shook her head and laughed. Well, that had shaken her out of her misery. Rachel would see everything from a more positive perspective and might even think of a solution for her upcoming court case. As she walked, she picked up her phone to call Gino and ask if it would be okay to bring Rachel to Becky's birthday party on Sunday.

He answered straight away. 'Hi, Laura, how are things?' he asked, his warm voice making her smile.

'Great, thanks. I'm still in Killarney but will be home

shortly. Vicky next door looked after Ken, by the way, so I decided not to bother you. They have become great friends.'

'So I saw this morning when I walked Anne-Marie on the beach. We had a great chat. So how was the party?'

'It was... Well, it kind of derailed slightly,' Laura said cryptically, not wanting to go into what had happened. 'I'll explain later.' She paused. 'The reason I called you is that my niece has arrived unexpectedly, and I was wondering if it would be okay to bring her to your party tomorrow?'

'Of course. I'll be looking forward to meeting her.'

'Oh great. I'm sure you'll like her.'

'If she is anything like you, I'm sure I will,' Gino replied. 'And I'm looking forward to seeing you again. You've been a bit of a stranger lately.'

'Yeah, well, it's hard to fit in dog walking or socialising with the new job,' Laura said evasively.

It wasn't the real reason. She had been avoiding Gino lately because of her feelings for him. What had begun as a spark that day, as they had walked up the hill to his house, was now a slowly burning flame in her heart. Adam's attentions had been very flattering, but she knew now that she could never feel for him what she felt for Gino. She knew that his possible relationship with Becky stood in the way of it ever becoming mutual. She had shied away from seeing him to spare herself even more pain. And with his strange insight into other people's feelings, she was sure she'd give herself away if they spent any time alone together.

Becky's birthday party would be difficult, but there would be a lot of people around her so she could push away her feelings and try to have fun. And Becky was becoming such a close friend, so Laura tried her best to be happy that she had found love with Gino. They were probably better suited to each other anyway. And then there was Adam... Laura shook her head and smiled. He had been so flirty and fun, but she knew it didn't mean anything except that he found her attractive. Well, wasn't he the real dream come true for a middle-aged woman? But the problem was the lack of chemistry between them. He was so polished and perfect in every way and seemed so keen on her.

'What should I do?' Laura asked Rachel as they drove down the road to Sandy Cove.

Rachel fluffed up her reddish blonde hair, newly cut very short, and touched up her lipstick, looking into the mirror on the sunshade. 'Do? About the men?' Rachel thought for a moment while she put away her lipstick. She looked out at the landscape that was whizzing by. 'I think you should forget about this Gino, who seems to be in some kind of relationship with your friend. That is bound to create problems. Then you should just have fun with this Adam guy. He seems so into you from what you've told me.'

'But there isn't much chemistry,' Laura argued. 'I mean I don't feel it, even if he seems to. Wouldn't it be unfair to just have fun with him when I know I could never feel that deeply?'

'You should think like a man,' Rachel declared. 'Men don't have any angst about having fun and going on dates with women they have no intention of committing to. And isn't Adam fantastic arm candy?'

'Oh please.' Laura rolled her eyes. 'At my age, I don't need arm candy.'

'Every woman needs arm candy,' Rachel retorted. 'In any case, you look way younger than your age.'

Laura patted Rachel's arm. 'Thank you, sweetheart, you're very kind.'

'It's not kindness, it's the truth.' Rachel looked out the window as they neared the village. 'Oh, this is so pretty!' she exclaimed. 'And I can see the ocean. And look at all those cute little shops and the houses and the pub,' she added as they drove down the main street. 'This is like a postcard.'

'I know. I love it.' Laura slowed down and pulled up outside the grocery shop. 'I have to get a few things for lunch. Do you want to come with me?'

'You bet,' Rachel said, getting out of the car as soon as Laura had turned off the engine.

They went into the shop together. Laura took a basket and started to pick out a few things, while Rachel wandered around and seemed to breathe in the atmosphere of the quaint little place. As Laura walked up to the checkout, she found Rachel deep in conversation with the lovely shop assistant. They both stopped talking as Laura arrived with her basket.

'I see you've met Pauline,' Laura said as she put her groceries on the counter to be checked through the till.

Rachel nodded. 'Yes, and she's told me so much about everyone already.'

'Pauline is the best source of information around here,' Laura said, smiling. 'She doesn't miss a thing.'

'That's true,' Pauline agreed with a grin. 'Everyone shops here, so there is quite a crowd at times.' She winked at Rachel. 'It's mad how they seem to want to tell me all the comings and goings in their lives. Not that I spread it around, though,' she added. 'Except if it's really interesting.' She looked at Laura. 'Oh, that reminds me. There was a man here earlier asking about you.'

'Really?'

'Could it be Adam?' Rachel suggested. She turned to Pauline. 'Was he drop-dead gorgeous?'

'No.' Pauline shook her head, making her dark curls dance. 'He was quite old with grey hair and pale blue eyes. And he wasn't really that nice, I thought.'

Laura looked thoughtfully at Pauline. It sounded like

Michael Monaghan, but what would he be doing here? 'What sort of things did he ask?'

Pauline checked Laura's groceries through the till. 'Just if you were settling in here and planned to stay on for good. Were you going to let your cottage and so on. But as he was a stranger, I didn't tell him anything. I mean, you're one of us now and we don't tell random people our business, do we?'

'No, we don't,' Laura said, touched by Pauline's remark.

'Isn't that so great?' Rachel said as they went out the door, having said goodbye to Pauline. 'I mean that you're now a part of the village and that they would never tell strangers your business. And also...' She paused and stopped by the car, staring at Laura. 'What was that guy doing here, asking questions about you? Who was he anyway?'

'I'll tell you when we get home,' Laura said as she got into the car. She was relieved that Pauline hadn't told Michael anything, but his visit worried her just the same.

They drove the short distance to the cottage, and then Laura gave Rachel a tour around the house that ended on the back terrace, where Rachel, speechless, looked in awe over the view of the bay, the cliffs and the glittering ocean all the way to the Skellig Islands.

'Wow,' Rachel whispered and turned to Laura with tears in her eyes. 'This is so beautiful it makes me cry. This view is truly heavenly. You just want to stay here forever and look at it.'

'I know.' Laura put her arm around Rachel's shoulder as they looked out across the bay together. 'It's quite distracting. But how about lunch? I got some soup and bread and then we can have a good chat.'

Rachel turned to Laura. 'And then you can tell me about what's going on with Josephine's son. I suppose he was the man Pauline talked about.'

'Yes. I think so. I met him yesterday by sheer accident. I'll tell you about it in a minute.'

'Great. I'll just wash my hands and meet you in the kitchen.'

'You can use my bathroom. The ensuite beside my bedroom. The door is open.' Laura took a last look at the view and went into the kitchen to put away the groceries and prepare lunch. Moments later, she heard Rachel give a shout from the bedroom.

Laura turned off the hotplate under the soup and rushed to see what Rachel was so excited about. She found her by the bed, staring at the painting that she had turned around. 'What's going on?' Laura panted.

Rachel didn't reply but kept staring at the painting. 'It's a de Barra,' she whispered, pointing at it, her eyes wide and her face pale. 'It's that painting that went missing years ago. *Girl on a Beach* by Louis de Barra. Holy mother, Laura, it must be worth a fortune.'

20

Her knees weak, Laura sank down on the bed. 'Wh-what?' she stammered. 'Louis de Barra? I don't think I've heard of him.'

'Of course you have. His work is in the National Gallery. You know, that huge painting of the Dublin Mountains and some fantastic abstracts too. He lived in Provence for years and did all his later work there before he died.'

'De Barra?' Laura said, the name ringing a very distant bell in her mind. 'Oh, maybe I've seen that one you're talking about. I kind of recognise the name. But how do you know all this?'

'I did an art course before I got into economics, if you remember. And we studied Irish contemporary art then.' Rachel turned to the painting. 'Is it the one Josephine left you?'

'Yes.' Laura went closer and looked at the little signature at the bottom. 'I thought it was someone called de Burgh or Burke, or even de Paor or Power. But now I see it says L de B and not P. But Josephine said it was connected to Starlight Cottages. How could that be? I've done some research and found out that the girl in the painting was called Oonagh Nolan and that she lived here in the mid-Sixties.'

'Yes.' Rachel nodded. 'That would fit. Louis de Barra lived

in Ireland then but later moved to the South of France, because his wife, Clodagh, was ill and the climate there would be better for her than the Irish rain.'

'He was married to a woman called Clodagh?' Laura felt a dart of disappointment. She had imagined a sweet love story between the painter and the young woman, but now it didn't seem so romantic, or even possible. Maybe the girl in the panting wasn't Oonagh but the wife, the one who had been ill? But then Laura looked at her again and knew that she truly was Oonagh, the same woman she had seen in the class photo.

'Yes, her name was Clodagh O'Brien before they were married. But we need to do a little more research into Louis de Barra's life, I think,' Rachel said and turned to leave the room. 'But now I feel hungry, so that soup smells really good.'

Laura didn't move; she kept staring at the painting. 'Where on earth did Josephine get this painting? I mean if it's a work by such a famous artist, wouldn't she have known about it? She was told it had something to do with Sandy Cove. But who told her?'

'That is very strange all right,' Rachel said.

'So many secrets,' Laura mumbled. 'So many unanswered questions...'

Over lunch in the kitchen, which Rachel declared to be 'super-cosy', they enjoyed fragrant tomato soup accompanied by walnut bread from Gino's bakery and a slab of local goats' cheese.

'So, Michael Monaghan,' Rachel said when she had nearly finished her soup. 'What is he up to?'

'No good at all,' Laura replied, and launched into what had happened the night before.

'Oh God.' Rachel shook her head. 'I thought he'd given up on that.'

'Me too. I've been lulled into a sense of security over the last few weeks. I haven't heard anything from him and I hoped he had dropped all this. My solicitor said he was gathering evidence to use against Monaghan. Witnesses who would swear Josephine was in her full mental health. But I hoped I wouldn't have to use them. Now it seems I may have to...'

'Maybe he was just playing to the gallery?' Rachel suggested. 'Trying to impress people? To seem powerful?'

'I think he meant it.' Laura shivered. 'He looked at me with such hatred.'

Laura pulled off a piece of bread, 'But why would he hate you?'

'He seems to think I didn't deserve the inheritance.'

'But you did,' Rachel said with feeling. 'You worked so hard and made Josephine's final years so happy.'

'I know.' Laura smiled at the memories. 'We did have fun. I think she appreciated that very much. It's why she wanted me to come here. She sent me a letter telling me so – it came as part of the inheritance. She told me she wanted me to find what she called "the rightful owner" of that painting.'

'Well, you've found the woman in the painting; maybe it's her? Maybe you need to search more to see where she is living now? Or at least if she is still alive.'

'Doesn't seem possible to find her,' Laura remarked. 'But maybe I haven't tried hard enough. I should ask around a bit more. All I came up with so far is a man who was a pupil in the primary school here when she was a teacher. But it seems she left after only one term and he didn't know where she went. Of course he was a small child then, so why would he?'

'True,' Laura agreed, helping herself to another slice. 'This bread is delicious.'

'From Gino's bakery.' Laura scraped the bottom of her bowl.

'You look strange when you say his name,' Rachel said, looking amused. 'You really do have a crush on him, don't you? Or more than a crush, I'd say.'

Laura got up from the table. 'I don't want to talk about it. Do you want more soup?'

'No thanks. It was delicious but I ate a lot of that yummy bread, so I'm full.' Rachel got to her feet. 'I should really unpack and make my bed. I brought my own sheets so you wouldn't have extra laundry. I suppose I can take one of the rooms upstairs?'

'Yes. The back bedroom has views of the sea, so I'd pick that one if I were you.'

'Fabulous,' Rachel said, and left the kitchen.

While she tidied up after lunch, Laura thought about what had happened earlier. Rachel was so sure that the painter Louis de Barra was the artist who had painted *The Girl on the Beach* and that it was a painting that had somehow disappeared. If that was true, it would cause a sensation in the art world when it came out. It would be best if Oonagh Nolan was found before then, to establish if she was indeed the young woman and, in that case, if the painting should be given to her. But had Josephine known who the artist was? And where had she got it? Those were the questions she found the most frustrating. She had a feeling she would never know the answer to either of them.

Laura stared out the kitchen window, deep in thought. Then she went into the living room to find her phone and called Adam's number. He had said he had an idea, by looking at that little drawing, so now he might have also discovered the identity of the artist.

But before she had a chance to call him, her phone rang and she saw it was him. 'Hi,' she said. 'How strange. I was just going to call you.'

'Oh? What about?'

'To thank you for last night. You rescued me from a very difficult situation. I hope your parents weren't offended.'

'Not a bit. I explained it all in a roundabout way. I think

they forgot all about it anyway. And I enjoyed last night too. We had a great chat, I thought.'

'We did,' Laura agreed. 'I also wanted to ask you if you had any more ideas about that artist. You said you had to look it up, so maybe you've found something?'

'I might have.' He paused. 'I'd love to see it, actually. Just to make sure. All I can tell you is that it could be big.' Laura felt a sudden chill. If it was as valuable as Rachel said it was, she suddenly felt very protective of it again. 'I can't come over right now, but I was wondering if you could send me a photo of it? That would be the easiest way to confirm my suspicions.'

'Eh, well, maybe later,' Laura stammered. 'I'm very busy at the moment. My niece is visiting, so I have to go and help her settle in. And then we're going to be out all day tomorrow. In any case, I'm not sure I want to send you a photo just like that. Who knows what could happen to it.'

Adam laughed. 'Don't you trust me?'

'Yes, of course I do. It's just that... well, the internet and cyber security and all that...' She stopped, wondering wildly how she could get out of this. 'Sorry, Adam, I have to go,' she said quickly. 'Talk soon. Bye for now.'

'Bye, Laura. See you soon.'

Laura hung up with a feeling of dread. She felt instinctively that she had to keep Adam from seeing the painting now. If it came out that Josephine had not only left her a cottage that her son desperately wanted, but also a painting that would prove to be extremely valuable, then Laura would be in even more trouble.

21

The following morning the weather was mild with bright blue skies and warm sunshine. Laura found Rachel on the window seat in the back bedroom, wrapped in a fleece blanket staring dreamily out to sea.

Laura knocked on the half-open door and stepped inside. 'Morning, Rachel. I brought you a cup of tea and there's breakfast in the sunroom, when you're ready.'

Rachel turned her head. 'Oh thanks, Laura. That's so kind. You don't mind if I drop the Auntie, do you? I feel the age gap is closing somehow.'

Laura laughed and handed Rachel the cup. 'That would be fine. The Auntie bit made me feel quite old, anyway, as you're an adult now.'

'Thank you for finally saying I'm an adult,' Rachel said and laughed. 'No more babying then, I hope.'

Laura squeezed in beside Rachel on the seat. 'No more babying,' she promised. 'But I'll always be there for you.'

'And I for you,' Rachel said with a tender smile. Then she sipped her tea while looking out the window. 'What a view to wake up to. You must feel you're in heaven every morning.'

'It's not always like this,' Laura remarked. 'Sometimes the rain is lashing up against the window and the storm-force winds make you wonder if you'll still have a roof the next morning. But that's what makes living here so exciting. The weather is always changing; you have to take every day as it comes and treasure the good days. Just like in life really,' she added.

'You've become so philosophical.' Rachel looked at Laura over the rim of her cup. 'But so am I right now. Maybe it's that heavenly view and the light on the water, but I've been thinking...'

'About what?'

'Josephine's son.' Rachel paused. 'It was just something Granny said to me the last time we visited her in Florida. She said that you should always be nice to people because we don't know what goes on in their lives.'

'I know. She said that to me too. Go on.'

'Well, maybe we should try to imagine where he's coming from. I mean... He didn't grow up like you and me, with a mummy who was always there, picking him up from school and making his lunch box and tucking him in at night and reading him a story. Could have left him with some kind of trauma if his dad wasn't that much into parenting either.'

Laura nodded. 'Could be. According to Josephine, his father was often away and he didn't remarry after the divorce, so there was no stepmother either. I think there was a series of nannies and au pairs and then he was sent to boarding school. Don't know why Josephine didn't get custody, but I'm guessing her ex-husband was as controlling with that as he was with Josephine.'

'Not a nice way to grow up, then,' Rachel remarked.

'No.' Laura got to her feet. 'But what do we do about that, then? He's still angry and plans to do his best to contest the will. Okay, so now we think he's suffering from this childhood trauma and that's what drives him. But I can't see how that helps us in any way, except we feel sorry for him.'

Rachel put the blanket on the bed. 'I'll think about it while I get dressed. I take it this lunch party is casual?'

'As casual as it gets,' Laura said with a laugh. 'We'll be hiking up the hill to get there, so I hope you brought your hiking boots.'

'I did, of course. I was hoping we could do some good walks up the hills here.'

'This one will be very good,' Laura promised. 'I'll get a move on myself and get dressed, then we'll have breakfast downstairs.'

'Great.' Rachel disappeared into the adjoining bathroom while Laura went downstairs to get dressed and finish making breakfast.

The doorbell rang just as she came to the bottom of the stairs. As she opened the door, she was surprised to see Edwina there, dressed in leggings and a T-shirt, her blonde hair ruffled by the wind.

'Hi,' Laura said. 'You're up early. Do you want to come in?'

'No,' Edwina replied. 'We just wanted to tell you that Gino invited us to the birthday party and thought we could walk up there together. It was such a lovely morning I decided to go for a run.'

Laura smiled. 'You're putting me to shame. I haven't even collected Ken from Vicky yet.'

'She's coming up the steps right now with Ken,' Edwina announced. 'And Peter, her husband, has just arrived, but they're going up the mountain road by car so they're taking the easy option. You could go with them if you don't feel like hiking.'

'I'm afraid I have to as my very fit niece is here and she's looking forward to a bit of exercise. And it's such a grand day, it would be a pity to miss it.'

Edwina nodded. 'Okay. We'll give you a shout when we're ready. See you later so.'

She had just closed the door when there was another knock and Vicky appeared with Ken, who greeted Laura enthusiastically.

'Enough.' Laura laughed, pushing away the excited old dog. 'I was only gone one night. Have you been a good boy?'

'He's been as good as gold,' Vicky declared. 'And happy to go to the beach with me. So don't you worry. We took good care of him.'

'That's wonderful.' Laura smiled at Vicky and opened the door wider. 'Do you want to come in? My niece arrived last night and we're about to have breakfast.'

Vicky shook her head. 'Thanks, but my husband Peter is inside expecting a Sunday fry. Must get going on that. We'll see you up at Gino's later.'

'Grand. See you then,' Laura said as Vicky left.

'This is turning into a huge party,' Laura told Rachel when she came downstairs. 'Everyone seems to have been invited.'

Rachel sat down at the table. 'Sounds great,' she said, as she put scrambled eggs on her plate and buttered a piece of toast. 'I thought about what we talked about earlier when I was in the shower,' she continued, licking her thumb.

'About Michael Monaghan?'

'Yeah.' Rachel bit off a piece of toast. 'I thought,' she said through her mouthful, 'that you could set up a meeting with him. He seems to be hovering around here so it wouldn't be too hard to find a moment to chat.'

Laura bristled. She put her mug of tea down on the table. 'Me, chat with him? Why would I?'

'Because it might help to talk to him. To let him know you understand how he feels and that you know what he went through as a small child. That Josephine might not have been the best mother and how hard that must have been.'

'I could never say that about her,' Laura protested. 'I think it was very difficult for her to look after her son because of her career. I'm sure she felt bad about it. Okay, so she did admit to not having been there for him a lot of times.'

'More like never,' Rachel stated. 'She even said so herself to me once. When she had had a few glasses of bubbly, of course, so she was a bit weepy. But I think she meant it.'

'I know she was feeling guilty about not being the motherly type,' Laura remarked. 'And now I'm beginning to see how that must have affected Michael. But I don't see how talking to him about it could change anything.'

'You might make him change his mind about the court case.'

Laura picked at her piece of toast and looked thoughtfully at Rachel. 'I don't think you're right. He seems so vindictive and set in his ways.'

'Why not give it a shot, though?' Rachel urged. 'What do you have to lose?'

Laura finished her toast and pushed her plate away. 'It might make him even more determined.'

Rachel sighed. 'I give up. You're so stubborn, Laura. Why can't you go with the flow a little? Meet Michael and talk to him. Tell him you know how hurt he must have been and how you think Josephine really failed as a mother.'

'That would be unfair to her. I would feel I'm betraying her memory.'

'Yeah, but if this is the only way to get him to back off, it would be worth it,' Rachel argued.

'I'd be lying if I said that,' Laura replied. 'I'd be pretending something I never felt was true.'

'Of course you'd be pretending, but if it works, wouldn't Josephine be happy that you get to keep your inheritance the way she wanted?'

'I don't know,' Laura said, torn between her loyalty to

Josephine's memory and her own wishes. 'I would be making things up in a way.'

'Of course you would,' Rachel said cheerfully. 'But in this case, the end truly justifies the means.' She winked. 'Fake it till you make it, dear Auntie.'

Laura laughed and shook her head. 'How did you get so bold? Come on, let's get ready for the hike and the party. Should all be great craic.'

Her tone was light but what Rachel had said stayed in her mind. Would it really be a good idea to try to talk to Michael Monaghan and pretend she thought Josephine had been a bad mother? Was there really a chance he might soften if she told her she understood how he felt?

While Laura considered this, she tried to imagine what it would have been like to grow up like he had. Like a lot of successful artists, Josephine had been charming and charismatic. She had totally captivated Laura. But she supposed success came with ego, with diva behaviour, and Josephine may have focussed on her career at her son's expense. Now she thought back, she remembered Josephine mentioning that she hadn't always been a very good mother. She had joked about it. But behind that, perhaps there was truth? And a feeling of guilt and loss?

As Laura walked through the house and saw the sun shining in through the windows, catching a glimpse of the glittering sea, she decided to forget about it for now. It would be a great party, even if she'd have to watch Gino and Becky together...

22

The glorious weather made Laura smile again as she started up the hill with Rachel, Shane and Edwina. The sun shone from a pristine blue sky and, despite the cool breeze, they were soon warm as they walked up the steep slope to Gino's cottage. Rachel and Edwina soon found each other and were deep in conversation while Shane walked ahead. Laura lagged behind, lost in the beautiful view of the coastline as they made their way further and further up.

She couldn't get enough of the view, the cool clean air and the sights of hawks hovering high above them in the blue sky, looking for prey. She was so at one with nature here, so completely relaxed and serene. The thought of losing the cottage that had become so dear gave her a dart of pain, before she pushed it away and tried to concentrate on the gorgeous day and the wonderful company.

Shane stopped and allowed Laura to catch up with him. 'Isn't this the best break from work?'

'Oh yes! It's such a glorious day.' Laura smiled at him and shaded her eyes against the sun. 'Can't believe it's only the end of March. It nearly feels like summer.'

'A pet of a day, as we say here,' he replied. 'The forecast for tomorrow is not as wonderful.'

'Oh?' Laura stared at him. 'Bad weather coming?'

'The worst. March went in like a lamb and now it's going out like a lion. Met Éireann warns of gale-force winds and heavy rain with a risk of flooding. Atlantic swells too. We could get power cuts as well.'

Laura made a face. 'Ugh. Not looking forward to that.'

'It's quite common to get weather like that at this time of year,' Shane remarked. 'But I kind of like it. I love watching the waves crashing in below the cottages. The spray hits the windows at high tide. Spectacular.'

Laura laughed and started walking again. 'You're such a kid, Shane O'Flaherty.'

He fell into step with her. 'I know. That's what Edwina says. But I love a bit of danger from time to time.'

'I know. I've seen you on that motorbike taking the bends at speed.'

'What do you mean?' Shane said with mock innocence. 'I have to drive fast to get to patients in need.'

'Yeah, right,' Laura scoffed. 'The elderly patients up the mountain road are really at risk from dying of their varicose veins.'

'Well, you never know what they might have got up to,' Shane retorted and started to walk again.

Laura followed his lead, panting as she laboured up the now steeper slope. 'Pull the other one. I know urgency of care isn't the reason why you drive *so* fast. But I understand that those patients do find it hard to get to the surgery and love to see you, to have a bit of a chat. It's like the old days when the family doctor used to take whole afternoons off to do house calls. Must be unique to this place.'

'I think it is,' Shane replied. 'And possibly not really what I should be doing, according to regulations. But we're lucky to be a two-doctor practice so we can do this. It's important for the mental health of some of those people. They often don't meet anyone except the postman.'

'That's so true,' Laura agreed and stopped again. This time to take off her jacket. 'It's getting very warm. And not a cloud in the sky. Hard to believe there's a storm coming.'

'I know, but the weather changes so fast,' Shane said as he helped Laura with her jacket. Then he looked thoughtfully at her. 'You know, I have been thinking about your position at the surgery. I know you're just filling in for Bridget, but would you consider working with us part-time when she comes back? I think Bridget needs to wind down on her hours a bit and look after Brendan. And herself, too, to be honest. Kate and I both think you're a wonderful nurse and a great addition to our practice. The patients love you, too, I've heard. You've only been here since the beginning of February, but after only two months you've settled in so well. And now everyone feels you're a local.'

Laura smiled, Shane's words giving her a surge of warmth and happiness. 'That's so nice to hear, Shane. I love working at the surgery, as you might have gathered. And a part-time job would suit me perfectly. But I'd hate to say anything before you talk to Bridget. She might not agree with you. But if she wants to reduce her hours, I'd be happy to take you up on the offer.' *If I'm not forced to leave after Michael has managed to claim ownership of the cottage*, she thought with a dart of fear.

'Grand. Let's decide when we've talked to Bridget.' Shane nodded and resumed walking.

A little further up they caught sight of Fidelma and Becky, who were nearly at the top of the hill. Becky turned when they caught up with them. 'Hey, Shane, please tell my mother to slow down. She's looking hot and tired and she's not exactly a spring chicken.'

'But still in good form,' Shane quipped. 'Still very much able to keep up with us all.'

Fidelma stopped and glared at them '"Still"? I hate that word. Everyone seems to insert it into every sentence when they talk to me. "You're still looking well," they say, or "Are you still going to keep fit?" They'll be asking if I'm still alive next.'

Laura had to laugh, even though she got the point. 'You're right, Fidelma, that's what most people do when they talk to someone older than them.'

'But Mam's seventy-six,' Becky protested, her face red with exertion. 'She shouldn't even attempt this kind of hike. Shane, please tell her to slow down.'

'Of course not,' Shane said. 'As her doctor, I can report that Fidelma has perfect blood pressure and takes no medication, so why should she slow down? She's as fit as a fiddle. See what I did there?' he added. 'I didn't put "still" into that sentence.'

'Thank you, Shane,' Fidelma said, beaming at him. 'You're a nice lad. Now tell Becky to get off my back.'

'Becky, get off your mother's back,' Shane said. 'You look a little tired, actually, and Fidelma looks as fresh as a daisy. What does that tell you about age?'

'It's true that age is just a number,' Laura cut in. 'It's all about lifestyle and a little bit about your genes. I'd say Fidelma has both on her side.'

Becky laughed. 'Oh, okay, I get it. You're all ganging up on me. And on my birthday and all. Shame on you!'

They all laughed and walked the last bit together, arriving at the top where Gino, dressed in jeans, a green T-shirt and a large apron, waited for them. He greeted them all warmly and kissed all the ladies on the cheek. As he kissed her, Laura tried to avoid looking into his eyes; they met hers with such warmth she felt her face flush. 'I'm so happy to see you,' he whispered into her ear before he turned away and enveloped Becky in a bear hug. 'Happy birthday, gorgeous,' he shouted and led her to the back of the terrace where a huge pan of paella simmered over a wood fire on the barbeque. 'I'm doing a Spanish theme here as you love that country so much,' he told a beaming Becky. 'We have sangria in jugs on the table over there.'

'Brilliant,' Becky exclaimed. She clapped her hands and kissed Gino on the cheek. 'You darling. You always do such a nice party for me on my birthday.'

'Why wouldn't I?' he said, giving her another squeeze. 'You're like the sister I never had.'

'More's the pity, you gorgeous hunk,' Becky retorted and extracted herself from Gino's arms. 'Where's that sangria? I need a drink after that monster hike.'

The sister I never had. The words resonated through Laura's mind every time she looked at Gino all through the lively party. And when their eyes met, she didn't avoid his gaze like she had before, but returned his smile with equal warmth while her heart sang. There was a ray of hope after all. Becky was just a dear relative, a kind of sister in spirit and not his girlfriend or secret lover. Why hadn't she realised this instead of imagining the worst? She chided herself for being stupid and having distanced herself from Becky instead of enjoying the friendship she offered. Gino was still a confirmed bachelor, and now she could at least feel less guilty about her attraction to him.

Laura piled her plate with paella and looked around for a place to sit down. Gino had organised a makeshift long table on the edge of the terrace, and there were also two smaller round tables around which some of the many guests had settled with their plates and glasses.

Becky waved at Laura from the edge of the long table. 'Laura! Come over here. I kept a seat for you between me and Mam.'

'Oh great. Thank you.' Laura looked around for Rachel and spotted her with Shane and Edwina and a group of younger people at one of the round tables. She could relax. Rachel, in her usual way, had found a group that seemed to be fun and chatty. Laura waved at her niece and then went to sit between

Becky and Fidelma. As she was about to sit down, she was startled to see Adam opposite her.

He grinned and waved his fork at Laura. 'Hi there. Surprised?'

'Yes, a bit.' Laura eased herself down on the bench. 'But happy to see you, of course,' she added, with a feeling of mounting tension. He was sure to ask her about the painting and push her to invite him home to see it.

'I invited him,' Becky whispered beside her. 'Although I didn't expect him to come; he normally doesn't.' She turned towards him. 'No party is complete without Adam,' she said out loud.

Adam grinned. 'That makes me feel I have to perform in some way.'

'Nah.' Becky laughed. 'Just being yourself is enough of a performance for us.'

Adam raised his eyebrow and looked at Becky. 'Was that a compliment or a veiled insult?'

'I'm not going to tell you,' Becky said with a cheeky look.

He laughed and raised his glass. 'Cheers to the birthday girl who never fails to challenge me.'

'Someone has to,' Becky quipped and clinked glasses with Adam. 'You're getting far too precious in your old age.'

Adam took a swig of wine. 'I would respond, but I'll let it lie as it's your party and I'm a guest.'

'The perfect gentleman,' Fidelma said, looking from Becky to Adam. 'But wouldn't you two make a lovely couple if you ever stopped sparring with each other?'

'Don't hold your breath, Mam,' Becky said, looking suddenly uncomfortable.

Laura looked at Becky and Adam in turn and saw that Fidelma was right. They were both exceptionally good-looking and matched each other in height and general appearance. Side by side they would be spectacular. But was this a possibility?

She could feel definite vibes between them like tiny sparks. There was something going on there that Laura had missed before. But how did Laura feel about it herself? Adam had paid her a lot of flattering attention lately and been hugely helpful and kind when she was upset. But was this simply because he was hoping to get to see the painting and perhaps cajole Laura to sell it to him? She had no idea, and when he winked at her across the table, she felt confused and flustered.

'Peter Pan,' Becky whispered beside Laura. 'I mean, he never grew up, did he?'

'I suppose,' Laura muttered back. 'He's gorgeous, but I find that kind of man difficult to deal with.'

'I know.' Becky glanced at Adam, who was getting up for a second helping of paella. 'Okay, we can talk now,' she continued as he walked away. 'I just want to ask if you're getting... fond of him?'

'Not the way I think you mean.' Laura pushed the food around her plate while she considered the question. 'Of course I was flattered and taken in by his charm and kindness. And his looks and the car and all that are all very seductive. But I'm fifty-two, not fifteen, and I've met men like that before. I know how it can end if I was allowing myself to get swept away. Actually,' she continued, after a moment's reflection, 'I'd prefer to be friends with him than get into anything else. I'm not the slightest bit in love with him and don't think I ever could be.'

'That's good to hear,' Becky said with a relieved sigh. 'Because I have been working on Adam for a long time now. I know he likes me and we've flirted quite seriously at parties and I've felt some vibes from him that said he's ready to commit. But then he seems to take fright and slips away again.' She laughed and shook her head. 'You must think I'm mad to lose my heart to a man like that at my age. But there you go. I'm the eternal optimist and an incurable romantic.'

Fidelma leaned across Laura and looked at Becky. 'Age has

nothing to do with romance, or romance with age, whatever way you want to put it. You can fall in love at any age. The trick is not to try too hard. Don't chase after love. Let love come to you. It will if you're patient and it's meant to be.'

Becky looked at her mother. 'Oh, Mam, that's beautiful. I never heard you say that before.'

Fidelma reached across to put her hand on Becky's cheek. 'It happens to be the truth, pet. Maybe I should have said it to you earlier, then you might not have been so frantic.'

'I think this is the right time,' Becky replied, her voice gentle. 'I wouldn't have listened before, but now I'm ready to heed your advice. I will sit quietly and wait from now on.'

'Good.' Fidelma patted Becky's hand. 'I just want you to be happy.'

'I know, Mam.' Becky smiled at her mother. 'Thank you.' She looked at her empty plate. 'You know what? I'm going to have some more of this and some of that sangria. What about you, Laura?'

'Thanks, but I'm happy,' Laura replied. 'It was delicious, but I had such a big helping it made me feel quite full.'

'I'll bring you some sangria, though,' Becky said as she walked off with her plate, smiling at Adam, who was on his way back to the table.

Fidelma turned to Laura. 'I'm sorry, Laura. I've been ignoring you. I had something important to tell you but then it flew out of my head. So, I've been trying to remember what it was and now it came back to me when we were talking about love and romance. I have been asking around about that young girl you were interested in... Oonagh Nolan, was that her name?'

'Yes, that's right,' Laura said, looking at Fidelma expectantly. 'Have you found out anything about her?'

Fidelma nodded. 'I have. It appears that she was indeed here for a term in the spring of 1965. And she left suddenly that summer when something happened that caused some kind of nasty gossip. That's all I know for now. But I'll do some more research. Pity I wasn't here that summer. Then I would have known more. But I'm trying to find some people of my generation who'll remember what happened. Sandy Cove was a different place then, of course. Very quiet and remote. Artists used to come here for the scenery, but not many tourists.'

'Do you know if Louis de Barra might have been here around that time?' Laura asked.

'Yes he was.' Fidelma looked thoughtful. 'You mean the one who did that amazing view of the Dublin Mountains? That de Barra?'

Laura nodded. 'Yes. I've heard he was in the area at that time. And I think that he and Oonagh might have been, eh... friendly.'

'Oh yes, I do remember hearing that he'd been here. But he wasn't that well-known then, of course.' Fidelma's eyes twinkled. 'Looks like I missed a *very* exciting spring and summer here when I was gadding about in England. Louis de Barra and Oonagh, eh? I will certainly follow up on that lead.'

'Great.' Laura leaned closer to Fidelma. 'But could we keep this quiet for now?' she muttered. 'I'll explain later.'

Fidelma nodded, looking even more intrigued. 'Of course. It stays between us. We wouldn't want to spread gossip if it isn't true, would we? I'll be very discreet. My lips are sealed from now on. Except when I'll be asking questions, of course.'

Laura laughed. 'Well, it would be a bit hard to ask questions with sealed lips.' Then she met Adam's curious gaze from across the table. Had he heard what they had been talking about? If he had, how would Laura deal with the questions he might ask later? She didn't want him to know that the painting might be by Louis de Barra and that it was so valuable.

But as their eyes met, she had an odd feeling he already knew.

23

To Laura's relief, Adam turned away to talk to the person sitting beside him. In an attempt to avoid talking to him, Laura got up to put away her plate in the kitchen, where she found Gino putting candles on a huge birthday cake with white icing and 'Happy Birthday, Becky!' in red letters.

He turned as she entered. 'Oh hi! Please, put the plate on the stack by the sink. I'll wash them all later when everyone's gone.'

'That's some pile of washing up,' Laura remarked, looking at the stack of plates. 'Do you have a dishwasher?'

'No, but I have plenty of helpers, so don't worry. Your lovely niece is helping out there, collecting plates. But perhaps you could bring the paper plates out so everybody has one? They're on the dresser by the window. Not so environmentally friendly, but I got desperate.'

'I'm sure they can be recycled.' Laura found the stack of paper plates. 'How about spoons?'

'Already on the little table where I plan to serve the cake. They'll all have to get up and help themselves.'

'Great. I'll go around with Rachel and collect the dinner plates and stack them in here,' Laura offered.

'You're a darling,' Gino said with a warm smile. 'And you look wonderful today. Any special reason?' His smile died and his eyes were suddenly serious.

'No, except I'm having a good time and it's a beautiful day.' She smiled.

He put the last candle on the cake and stepped closer. 'And your niece is here and you're very fond of her, I can tell.'

'That too.' Laura suddenly felt self-conscious under his intense gaze.

'I've noticed that you've settled into village life so well,' he remarked. 'It's easier to be single here, don't you think?'

'Oh yes,' Laura agreed. 'I don't ever feel lonely here like I did in Dublin. There are people around everywhere and things going on all the time.'

'I know.' He nodded. 'You can pick and choose and be on your own when you want to and then meet people whenever you feel the need. Quite perfect really.'

'I had been wondering why you seem so happy to live on your own,' Laura said, leaning against the counter. 'But now I see how it works.'

'Seems to suit us both. Happily single, right?' Gino said, still looking at her in a way that seemed to contradict his words.

'Yeah, well...' Laura mumbled.

'Except if you meet someone you like more than you thought you ever would...' Gino continued, stepping closer. 'A special person you just want to be with all the time...'

'Yes,' was all she managed, and then didn't know how to go on.

'And perhaps that special someone happens to be out there on the terrace?' he asked.

Laura shook her head and looked into his lovely grey eyes. She took a deep breath. 'No,' she said quietly, meeting his gaze.

'The person I want to be with all the time is right here. Right in front of me. Right now.'

'Right now?' Gino asked, a smile forming on his lips. 'In this kitchen?'

'Yes,' she whispered as he leaned forward, his mouth nearly touching hers. It could have ended in a kiss if they hadn't been interrupted by Rachel storming into the kitchen. They flew apart and Gino went back to the table with the cake.

'There you are,' Rachel exclaimed. 'I was looking for you all over the place. I need to talk to you about... something,' she said.

Laura tried to pull herself together. 'I'll be out in a second.'

'Okay,' Rachel said, looking from Gino to Laura and then walking out of the kitchen again.

'Can we talk about this – us – later?' Gino asked.

'We can,' she said and ran outside, forgetting the stack of paper plates, so she had to run back in again and pick them up. 'You make me forget everything,' she said, laughing.

He kissed his fingers at her. 'Go out there and we'll sing "Happy Birthday" for Becky. It's her day, after all.'

'It feels like my special day,' Laura said. 'The most special day in my whole life.'

'And mine.'

'See you later.'

'Yes, when things are quiet. Bye,' she heard him say before she went back outside, into the sunshine and a day that now seemed even more beautiful than before.

Heading back outside, Laura noticed Adam talking to Rachel, and they seemed to be chatting animatedly for a while. Then they parted company and Adam went to talk to Becky. Laura wondered if Rachel found him as charming as everyone else did. It would be interesting to hear her comments later.

. . .

The birthday celebrations continued with the cake and everyone singing to Becky. And then when the cake had been eaten, the coffee drunk and the skies darkened, the guests who had stayed behind to help with the washing up decided to walk down the slope before it got too dark. Laura didn't get another moment alone with Gino, but he managed to whisper to her he'd call her later. Then as they all made their way down the hill in dribs and drabs, they could hear Gino on the terrace playing a beautiful Irish ballad on the tin whistle, the sound echoing over the still landscape and the gently lapping waves below them. It was hard to believe the weather was about to turn nasty, but Laura was told the storm would arrive in the middle of the night and to have candles ready as they were sure to have a power cut.

'What a beautiful day,' Rachel sighed as she linked arms with Laura.

'It's heavenly,' Laura agreed. 'But I'm afraid I've heard the weather is about to turn nasty later. A storm that wasn't forecast earlier is on its way.'

'What?' Rachel exclaimed, looking alarmed. 'But I thought they said we'd have nice weather for the next few days.'

'I know. But these things happen often in Kerry. The Atlantic storms can veer towards us at the drop of a hat. Hopefully the storm won't last long.'

'But we can still enjoy what's left of this day,' Rachel said. 'And just listen to that lilting ballad. It's magical.' She cocked her head and listened to the music that still floated in the air. 'He's playing "An Cailín Álainn". "The Beautiful Girl". A love song that is a bit sad at the end.' She glanced at Laura. 'But I have a feeling it's not the end he's hoping for. And that this is a message to... someone...'

'I have no idea what you mean,' Laura said airily.

'Yes, you do,' Rachel argued. 'I wasn't going to say anything, but I saw you through the window when I was helping with the tidying up. You and Gino. Nearly kissing. That seems so perfect.'

'It wasn't a kiss... It didn't really mean anything,' Laura tried, flustered at the thought of Rachel having seen them. 'Just a bit of fun, really.'

'I'd say it meant more than you let on,' Rachel teased. 'If it did, I'm happy for you. I didn't really take to that Adam guy. I had a chat with him when we mingled at the end of the party. Very sweet and charming but too into himself, to be honest. And he asked a lot of questions about the painting. Told me he's an art expert and that he would be very interested to see it. But I played the innocent and said I had only glanced at it and that it looked like the work of an amateur to me.' Rachel laughed. 'I didn't feel a bit guilty about lying. He was too smooth for my liking.'

'Oh, that's such a relief,' Laura said with a sigh. 'Thank you for not telling the truth.'

'I just didn't trust him. I'm sure he's not all bad but I didn't take to him at all.'

'Becky is fond of him.'

'She can have him. Gino is more genuine. More down to earth and trustworthy. Much more your type, Laura.'

'And this you have decided after meeting them just once?' Laura asked incredulously.

'I am a very good judge of character,' Rachel stated. 'I can read people very quickly.'

'Okay then. What about the others?'

'Well...' Rachel thought for a moment as they neared the bottom of the hill. 'Becky is a good friend who will never let you down. And she's fun but a little nervous and perhaps lacks self-confidence.'

Laura nodded, impressed. 'True, I think. Go on.'

'Fidelma is very solid, and has a sunny disposition. Kindness personified with a bit of an edge. Doesn't suffer fools gladly.

Not sure how she feels about Adam and Becky but is willing to go with it if it makes her daughter happy. And if he hurts her, she'll be like an avenging angel with a flaming sword.'

Laura laughed. 'Yes, I'd say she would be. But Adam is also kind, you know. He'll be careful with her. But their relationship is none of our business.'

'Of course not,' Rachel agreed. 'I'm sure they'll work it out.'

'They will. But go on with your analysis,' Laura urged. 'It's very interesting. So far, you're doing well.'

'Okay. And then, of the people I met coming up the slope,' Rachel continued, 'Edwina is stylish, smart and hides a vulnerable side. Shane is confident, caring with huge empathy and possibly a very good doctor.'

'He is.' Laura nodded. 'I'm so happy to work with him and with Kate, who's terrific too. Never had such a great work environment.'

'Which will end when that other nurse comes back,' Rachel remarked.

'It might not.' Laura stepped onto the path that led to the cottage. 'But I'm not going to think about that at the moment.'

'Good idea,' Rachel agreed. She looked out to sea, where the sun was slowly sinking behind the peak of Skellig Michael. 'Such a heavenly evening. Hard to believe there is bad weather on the way.'

'I know.' Laura stood with Rachel for a moment and looked out across the bay. 'Such a beautiful vista. Not surprising it inspires artists.'

'Like Louis de Barra,' Rachel said. 'Oh, that painting is amazing. The beach, the light, and the look in that woman's eyes, it gave me goose bumps. I can't wait to track down that woman. She has to be around Fidelma's age. Have you looked up any of the historical archives? There must be something in the library here.'

'The library has been closed for renovations the past

month,' Laura replied. 'And their website doesn't have much on the 1960s. But I've asked a few people who'd have been around then, like Fidelma.' Laura paused. 'She actually told me she had heard that there was some kind of nasty gossip about Oonagh and that was why she left after only a term at the school.'

'Ooh!' Rachel exclaimed. 'That sounds very interesting.' She started to walk to the cottage. 'I want to do a little research online while I have the chance. If we have a power cut, it'll be impossible later. And we have to charge our phones.'

'Yes.' Laura walked ahead. 'I'd better get ready for all that. I'll go and find the candles Gino said he put in the kitchen and get the stove and fire going. We could be cut off for days, I've heard, if the storm lasts.'

'I hope not,' Rachel said as they reached the front door. 'I need to get back to college by the end of next week. I have exams and lectures that I can't miss.'

'I'm sure you'll make it back in time,' Laura reassured her as she opened the door to be greeted by Ken, who jumped all over them as if they had been gone for weeks instead of a few hours.

Rachel went upstairs to get her laptop. Laura went into the kitchen to feed Ken and to get ready for a potential storm and loss of electricity. She wondered if Rachel would be successful with her research and thought that she probably would, as she would be more at home with the internet than Laura, so she'd know exactly where to look. And Rachel's interest in art and history would also be a great help.

Laura busied herself with preparing to batten down the hatches as Gino had told her, by closing all the windows, stacking firewood and making sure all outside items lying around on the terrace were put away. She stood for a moment with a bundle of logs in her arms and looked out over the quiet bay. All was still and a full moon rose above the bay with stars twinkling in the dark sky. A gentle breeze brought with it the salty tang of the sea and a wisp of woodsmoke from the cottages next door. Both Shane and Edwina and Vicky and her husband were getting ready, and it felt comforting to have neighbours so close. Laura thought of Gino on top of the hill and wondered how he'd manage as the winds were sure to be worse up there. But he had seemed calm and sure of being secure as his house had seen many storms and he knew how to stay safe.

Laura smiled as she remembered the kiss that had nearly happened and how it had made her feel. It had been so unexpected, but she knew it had been building up for a while. Gino, who she had thought to be a kind of hermit living alone and happy to remain single, had responded to her in a way that had surprised and delighted her.

What would happen now? Was their brief embrace just a passing fancy or would it develop into something solid and enduring? How would that work with a man who lived in a log cabin and had very few possessions? *How weird to have fallen for the village baker*, Laura thought. *But Gino is much more than that... So much more*, Laura told herself, thinking of his books and his love of music and his kindness and empathy. But was he going to change his ways and want to commit? If he didn't, Laura knew she couldn't stay on in Sandy Cove. It would be too painful.

She was startled out of her daydream when Rachel suddenly gave a shout in the living room where she was sitting at the small desk with her laptop.

'Here it is! The most important clue to the identity of the artist. I knew I was right. This confirms my suspicions without a doubt. Come and look at this, Laura!'

24

'What?' Laura asked as she ran inside, dropping the stack of wood she had been carrying to the fireplace. 'Have you found something?'

'Yes. This.' Rachel pointed at the screen. 'I just came across it on an art website. Listen!'

Louis de Barra spent the spring and summer of 1965 in Sandy Cove, a small village on the Ring of Kerry. He and his wife, Clodagh, rented a coastguard cottage on the edge of the Atlantic, hoping the sea air would be good for her as she suffered from a lung disease. During his time there, he produced the bulk of his seascapes, inspired by the beautiful views and the unique light in this part of Kerry.

'That proves he was here during this time,' Rachel interrupted her reading. 'And then this—'

One of the seaside paintings, The Girl on the Beach, *which was in private ownership, mysteriously disappeared but it is*

now known that Louis de Barra sold it in order to pay for his
wife's medical bills.

'Wow.' Rachel's eyes sparkled with excitement. 'But now
we've found it. And you are the legal owner of the painting as
the artist sold it himself.'

'But how did Josephine get it?' Laura asked. 'Where did it
disappear from and how did it end up in her house?'

Rachel looked thoughtful. 'Well, you know. These things
happen. Someone is moving house and sees a painting without
knowing what it's worth and sells it on some flea market or car-
boot sale. Or they find it in an attic years later. Happens all the
time. I've seen stories like that on *Antiques Roadshow*.'

Laura nodded. 'I suppose you're right. Josephine liked going
to markets and charity shops. It was one of her hobbies. She
didn't always buy anything but she loved having a good browse.
So she must have seen the painting and liked it and then bought
it for a song. I don't know if she would have known its value at
the time. But she seemed to have found out about it later.'

'Must be what happened.' Rachel turned back to the laptop.
'I'll keep looking and see if I can find out something else.'

'Okay.' Laura started to pick up the logs she had dropped.
Then she straightened up as there was a rumbling outside.
'What's that?'

'Sounds like thunder,' Rachel said, as she went to the
window of the sunroom and peered out. Then there was a
sudden flash and the whole bay was lit up for a second before
another roll of thunder erupted. 'Holy mother, just look at the
sky,' she exclaimed. 'Black clouds are rolling in and there was
just a fork of lightning over Skellig Michael. Spectacular!'

'Get away from the window,' Laura ordered. 'It could be
dangerous.' Her voice was barely audible as heavy rain smattered against the windows, and then the wind started with a
roaring sound.

'Better get ready.' Rachel turned off her laptop and unplugged it as the lights started to flicker. 'Here we go.'

Laura's phone rang suddenly in the bedroom. She ran to answer it, unplugging it from the charger at the same time. 'Hello?' she said in a shaky voice.

'Laura?' Gino's voice on the phone was oddly reassuring. 'Just wanted to check that you're okay. The storm is here and it will be wild. You'll be fine in the cottage. The roof is solid and the windows will hold. Just don't go outside under any circumstances. Try not to worry. This one won't be worse than any we have seen here during the winter.'

'Oh, Gino,' Laura exclaimed. 'How kind of you to call. We're fine. I'm only worried about you up there in the hill.'

He let out a laugh. 'I'm not up there. I'm in the bakery. I drove down here in my van just as it got dark. I always go down here during a storm. Now you'll think I'm a bit of a chicken.'

'Of course not.' Laura heaved a sigh of relief. 'I'm glad you're not up there. Then I don't have to worry.'

'Not at all. I'm safe and so are you. Only...' He stopped. 'I'd love to be there with you. Can't imagine anything more exciting than watching a storm from Starlight Cottages.'

'I know,' Laura whispered. 'It would be... I mean after what happened...' She didn't know what to say next; she only knew she wanted to keep hearing his voice. 'Sorry,' she said, feeling suddenly awkward. 'Maybe I read too much into that?'

'A bit of momentary madness, would you say?'

'Yes. Maybe.' Laura drew breath and laughed, to cover up her confusion. Of course, that's what it was. Just an impulse from his side, a little bit of flirting or something... She shivered as the storm gathered force outside and the windows rattled in a gust of wind. 'It's getting worse.'

'The thunder has rolled away,' Gino remarked. 'But now the wind is stronger. Anne-Marie is shaking like a leaf. How about Ken?'

'I don't know where he is. I think he's with Rachel in the living room.' Laura jumped as the lights flickered again and then went out. 'The power's gone and it's pitch black here. I'd better go and light a few candles. And the fire.'

'There's a torch in the bottom drawer next to the stove,' Gino said. 'The light's gone here too. But I have candles and I lit the fire in the office earlier. I can sleep on the sofa bed in there.'

'Sleep?' Laura asked with a hollow laugh. 'How would that be possible with this noise?'

'I'm used to storms. I like the sound of the wind, strangely enough. Anyway, I'd better go. I want to call Fidelma and see if they're all right. Try to get some sleep. All will be well in the morning. Goodnight, Laura.'

'Goodnight,' Laura whispered. 'See you soon, Gino.' She hung up and sat staring into the darkness for a while. She felt a surge of sadness as she went through what Gino had said. She realised it hadn't meant as much to him as it had to her. He liked her as a friend and that was all it was. But she knew she liked him more than that.

But there was no use moping. Laura got up and walked gingerly across the room, her arms outstretched in front of her, trying not to bump into anything in the dark. She opened the door and saw the flickering light of a candle in the living room.

'I'm lighting the fire,' Rachel said. 'Maybe you could find more candles?'

'Yes. Give me that one,' Laura said, walking to join Rachel as flames sprang up around the logs in the hearth. 'I'll go and find that torch in the kitchen.'

'Okay.' Rachel gave Laura the candle that sat in a silver candlestick. 'I'll wait here until you come back.'

'Is Ken here with you?' Laura asked.

'No, I thought he was with you,' Rachel replied.

'What?' Laura looked wildly around the dark room but there was no sign of the dog as far as she could tell. 'Well, he's black so very hard to see,' she remarked. 'I'm sure he's around somewhere. Ken?' she called. 'Come here, boy!'

'Here, Ken,' Rachel shouted and got to her feet. 'He has to be here somewhere.' She gave a shriek as a gust of wind blew the front door open and then it blew shut again with a bang.

'Oh God,' Laura exclaimed. 'Did he run out the front door just then?'

'No, he can't have,' Rachel protested. 'He wouldn't run outside in this weather. Would he?' she said, her voice shaking.

'He might have panicked.' Laura ran into the hall and tried to look out through the small window, pressing her face to the glass. She saw nothing but the bushes bent over in the now near-hurricane-force wind. 'It's lashing rain out there too. If Ken is out there, he will not survive.' She wrung her hands, feeling utterly helpless.

Ken is my last link with Josephine, she thought, as tears welled up in her eyes. *He felt like a bit of a nuisance when I got him but now he's become my best friend and companion.* She imagined the poor dog out there in the roaring wind and rain and knew he'd be dead if they didn't find him soon. 'We have to go out and find him,' she said, trying to wrench the door open.

'You're mad.' Rachel held her back. 'You can't go out there. It's too dangerous.'

'But I have to find Ken,' Laura sobbed. 'I can't just leave him out there to die.' Ken's lovey doggy eyes flashed before her, his comforting presence, always by her side, his silky fur and his paw on her knee when she was feelings sad, all came in a wave of memories. 'What am I going to do if I lose him?'

Laura shook off Rachel's hands and finally managed to open the door, and ran out into the wild, dark night, shouting Ken's name.

25

Laura was soaked to the skin in seconds. But she didn't care. Bent double against the strong wind that threatened to push her down, she kept walking. She managed to get up the path towards the village, while she kept shouting for Ken. There was no sign of him, but even if he had been anywhere around, she couldn't have seen him. She knew she should make her way back to the cottage, but something drove her to keep going up the village street where the houses were mostly in darkness, except for flickering lights from candles or fireplaces.

She wondered if Ken might have sought refuge in one of them, but it didn't seem very likely. 'Ken!' she kept screaming into the wind. 'Ken, come back! Oh God, please help me find him,' she sobbed, the thought of losing him even more horrible than before. The dear, darling old dog who seemed to know how she felt, who was always by her side, who... Laura screamed as someone suddenly grabbed her and dragged her towards a house. A man in a dripping wet raincoat. When they were inside the house, she discovered that it was Gino and she was in the bakery, lit by several candles.

'You crazy woman,' he chided, shaking her. 'Didn't I tell you to stay indoors?'

Laura stared at him in the dim light. 'I've lost Ken,' she wept into his wet jacket. 'He's somewhere out there...'

Gino grabbed Laura by the shoulders. 'No, he's not. Rachel just told me. She found him.'

'What?' Laura stared at him. 'Found him? Where?'

Gino let go of her and laughed. 'Under your bed. He must have hidden there when the thunder started.'

'How do you know this?'

'Rachel answered your phone when I rang you back.'

'Oh.' Laura went limp with relief. 'So he was there all the time? Why didn't he come out when we called him?'

'Probably traumatised and terrified.'

'The poor thing,' Laura said, full of pity for the old dog. 'And now here I am, soaked to the skin and feeling foolish.'

'It was a bit mad to go out there,' Gino chided.

'Yes but I had to try to find him. He means so much to me,' Laura said, trying to explain how she felt. 'Josephine adored him. She'd never forgive me if I let him die out there in that storm.'

'I know,' Gino soothed. 'He's your last link to her, isn't he?'

Laura nodded. 'Yes. But I also love him. He's been such a wonderful companion.' She suddenly shivered. 'I'm so cold. Maybe I should try to get back home?'

'Don't be silly. Come into the office,' Gino said. He pulled her behind the counter and through a door that led into a cosy little room, with a desk and an armchair beside the fire that glowed warmly through the darkness. A sofa stood at the back wall and there was a multicoloured carpet on the floor. As Laura came in, Anne-Marie jumped up from the rug and let out a bark, then wagged her tail and sniffed at Laura's leg.

'Hi, Anne-Marie.' Laura patted the dog and then held her

hands out to the fire. 'This feels lovely. But I don't want to sit down in my wet clothes.'

Gino pulled off his dripping raincoat and hung it on the door handle. Then he took off his sweater and handed it to Laura. 'Take off that wet shirt and put this on. In fact you should take everything off or you'll freeze to death. There's a blanket on the sofa. You can wrap that around you. I'll go into the bakery until you're done.'

'Thanks.' Laura grabbed the sweater and looked at the T-shirt Gino was wearing. 'But now you'll be cold.'

'I'm grand. Put it on and stop arguing,' he ordered gruffly before he went back into the shop, closing the door behind him.

Laura quickly took off her wet shirt and put on Gino's sweater, pressing it to her nose to smell his scent she knew so well by now. Then she peeled off her jeans and hung it all on the radiator that was still warm. Once she was wrapped in the blanket, she sat down on the chair and stared into the fire, absentmindedly stroking Anne-Marie, who had settled back on the rug. The blanket and the sweater were warm against her chilled skin and she was soon more comfortable. 'Ready!' she shouted.

'Feeling better?' Gino asked as he came back in and sat down on the couch at the far wall.

'Yes. Warmer but still foolish. Why didn't I look under the bed for Ken? When the door was blown open, I thought he had panicked and run outside.'

'But instead he had panicked earlier and crawled under the bed,' Gino said, his voice light. 'Anyway, all is well.'

'I know. Except here I am wearing your sweater and you're sitting there in just a T-shirt.'

'I'll survive. At least I'm not wet.'

'Lucky Rachel answered my phone,' Laura remarked. 'Why did you call me back?'

'I was going to say something important to you. Something I should have told you earlier.'

Laura pushed back her still wet hair from her face and turned to look at him. 'What?'

'About what happened between us in the kitchen.'

'Yes?' Laura said, staring into the fire, suddenly shy and awkward. What was he going to say? That it didn't mean much and that it was just a passing fancy, a bit of flirting that she should forget about... She closed her eyes and waited for him to speak. 'Go on,' she whispered, glad that he was sitting behind her and couldn't see her face. 'Maybe I was wrong when I thought you were going to kiss me,' she said to soften the blow.

But Gino got up and went to her side, kneeling on the floor beside the chair, taking her cold hands. 'No, you weren't.' He took a deep breath. 'Laura, I want you to know that you have come to mean so much to me ever since the day we met on the beach and you gave out to me about my dog.' He laughed softly. 'You were standing there, your amazing blue eyes blazing and your wild curly hair blowing around your face. *Coup de foudre*, the French say about love at first sight. A bolt of lightning. And it truly was. I never thought it would happen to me, but there you were, like a vision on the beach.'

'Oh,' she said, her heart beating. 'You had the same effect on me. Your eyes, your smile... And then you quoted that beautiful poem by Byron. I couldn't get your out of my mind for a long time afterwards. And then... well, we chatted and you gave me the impression of a man who was happy on his own and didn't need anyone to share his life with.'

'Is that why you said you were happily single?' he asked, his voice light.

'Yes, I suppose it was. I'm single but not happily, really. I mean I'm quite content, but I always dreamed of finding someone to share my life with.' She stopped and cleared her throat. 'I haven't told you this, but now I feel I need to. Ever since my dad left my mum, I've felt a distrust towards men. Especially ones as good-looking as you are.' She stopped and saw him smile. 'So every relationship I've had has been tainted with that. I did want to find someone but then I've always had that doubt in my mind.'

'And now you have that about me?' he asked, looking worried.

'At first I did, but not any more,' she assured him. 'Before, when I thought I'd never find that special someone, I occupied myself with nursing. First it was hospital work and, later on, I came to love looking after older people. I liked making a little bit of a difference and making them feel less lonely. It seemed to fill that space for me.'

'Because you were lonely too?' he asked gently.

'Yes.' She touched his face. 'You understand me so well.' She was taken aback by his deep understanding.

'Because I love you.' He took her hand and kissed it.

Laura couldn't believe what Gino was saying. She'd felt so much for him, but she hadn't let herself admit it. 'Oh, Gino, I love you too,' she said with a deep sigh. 'So very much. From the very beginning.'

Without a word he got up and pulled her to her feet and kissed her, gently at first, and then harder as she responded with a fire she hadn't known she possessed. Laura closed her eyes and felt as if she was being wrapped in warm cotton wool, his scent in her nose and his warm, strong body against hers. It was like a dream come true. She was finally in the arms of the man she felt she had been waiting for all her life.

'Well, here we are,' he said when they drew apart. 'You in a state of undress and we're all alone and the storm is raging and...'

'And we can go and sit on the couch and maybe you could kiss me again?' Laura suggested.

'I could do better than that,' he said. She heard him pull out the sofa bed.

She reached out and pulled him down beside her. 'Come here,' she whispered. He did as he was told and kissed her again. As the fire glowed and Anne-Marie snored, Gino and Laura lay under the duvet and whispered words of love to each other. And then they fell asleep, a little awkwardly and uncomfortable in each other's arms, while the storm raged outside.

26

A ray of sunshine woke Laura up early the next morning. She looked at Gino, still asleep, and wondered if she had dreamed it all. Then she looked around and saw Anne-Marie curled up on the rug in front of the fire, the burned-out candles around the room and her clothes draped on the radiator.

The events of the night before, beginning with her mad dash out into the storm to find Ken, and then what had happened between her and Gino, went through her mind. It had really happened. They had made love in front of the fire and then gone to sleep... Gino had declared his love for her and she had told him she loved him too. It felt like a miracle that they were finally together and that she had found true and lasting love after all the years of dreaming and searching.

But now she had to go home and make sure Rachel and Ken were okay. If it was safe. She listened for a while and heard the wind still roaring outside. The storm was still going strong, but it was daylight and maybe it would be possible to walk home if she was careful.

With the blanket around her, she eased herself out of Gino's arms and went to get her clothes that were now thankfully dry. She quickly dressed and then tucked the duvet around Gino and tiptoed to the door, casting a final look at him, then walking out and closing the door softly behind her. Better let him sleep or he'd try to stop her going out. She'd call him later.

Outside, the storm was still in full swing, but as she could see where she was going, Laura was able to slowly make her way down the street, dodging bins and post boxes that had blown over, along with branches and even the sign over the grocery shop that had been torn down by the strong gusts. There would be a lot of tidying up to do later.

Then, finally, she was at her own front door; she had never been happier to get inside. The door banged shut behind her and she stood in the hall for a moment to catch her breath before Ken hurled himself at her, barking and whining and nearly tying himself in knots with delight to see her again.

Rachel rushed into the hall. 'Oh, you made it back. It's still really bad out there.'

'Yes, but I could see where I was going. Get down, you eejit,' she said and pushed Ken off her. 'You're the cause of all the trouble.' Then she suddenly laughed out loud with happiness as she realised he was also responsible for what had happened between her and Gino. 'But I forgive you,' she said and ruffled his fur. 'I'm sorry I gave you a fright,' she said to Rachel.

'I was really scared when you ran out into the storm,' Rachel chided. 'That was a stupid thing to do. Lucky you were able to call me to tell me you were safe with Gino.' She gave Laura a cheeky look. 'And then I found that big chicken under the bed so it was totally unnecessary.'

'I know. I didn't think,' Laura apologised. 'Sorry I scared you.'

'It's okay. It all ended well. I lit the stove in the kitchen,'

Rachel said. 'So I can make tea and even boil some eggs if you're hungry.'

'Starving,' Laura said, and followed Rachel down the corridor. 'But let me change into something less wrinkly and a little warmer.'

Rachel turned and looked at Laura. 'Yeah, you look little dishevelled, even though there is a strange glow about you. I'm guessing here, but I have a feeling there is romance in the air.'

Laura giggled. 'You could be right.'

Rachel smiled, her eyes twinkling. 'That's fabulous! I'm dying to hear what happened.'

'That's all I'm going to say for now.' Laura winked and disappeared into her bedroom to change. She glanced at herself in the mirror and laughed at her wild hair and wrinkly clothes. She did look a mess, but there was that glow in her cheeks. The expression in her eyes said she was hiding a delicious secret that she wasn't going to share with anyone. It was too new and precious and she needed time to get used to the idea. To remember their first night together that had been strange and awkward and faintly ridiculous but so, so wonderful.

The shower was cold but felt nice and refreshing. Laura wound a towel around her hair and put on several layers of warm sweaters, a pair of tracksuit pants and two pairs of socks. Then, in her sheepskin slippers, she padded out to the kitchen, warmed by the woodburning stove, where Rachel was setting the table while water and eggs boiled on the stove.

'Thank God for woodburning stoves,' she said as Laura sat down. 'What would we do without them in a storm?'

Laura took a slice of bread from the bread basket. 'I know. Very clever of Edwina to make sure the stove stayed in the kitchen instead of making it all modern and electric.'

Rachel went to fish two eggs out of the saucepan. 'We're still without power. But I'm guessing the ESB boys will be out in force once the wind drops. Aren't they the real unsung heroes?'

'Absolutely,' Laura agreed. 'Do you want me to make the tea?'

'No, I have it all organised.' Rachel put two egg cups on the table, poured boiling water into the mugs and then sat down, looking at Laura. 'So, are you going to tell me, or do I have to keep guessing? You and Gino have realised you're mad about each other and... whatever happened was wonderful?'

'Yes.' Laura's cheeks turned pink. But then she shot Rachel an irritated glance. 'And that is all I'm going to tell you. The rest is private. You young things want everything spelled out and shared all over social media, but us old folk like to keep things to ourselves. Yes, Gino and I are getting closer but I feel that talking about it would spoil it. So let's change the subject, okay? How did you cope here all by yourself?'

Rachel smiled. 'I slept through the storm once I had found Ken and knew you were all right. Then I was so tired after the party and everything I just got into bed and didn't wake up until around seven.' She shrugged and smiled sheepishly. 'I know I should have been terrified and worried the roof would blow off and stuff, but storms make me sleepy.' She took a bite from her slice of soda bread. Then she looked at Laura again. 'Oh, God, I completely forgot to tell you something. I think I found this Oonagh Nolan.'

'You found her?' Laura's hand holding her mug froze as she stared at Rachel. 'How? When?'

'Hang, on, I didn't find *her*, I found someone who could be her daughter. On Facebook. In my yoga group.' Rachel hit her forehead. 'I *knew* I recognised those amazing eyes and that heart-shaped face. Why didn't I realise it from the start? I've been looking at her on Facebook for over a year. And we've been chatting online too. Her mother was from Ireland, she told me a while ago. So that was the reason we connected. But now I'm sure she's related to the woman in the painting.'

'What?' Laura nearly choked on her bread. 'That's not possible,' she said, staring at Rachel. 'I mean... it seems so completely unbelievable. Maybe it's just wishful thinking on your part.'

'I don't think it is,' Rachel argued. 'She is the absolute spit of the woman in the painting.'

'That, of course, is amazing, even if she's not who you think,' Laura remarked. 'So where is this woman? Can we meet her? Is she nearby or do we have to drive somewhere to see her?'

'No.' Rachel shook her head. 'We can't drive there. She lives in California. And I only just realised her connection with the woman in the painting.'

'How?' Laura asked, her heart racing.

'I managed to connect to the internet this morning,' Rachel explained, taking a sip of tea. 'I used the hotspot on my phone as the masts are miraculously still standing. I was bored so, at around seven o'clock, I did the online live yoga class this woman does. Her name is Rosemary Nolan, by the way. And as she was talking and showing the poses, she looked straight at me and her face resonated with someone I'd seen recently. And then in the middle of the tree pose, it came to me in a flash and I fell over. It was a live class on Zoom, so she could see me. We were nearly at the end of the class and then, when we all said "namaste", she looked into the camera and asked if we had any questions. So I immediately shouted "yes!" and then we went on FaceTime and I asked her if her mother's name was Oonagh. She said yes, looking both shocked and sad. And she said her mother had died about a year ago. Then she asked where I was and I said Kerry and she nearly fainted. Then the connection broke.' Rachel drew breath.

'Oh no,' Laura said, disappointed. 'So you couldn't ask her anything else. Like her father's name?'

'No. But...' Rachel thought for a moment, staring into her mug. Then she lifted her gaze and looked at Laura. 'I know what you're thinking. But Louis de Barra died in 1979 and this woman, Rosemary Nolan, is only thirty-six, it says in her bio on her website. So Louis de Barra can't have been her father.'

'No, I suppose not,' Laura said, feeling deflated. They were so close but still not able to establish if this woman was truly Oonagh Nolan's daughter. 'We have to talk to her,' she said. 'Is there any way we can contact her?'

'Yes, we can call her through Messenger on Facebook. Or WhatsApp or just a simple FaceTime on our phones like she and I usually do. When we get internet connection back. It's better than the phone signal.'

'I know,' Laura agreed. 'I hope we can get it back soon.'

'Me too.' Rachel listened for a moment. 'I think the wind has dropped. It seems much quieter now.'

Laura went to the window. 'Yes, it's fairly calm. Just a strong breeze, which is like a whisper compared to the storm. I wonder if I should go to the surgery?'

'Maybe just to see if they're open today,' Rachel suggested. 'I'd say it's a bit difficult to do any work there today with no power.'

'I'll just go and see.' Laura put the mugs and dishes on the sink. 'We'll tidy up later.' She went into the hall, put on her jacket and went outside. The chilly wind made her button up. The sky was still overcast, but there were blue patches here and there through which the sun shone intermittently.

Shane came out of his front door and smiled at Laura. 'Hi, I was just going to call in to tell you we're not opening the surgery until after lunch. No power yet and everyone is too busy tidying up to be sick. But I'm going to go up the road and check on the old people up there to make sure nobody's been injured. And Kate will answer the phone in the surgery if anyone calls. Edwina is going up to the village to help clear the

debris with everyone else. That's what we usually do after a
storm.'

'Oh great,' Laura said, as Edwina emerged dressed in jeans
and a down jacket. 'I'll go with you so.'

Shane nodded. 'The more the merrier. All hands on deck.'

'But get yourself a pair of gloves to protect your hands,'
Edwina cut in.

'I will. And I'll get Rachel to come with us.'

Shane nodded. 'Great. See you later. And we'll be in the
surgery this afternoon, even with no power. Just to see to
anyone who might have been hurt or come down with anything
during the night.'

'I'll be there,' Laura promised.

The village was a sea of debris; branches and twigs littered the
main street along with the contents of upended bins, bits of
paper, plastic feed bags from farms up the road and broken glass
here and there. Everyone was outside helping to clear up the
mess, and there was a jolly, friendly vibe as they all chatted and
formed groups for different cleaning-up tasks. Rachel joined the
group that was knocking on doors to offer help with clearing
gardens, while Laura started picking up sticks and branches.

Gino was at the top of the street with Fidelma, helping her
to put back the gate on her fence. He shot Laura a smile as she
passed carrying branches to be put on a pile outside the library.
Then he ran after her, took the bundle from her and ran to
dispose them on the pile. He turned to her with a tender smile.

'Hello, lovely. You snuck out while I was still asleep.'

'I didn't want to wake you.' Laura felt suddenly shy as she
looked at him, remembering what had happened between them.

'That was sweet of you. I tried to call you but there was no
signal. But I knew you'd be here with Rachel to help with the
clearing up.' He stepped closer and put his arms around her,

kissing her before he let her go again. 'Just to show everyone we're together. I think they've been expecting it for a while.'

'Have they?' Laura stared at him. 'Why?'

'Because we've made it pretty obvious except to ourselves.' He laughed and turned her around so she could see everyone in the street behind them. They were all beaming at them and then someone shouted: 'There they are, together at last!' Everyone applauded and someone even let out a wolf whistle. Laura blushed and waved.

'How amazing,' she said, once she had recovered and they were walking back to Fidelma's garden. 'It's like being part of an enormous family.'

'Not all the time,' Gino remarked. 'What do you say, Fidelma?'

'Oh, there are ructions from time to time,' Fidelma declared from the front garden. 'And fisticuffs outside the pub on a Saturday night, arguments in the tidy towns committee, dirty looks between the mothers in the after-school activity group. All part of the rich tapestry of life, I suppose. But when the chips are down, we all pull together and do what we can.' She massaged her back. 'Not much at the moment in my case. The old back is giving out. Must be the big branch across the street I lifted earlier.'

'I told you to leave it alone,' Gino chided. 'I was on my way to help you.'

'I know,' Fidelma soothed. 'But this old girl needs to feel she can still do it.' She looked at them and smiled. 'And now I'm going to do something even more useful. I'm going to go inside and put the kettle on the wood burner. Good to have these so-called old-fashioned things still in our houses. I'll bring you both a mug of tea when you've finished fixing the gate.'

'Thanks, Fidelma,' Gino said, beaming at her. 'Just what I need.'

'Where is Becky?' Laura asked, looking around.

'Oh, Adam came to pick her up this morning,' Fidelma replied. 'He managed to get here despite warnings of fallen trees and power lines. He was worried about her, he said.' Fidelma let out a snort. 'That's the first time I've seen that boy worried about anything. Anyway, he whisked her away to Killarney, which hasn't been badly hit at all. They even have power. Becky looked as if she had won a million euros in the Lotto as she stepped into his fancy car.'

'That's wonderful,' Laura said, feeling a surge of happiness for Becky. She suddenly realised that Becky was a much better match for Adam than Laura had ever been. 'I have a feeling they'll be happy together.'

'That remains to be seen,' Fidelma muttered as she went inside.

'She doesn't trust him,' Laura said to Gino, as she held the gate while he screwed the latch back in place.

'She'll be cursing him forever if he breaks Becky's heart.' Gino gave the screw a last twist with the screwdriver. 'There. Should hold through the next storm.'

'Looks great,' Laura said, impressed with his handywork. 'DIY, cooking and baking. You're a good man to have around.'

'You want me around?' Gino smiled at her.

'I do.' Laura reached up and kissed him.

'Last night was a little strange,' he muttered in her ear.

'We can remedy that very soon,' she whispered back.

'When is your niece leaving?' he asked with a twinkle in his eyes.

'The day after tomorrow. Hopefully the roads will be clear by then.' She stood back. 'I forgot to tell you. We think we've found Oonagh's daughter.' She went on to tell him about the woman in California and how Rachel had known her all along.

Gino looked stunned. 'That's incredible. What a weird coincidence. I mean such a random thing and then someone halfway across the world sees you and knows who your mother was.' He shook his head. 'But maybe she isn't who you think? Her mother was from Kerry and was called Oonagh. Could be a thousand other women.'

'That's true. And as the connection broke and we couldn't go online, we can't speak to her or even see her picture. Rachel didn't save anything on her phone. So we'll see. Hopefully we'll get the power back soon and can talk to her.'

'Let me know what happens.'

'Of course,' Laura promised. 'I have to go to work after lunch. Shane said they'll be in the surgery after lunch, even without electricity.'

'Good idea,' Gino agreed. 'Even if there's no power you can see to patients while there's daylight. But it should be back soon. Most of the damage was around here so there wouldn't be a huge amount of wires to fix.'

'I hope you're right.'

They finished fixing the gate and had a mug of tea with Fidelma. Afterwards, they had to part again, but Gino promised to call Laura as soon as there was a signal. He had to go up to his little house to check if there was any storm damage, and then he'd go back down to the village and the bakery. 'So we're both busy,' he remarked as they said goodbye.

Laura watched him walk away, with Anne-Marie trotting by his side, and felt a surge of warmth for this unusual, wonderful man she loved with all her heart. Then she sent a little whisper of thanks to Josephine, whose legacy had not only brought her here to this village but also helped her find true love at last. Now all that remained was to find 'the rightful owner of the painting', as she had put it. Was she the woman in California? Laura couldn't wait to find out. It would tie up that loose end at least.

The only cloud on the horizon was Michael Monaghan and his threat to contest the will and take possession of the only home Laura had ever owned. How was she going to win that case? He had been threatening to bring the case to court for over two months, and now it was going to happen very soon, she felt. She just had to do something to stop him. But what? She stood by Fidelma's gate for a moment, thinking hard. Then an idea came to her. It might not work, but it was worth a shot. And she wouldn't tell Rachel or anyone else what she was planning to do.

27

The power came back in the early afternoon. Laura was in the surgery when she heard the central heating starting. Some of the lamps flickered for a while and then shone steadily in both the treatment rooms and in the nurse's office. It was a huge relief to get back to normal, after hours spent in the ice-cold building. They had handed blankets to the elderly patients in the waiting room and tried to see them as soon as possible. But now all was well, and the afternoon continued in a more positive manner. Rachel sent a text saying Rosemary Nolan would talk to them on Messenger at seven o'clock Irish time, which would be early morning in California. Excited, Laura ran home just after six, to find Rachel at the desk in the living room, setting up her laptop and arranging chairs in the right position for them to both to see the screen.

'She said she prefers to talk to us on Google Meet,' Rachel announced. 'Which might be better than Messenger. In any case we have power and heat and the internet all back and I made a casserole with some lamb and potatoes and other stuff I found in the fridge.'

Laura laughed. 'What would I do without you?'

'I don't know, starve to death?' Rachel replied. 'I fed Ken too and took him out for a little spin around the village just to show him everything is back to normal. All that knocked him out and he's fast asleep by the fire, as you can see. Snoring his head off, actually, if you were wondering what the noise was.'

'I thought the wind had started up again.' Laura kicked off her shoes and put on her slippers. 'So let's go and eat before we talk to Rosemary.'

'Okay.' Rachel led the way to the kitchen, where she had set the table. The steaming pot of lamb casserole filled the kitchen with a delicious smell.

'Lovely.' Laura sat down at the table. 'Gino is very doubtful that this woman truly is who we think. He said it was too much of a coincidence.'

'Coincidences do happen,' Rachel said as she piled food onto a plate for Laura. 'I believe in karma and this smells like karma to high heaven.' She put the plate in front of Laura. 'It was meant to happen, I'm sure of that.'

'We'll see.' Laura picked up her knife and fork. 'This smells divine.'

'Granny's recipe,' Rachel explained, helping herself. 'She gave it to me when I was in Florida last time. She said the recipe was not to be shared.'

'That's a family secret,' Laura said. 'So please don't give it to anyone.'

'I swear.' Rachel sat down at the table. 'So, I was thinking,' she said as she started to eat, 'that we should ask Rosemary questions about the area around here and Kerry in general. And if her mother told her anything about her friendship with a certain artist, without mentioning his name. Just to see if she told her daughter anything.'

'She might not have,' Laura argued. 'But let's wait and see.'

'Okay. But I have a feeling she'll have at least something to tell us.'

Laura felt a knot in her stomach. 'I'm beginning to feel nervous. What time is it?'

Rachel glanced at her phone beside her plate. 'Quarter to seven. We'll be talking to her soon. I'm really excited.'

Laura finished what was on her plate, mopping up the gravy with a piece of bread. 'This is delicious, but I'm afraid I'm too nervous to do it justice.'

Rachel got up. 'Me too. Let's have a second helping when we've talked to Rosemary. Come on, it's nearly time.'

They left everything in the kitchen, went into the living room and sat down in front of the laptop. 'Five more minutes,' Rachel said. 'Is there any way we can stop Ken snoring? It's very loud.'

'I'll put him in my bedroom.' Laura called Ken, who slowly got up and followed her into the bedroom, where he collapsed on the rug beside the bed with a grunt. Then she joined Rachel, sitting down on a chair, already chatting to someone whose image appeared on the screen. 'Here's my aunt now,' Rachel said. She turned to Laura. 'Say hi to Rosemary. I've already explained to her why we're interested to hear what happened to Oonagh.'

'Hi, Rosemary. Nice to meet you.' Laura stared at the woman, whose long jet-black hair tumbled to her shoulders like a gleaming curtain, taking in her amazing hazel eyes, heart-shaped face and wide mouth. She truly was the image of Oonagh Nolan, both in the photo and the painting. 'God, you're so like your mother.'

'What?' Rosemary said, frowning. Then she smiled. 'Hi, Laura,' she said in an American accent. 'Nice to see you. How are you both?'

'We're fine,' Rachel said. 'And, well, you know why we want to talk to you.'

'Well, yeah, maybe,' Rosemary replied. 'You think you saw my mother in a painting?'

'That's right,' Laura cut in. 'We... oh, this is hard to explain.'

'Give it a shot,' Rosemary urged. 'If you can tell me what you want to know and why, I'll decide if I want to share anything. I mean,' she continued. 'I know Rachel as an online friend through my classes but that's all. You're in Ireland, right? And Kerry? That's where my mom was from. Valentia Island to be precise.'

Rachel nodded, looking excited. 'Yes, that's what we heard.'

'But she worked in our village for a bit,' Laura started. 'I mean she spent the spring and summer here in the mid-Sixties. The village is called Sandy Cove and Oonagh was teaching at the primary school here. Do you know anything about that?'

Rosemary stared at them for a while, looking stunned. 'Yes,' she said. 'It was a very special time in my mother's life. She was a teacher and came to America just after that summer in Sandy Cove. She had a cousin in California and she came here and managed to get a green card. And then she did some kind of training course and got a job teaching kids in a school here in LA. Then she met my dad and they had me a long time after they met.' Rosemary smiled. 'She always said I was the best Christmas present ever.'

'But they weren't married?' Rachel asked. 'I mean that's why you have the same last name as your mother?'

Rosemary smiled. 'Yeah, that's right. They were free spirits, kind of hippies really. Flower-power and all that. Against the establishment and organised religion. Neither of them believed in marriage. They were like kids until they were old. My dad was a poet and a teacher too. Taught English lit at UCLA. They inspired me to choose this career as yoga teacher and therapist. A great gift that I'm very grateful for.'

'That's wonderful.' Laura smiled at the young woman, who exuded a kind of spiritual harmony she wished she had herself. 'But back to your mother. Tell me what she said about her time here. If you don't mind talking about it with us.'

'Oh.' Rosemary paused and there was suddenly a sad expression in those lovely eyes. 'Well, I guess it's okay to share this with you.' She paused for a moment. 'My mom told me years ago that she had a kind of love affair with an artist. He later became famous in Ireland.'

'A love affair?' Laura asked.

'Well, not quite,' Rosemary explained. 'It wasn't physical, more like a meeting of spirits. He was married, she had just landed her first teaching job. His wife was very sick and bedridden and he looked after her. And when she was resting, he went out and painted the lovely scenery, setting up his easel on the beach below the cottage where they were staying. A beach surrounded by slopes covered in wild roses, Mom said.'

'Wild Rose Bay?' Laura cut in.

'That's it,' Rosemary replied. 'It sounded so lovely. And they met there when she was walking at sunset and he was painting. They began to talk and then they started to meet there regularly. Nearly every day, I think. And one day he asked if he could paint her. She was wearing a white summer dress that first time and he wanted her to wear it when she posed for him on the beach. Is that the painting you were talking about?'

'Yes,' Laura said in a near sob. 'I can see it in front of me. Lovely and sad at the same time.'

'Yes, I think it was,' Rosemary said. 'Like they were meant to be together but never could. His wife was sick, so he could never leave her. In any case, divorce was impossible in Ireland then.'

'So they met in secret on the little beach?' Rachel asked. 'Right below the cottages where we are now.'

'You're in the cottage?' Rosemary asked, her face suddenly pale. 'That coastguard place Louis rented that summer?'

'Yes,' Laura replied. 'Did your mother talk about the house? Did she know it?'

Rosemary shook her head. 'No, she never went there. She

knew of the coastguard station, of course. But they only met down on the little beach and then sometimes they walked out to the headland to watch the sunset. And she said she brought the children from her class down to the main beach when he was painting there and he gave them tips about painting and drawing. Their friendship grew during that time and they were very close by the end of the summer.'

'Then what happened?' Rachel asked.

'Someone spotted them together,' Rosemary said in a low voice. 'I think they might have been kissing or something. Just a kiss on the cheek to say goodbye one evening, Mom said. And then the gossip started. This was in the Sixties. So things were a little different then.'

'To put it mildly.' Laura tried to imagine what had happened. 'I'd say whoever saw them started to read things into that little kiss. And then once it was out there, the story got more and more dramatic. I mean... a young woman and an older man with a sick wife. Long walks in secluded places. It had to become something immoral in people's wild imagination.'

Rosemary nodded. 'Exactly. So my mom went back to Valentia Island first and then, as she had practically no family, being an only child, she started thinking of leaving. She asked her cousin here in LA if she could come over and then... Well, the rest is history, as they say.'

'Yes.' Laura looked at Rosemary. 'That painting... The one Louis painted of your mother. Do you know what happened to it?'

Rosemary shook her head. 'No idea. I'd love to see it, though.'

'Well, you know what?' Rachel said. 'You can see it. Right now. It's here in the cottage.'

Rosemary's eyes widened with shock. 'Are you serious? You have that painting? How come?'

'Long story,' Laura replied. 'It was bought somewhere by an

old lady I was looking after. And when she died, she left it to me in her will, saying it had a connection to the cottage. Do you want to see it?'

Rosemary brought her hands to her cheeks. 'Oh yes, please, please show it to me.'

'Of course. Hang on.' Rachel got up and took the laptop, carrying it to the bedroom door.

Laura ran to open it, then turned on the light in the bedroom. Then she turned the painting around and Rachel held the laptop so Rosemary could see it. 'Here it is,' Rachel said.

'Wow,' Rosemary whispered and started to cry. 'I have never seen it before. Oh, how beautiful it is.'

'It's gorgeous,' Rachel said. 'And such a typical work of Louis de Barra. You can just see his signature on the bottom left-hand side.'

'Oh.' Rosemary seemed suddenly stuck for words. 'Could... could you take a photo of it and send it to me? I want to print it and hang it on my wall.'

'Of course,' Rachel promised.

Laura sat down on the bed and Rachel joined her, holding the laptop. Rosemary's cheeks were wet with tears. She dabbed at her eyes. 'This has been such a shock. I can't believe it's happening. To see that painting... Oh wow, it's like a dream. I wish my mom had seen it too.'

'So do I,' Laura agreed. 'So sad she couldn't see it. But...' She paused. 'As I said, I was left this painting in someone's will. And it wasn't meant to go to me, but I was given the task of finding the rightful owner. And now I feel I have.'

Rosemary's hand flew to her mouth. 'You mean...? No, you don't have to.'

'I feel I do,' Laura said with a smile. 'You should have the painting. I will keep it here for you until you can come and collect it.'

'Oh, but...' Rosemary's eyes filled with tears again. 'That's so kind of you, Laura.'

'It feels right,' Laura replied. 'It's as if we've been waiting for you all this time.'

'Do you think you could come over here and collect the painting?' Rachel asked.

Rosemary nodded. 'Yes. I'd love to. I've always wanted to go to Ireland and now I can afford it. When would be the best time to come over?'

'Come in late May,' Laura said. 'When the wild roses bloom. I'll be here, waiting for you.'

'When the wild roses bloom,' Rosemary said and brought both her hands together. 'How lovely. I will see you then. Please keep in touch. And now I have to go and teach my first early morning class.' She bowed her head. 'Namaste, to you both.'

'Namaste,' Rachel said as the session ended. Her eyes were full of tears as she turned to Laura. 'That was so perfect, don't you think?'

'Like the very happiest of endings,' Laura said. 'Or maybe the beginning of a new friendship? But I feel so happy now. We found her and she truly is the rightful owner to the painting.'

'That's for sure,' Rachel agreed.

'I'm just going to hang on to the painting until Rosemary comes,' Laura declared. 'And Adam can see it if he wants. Now that I know who the rightful owner is, I don't mind if he knows about it.' She paused. 'I do have the right to give it away, don't I?'

'Yes,' Rachel said. 'Because Louis de Barra sold it and whoever bought it became the legal owner, and then Josephine was when she bought it and left it to you.'

'But she wanted me to give it to the *rightful* owner,' Laura cut in. 'And that is Oonagh's daughter, which I'm sure Josephine would agree with.'

'I'm sure she would. You might want to insure it, though,' Rachel remarked.

'Yes, I'll do that as soon as I can. I'll contact my insurance dealer and he'll point me in the right direction.'

Rachel got up from the bed. 'Let's go and finish dinner. I'm suddenly hungry again.'

'Me too.' Laura rose and followed Rachel into the living room. They switched on lights as they went, delighted to have the power back.

'So,' Rachel said as she reheated the lamb casserole, and Laura found a bottle of wine in the larder. 'All that remains now is to get Michael Monaghan off your back, which seems impossible at the moment.'

Laura pulled the cork out of the bottle. 'Nothing is impossible if you look at it from a different angle. And I think I know what to do now.'

Rachel looked up from stirring the casserole. 'What?'

'I'm going to write him a letter. But that's all I'm going to tell you right now. I'd like to solve this on my own. I'm the person who knew Josephine's state of mind during her last few months. So maybe if...' Laura stopped. She suddenly didn't feel like talking about it. She wanted to do this her way, and Rachel might have different ideas. 'I don't really feel like talking about it right now,' she said. 'Let's enjoy your lovely casserole and talk about something else.'

'Of course,' Rachel replied, as she carried the casserole to the table. 'It's too much on top of everything else.'

They sat down and started to eat and chat about other things, while Laura silently planned what she was going to say to Michael. It wouldn't be easy, but if she put it right, she might have a chance to keep her cottage and stay here, in this place she had come to love so much, where she had found love at last after so many years of dreaming.

· · ·

Much later, when Rachel had gone to bed, Laura sat down at the desk in the living room, where the dying embers of the fire still cast a warm glow around the room. She looked at Ken lying at her feet and smiled. 'This is it, boy. My last chance at rescuing us from having a drawn-out battle in court.'

Ken lifted his head and wagged his tail before going back to sleep. Laura felt he was wishing her good luck. Then she looked at the blank screen of her computer and wondered how to start. Maybe she should try to understand what Michael had been through as a child... She fleetingly thought of Josephine and wondered if she would approve. But she had been feeling guilty about not being there for her son when he was a child, so maybe this would be asking forgiveness in her place and let her rest in peace at last.

Laura imagined Michael as a little boy without a mother to care for him, to pick him up from school and give him milk and cookies and ask how his day had been. A mother who had never stood freezing watching him play soccer, or put plasters on his scraped knees or read him stories at bedtime, tucking him in and kissing him goodnight. No mother to call for in the middle of the night when he had nightmares or making him banana sand-wiches for his lunch. All these things Maureen had done for her children, and Laura, too, when she was minding her niece and nephew. Poor little boy who had grown up without much love, and feeling like his mother had put her career first. But Laura could understand why Josephine had put her career first. Her voice, her amazing talent, had given the world so much. But her little boy had paid for all of that. And it seemed suddenly to be a very high price to have to pay.

Laura felt tears well up as she thought of Michael's child-hood. And she suddenly understood where he was coming from. He didn't want Josephine to get her last will because he was still angry and wanted revenge. But that would mean that Laura had to give up a cottage she had come to love and people that had become so dear to her, in a place where she had found true friendship. She knew she wanted to stay here for the rest of her life.

Laura nodded to herself. Now she knew what to write. His response would decide her future with the man she loved, and she wanted to fight for it with everything she had. She took a deep breath and started to write.

Dear Michael...

EPILOGUE

Rosemary didn't come to Sandy Cove to claim her painting until two years later. But, when she finally arrived, it was with fanfare and celebrations.

Adam had finally managed to organise an exhibition in the communal hall in Sandy Cove of Louis de Barra's seascapes, and *The Girl on the Beach* would be the star of the show, so to speak. And then he was allowed to exhibit this important work by Louis de Barra in his gallery for a few weeks. He had tried his best to get it for months, but Laura had resisted until Rosemary had agreed to lend it to him for a limited time. Then it would be on permanent loan to the National Gallery until Rosemary decided what to do with it. She would probably let them keep it under that arrangement, she had told Laura. It would be too awkward to ship it to California, and then she would have to insure it and install security doors and windows and be constantly worried it would be stolen.

The opening of the exhibition was held on a beautiful day in late May, the day after Rosemary's arrival. Laura and Gino had met her at the airport and brought her to Starlight Cottages where she would stay for the duration of her visit. After a short nap, Rosemary came downstairs and declared it was too beautiful a day to miss, so they took the dogs and brought her for a walk on the beach at Wild Rose Bay.

As she stepped onto the sand below the steps, Rosemary looked across the beach to the slopes covered in wild roses in full bloom, her eyes full of tears. 'I can't believe I'm here,' she said. 'In the place where my mom spent such a happy time. It's like a dream.'

Laura pointed at a rock. 'I imagine that she sat there when he painted her.'

Rosemary nodded as she looked at it. 'That looks like the right place.' She walked to the rock and sat down, staring out to sea. Laura could see that Rosemary's grief was still fresh, but that this trip and the painting were helping her to heal. 'I'll sit here for a while if you don't mind.'

'We'll walk ahead,' Gino said. 'You need some time alone.'

'I won't be alone,' Rosemary said softly.

'We know.' Laura took Gino's hand and pulled him away. 'We'll take the dogs for a walk and meet you on the way back.'

'Thank you.' Rosemary nodded, and they left her sitting there, deep in thought, possibly connecting with her memories of her mother, their spirits meeting in some strange and wonderful way.

'It's like it's come full circle,' Laura said as they walked on, the dogs running ahead. 'A lovely end to a sad story.'

'Just like yours,' Gino said, kissing Laura's hair. 'You had a happy ending after a lot of sadness and worry.'

'I know.' Laura stopped walking and looked at Gino. 'I even tamed Michael Monaghan.'

'He dropped that case so suddenly,' Gino remarked. 'Will you ever tell me what you said in your letter to him?'

'That's between me and him – and Josephine.'

'I admire your reticence.' Gino smiled apologetically. 'But

I'm still curious. You have kept this secret for the past two years.'

'The best two years of my life,' Laura said, feeling a surge of joy as she thought of all that had happened since the day after the storm, when she had written that letter to Michael Monaghan.

The letter had taken all morning to write but, when she finally signed it, she felt she had said what was in her heart. She had told Michael that she understood where he was coming from, and that the trauma of his childhood must have left scars that he was trying to heal. But she had also said that revenge and anger were not the way to go – that forgiving Josephine might be a better option, even if his mother was now dead. Then she explained her own situation and that he would be taking out his anger on her, which would only cause more misery. Would it really give him a good feeling to deprive her of a house she had come to feel was her home and a place where she was so happy?

Laura went on to tell him that she had been devoted to Josephine but had also been aware of the flaws in her character, and that her failure as a mother had been something Laura had found hard to accept. At the end of the letter, she offered him an open invitation.

> The cottage is not really suitable to be lived in only for a week or two during the gap between Marbella and the Bahamas; it's a place that should be a home with the fire lit and someone there to say welcome to anyone who wants to come. And, of course, you would be welcome any time should you feel you want to talk or just enjoy the view. My door will always be open.

There had been no reply, but only a week after sending the letter, Laura's solicitor had called to say that the will would no longer be contested. Giddy with joy, Laura had wanted to contact Michael to thank him, but Gino had had advised against it. 'Better to close the chapter,' he said. 'But if he wants to visit, we'll welcome him and give him a cup of tea.'

'We?' Laura looked at Gino as they stood on the terrace, knowing what he meant but wanting him to say it out loud.

'Yes, we,' Gino said with a laugh. Then he groped in his pocket and produced a scuffed leather box. 'If your answer to my question is yes.'

'Ask it, then,' Laura said between tears and laughter.

Gino crushed her to his chest in a tight embrace. 'Will you marry me, my darling Laura?' he whispered in her ear.

'Yes, of course I will,' she said and pulled away from his arms. 'Show me the ring, then, you silly man.'

Gino put the box in Laura's hand. 'It was my mother's ring,' he said hoarsely. 'One of the few things I have of her.'

'Oh,' Laura said, her heart breaking for him. 'That makes me sad.'

'But if you wear it you will make me happy,' Gino told her, while she slowly opened the box.

Laura looked at the ring: a square aquamarine set with tiny diamonds in white gold. 'It's beautiful. Will you put it on for me?'

Gino took the ring out of the box and slid it onto Laura's ring finger. It fit perfectly. 'It looks lovely there,' he said, and kissed her hand.

'I love it. And I love you. And I want you to move in here with me and we'll be happy ever after.'

'Of course I will,' he said, his eyes dancing. 'Thought you'd never ask.'

'What about the cabin?'

Gino shrugged. 'We'll go and stay there on summer nights and just use it as a little getaway when we feel like it.'

'That's a great idea. And you can move your books and stuff down here and we can make the living room...'

'Never mind all that. Those are just things.' Gino put his arms around her and let out a long sigh. 'I thought I'd never get the nerve to ask you. But now that I have, I feel at peace.'

'So do I.'

Laura smiled as she remembered that day two years ago. They were still not married but had a wedding planned for August. But, married or not, she knew they were together for life.

The opening of the exhibition was attended by nearly everyone in the village. It was also broadcast on national television as the discovery of *The Girl on the Beach* had caused a sensation in the art world. Adam unveiled the painting and there was gasp of admiration as everyone could finally see it in real life. The colours glowed in the light from the spotlight. The girl looked so real it was nearly as if she could speak. Rosemary posed in front of it, and everyone remarked on how like her mother she was.

Adam, with Becky by his side, made a short speech. Then the exhibition was open and they could walk around and admire the other works Louis de Barra had produced during his stay in Sandy Cove all those years ago. They were nearly all seascapes, some with distant figures in them, like the one with a curragh rowed by six men across the bay at sunset.

'Isn't it fabulous?' Becky asked Laura as they enjoyed a glass of wine later on. 'Oonagh's daughter reunited with her mother's image, even though it's sad she is no longer alive.'

'I think Rosemary found it a great comfort,' Laura replied. Then she smiled at Becky. 'Another fabulous thing is you and Adam. You look so great together.'

'I know.' Becky laughed. 'That's what everyone says. Adam thinks I'm a great accessory to his image.'

'And he obviously adores you,' Laura stated.

Becky looked doubtful. 'Does he?'

'He looks at you as if he can't believe his luck.'

'And Gino looks as if he's won the jackpot in some lottery,' Becky replied. 'Totally besotted with you.'

'And I with him.' Laura looked across the room at Gino. He was talking to Fidelma and Bridget, who had recently retired, which gave Laura a full-time job as surgery nurse.

'He's a dote,' Becky said affectionately. 'And the painting has found its rightful owner, and you are secure in your cottage and Oonagh's daughter was connected with her mother's Irish roots, and...' She stopped and laughed. 'It is the perfect happy ending to your story that is now only beginning.'

Laura laughed. 'Sounds a little weird but I like that.'

Becky raised her glass. 'Let's drink to that. Here's to all our new beginnings.'

Laura clinked glasses with Becky. 'Cheers to that. And to us and our friendship.'

'Love all around,' Becky said, winking at Adam across the room.

Much later that evening, Laura, Gino and the dogs climbed up the slope to the cabin in the light of the setting sun.

They had nearly reached the top when Laura stopped and turned to look at the view. The glittering water of the bay had a pinkish hue, and the outline of the islands shimmered in the late evening light. In the darkening sky to the east, the crescent of a new moon slowly rose above the mountains, and the evening star could be seen beside it. And then more and more stars appeared as the sun slowly sank into the sea.

'This,' she said, 'has to be the most beautiful spot on earth.'

Gino stopped walking. 'It is to us anyway.' He walked down to meet her and took her hand. 'There are so many beautiful places to see in the world. I'd like to go and discover them with you. Maybe we could take some time off and travel when things calm down a bit after the wedding? Just to see the world together.'

'Oh yes,' Laura replied, her heart soaring. 'I've wanted to go and see a few places but I didn't want to travel on my own. With you it will be wonderful.'

'Where do you want to go?' Gino asked.

'I don't know where to start.' Laura thought for a moment. 'Maybe the Amalfi coast? We could hire a car and drive from Rome. I've seen it in so many movies and I've always wanted to go there.' She paused. 'Don't argue now, but I want to use Josephine's money to do things like that. We can afford to stay in nice hotels then and have a bit of a blast.'

Gino laughed. 'Why would I argue? Great idea, sweetheart. It'll make a perfect honeymoon. And then we could go to Sicily and meet my family. They'll love you.'

'I'm sure I'll love them too.' Laura smiled at him. 'I'm glad you want to do this and to use that money for our honeymoon.'

'Josephine would approve. She always said life was for living and having as much fun as possible.'

Laura nodded, leaning against him, staring up at the starlit sky. 'She did. And maybe she is up there, among the twinkling stars, looking down and smiling.'

Gino put his arms around her. 'And she's happy that all the things she meant to happen actually did. It was all in her plan.'

'I have a feeling you're right.' Laura leaned her head on his shoulder. 'All of it. Finding Rosemary, meeting you, even making peace with Michael. Everything has finally fallen into place.'

'And now she can rest in peace.'

'Yes.' Laura laughed as the dogs started to bark above them. 'And those rascals want us to come up before it's pitch black.'

'Or they've found a rabbit,' Gino suggested. He let her go and took her hand, pulling her up the slope. 'Just a few steps and we'll be up there. We can dine under the stars as it's such a warm evening.'

'Perfect,' Laura said. 'We can plan our trip. And you know what I'll look forward to the most during our travels?'

'A real Italian pizza?'

'No.' Laura glanced behind her and looked at the village where the lights were coming on in all the houses. 'To coming back home. To Sandy Cove.'

A LETTER FROM SUSANNE

I want to say a huge thank you for choosing to read *The Lost Mother of Ireland*. If you did enjoy it, and want to keep up to date with all my latest releases, just sign up at the following link. Your email address will never be shared and you can unsubscribe at any time.

www.bookouture.com/susanne-oleary

I hugely enjoyed writing this book as I was so inspired by the beautiful views and vistas along the coast of Kerry. The people I meet there are so similar to the inhabitants of Sandy Cove in my novels: fun, lively, quirky and incredibly kind. You might think they are too good to be true, but even if they're not quite as perfect, they are the kind of people you'd love to have as your neighbours! Writing these stories takes me away from all the worries of the world out there and I hope it will do the same for you.

I have been overwhelmed with kind messages from readers and I am so happy my novels are read and enjoyed all over the world.

I hope you loved *The Lost Mother of Ireland* and, if you did, I would be very grateful if you could write a review. I'd love to hear what you think, and it makes such a difference helping new readers to discover one of my books for the first time.

I love hearing from my readers – you can get in touch on my Facebook page, through Twitter, Goodreads or my website.

Thanks,

Susanne

www.susanne-oleary.co.uk
www.goodreads.com/author/show/837027.Susanne_O_Leary

facebook.com/authoroleary
twitter.com/susl

ACKNOWLEDGEMENTS

There are so many people to thank for their huge help and support during the writing process of this novel. My interim editor, Jess Whitlum-Cooper, did a wonderful job with the first edits and my editor, Jennifer Hunt, then continued with an equally outstanding edit when she was back from her maternity leave. Both deserve a huge thanks for all their hard work.

Also all at Bookouture, and Kim, Noelle and all the publicity and marketing teams.

My friends and family have been hugely supportive and they also deserve a mention.

And then, I must thank my readers, especially those who leave reviews and take the time and trouble to contact me. I really appreciate it!

Made in United States
North Haven, CT
26 August 2024

56582350R00146